MEMORY'S TAILOR

Memory's Tailor

Lawrence Rudner

University Press of Mississippi Jackson

Manufactured in the United States of America

01 00 99 98   4 3 2 1

The paper in this book meets the guidelines for permanence and durability of the committee on Production Guidelines for Book Longevity of the Council on Library Resources.

Library of Congress Cataloging-in-Publication Data

Rudner, Lawrence Sheldon, 1947–1995

    Memory's tailor / Lawrence Rudner.

       p.   cm.

    ISBN 1-57806-090-7 (cloth : alk. paper)

    I. Title.

    PS3568.U333M35   1998   98-15895

    813'.54—dc21   CIP

British Library Cataloging-in-Publication data available

After the final no there comes a yes
And on that yes the future world depends.

Wallace Stevens,
"The Well Dressed Man with a Beard"

During the terrible years of Yezhovshchina I spent seventeen months in the prison queues in Leningrad. One day someone recognized me. Then a woman with lips blue with cold who was standing beside me, and of course had never heard of my name, came out of the numbness which afflicted us all and whispered in my ear—(we all spoke in whispers there):

"Can you describe this?"

I said, "I can!"

Then something resembling a smile slipped over what had once been her face.

Anna Akhmatova, *Requiem*

PART ONE

I

You saw them, didn't you? Such an amazing and sad spectacle. They say a hundred thousand marched down Kalinin Prospekt behind the coffins draped with the old czarist flags and the huge photos of the three dead. "Let them sleep peacefully," Hero-Yeltsin told the weeping Moscow crowd at our Square of Free Russia. "We will not forget." Gorbachev spoke at Manezh Square. He wore a black armband bordered in red. Pale as rice after those three days in his Crimean dacha when he saw Stalin's ghost appear, Mikhail Sergeyevich declared the three dead men—Komar, Usov, and the Jew, Krichevsky—"Heroes of the Soviet Union." The patriarch Aleksy II, waiting at Vagankovskoye cemetery, presided over the final Orthodox rites for Dimitri Komar and Vladimir Usov, while, in full view of the Soviet Union's television cameras, a rabbi and a good violinist took care of Ilya Krichevsky, who was twenty-eight, and, because of the press of events, was buried on Shabbes. Incredible!

But, as you know, a camera's lens takes in more than the center of any scene; life also seeps into view from the bottom and sides. So to absorb everything that happened on this amazing day, you must replay the videotape of the

3

funeral. Watch for the moment when the violinist next to the Moscow rabbi begins to play. If you look quickly toward the lower half of the screen, you'll see our Berman, perched atop a wooden box like a skinny crow, the rounded top of his large black hat moving up and down because he's doing a frantic Hasidic dance on a very small stage. He cradles a portable Victrola in his arms. He appears to be a crazy man, doesn't he? Notice how the Russians closest to him give him some room when he swings about; they think this old Jew is drunk, maybe worse. Just before the camera loses sight of him, the dancer, twirling a bit too fast for his advanced age, loses his balance, and the crowd closes in. No more Berman!

Ladies and gentlemen of the rational persuasion, now that the recent history of Mother Russia is, by God's grace and the party's arch stupidity, no longer being written by criminals and policemen, the story of master tailor and reborn mensch Alexandr Davidowich Berman—he's the strange one on the box—can, like a dill seed in heavy brine, float to the surface for your full inspection. Given the circumstances, there's no reason to hold back on the simple truth: after many years of quietly surviving the killers of his time, Alexandr Davidowich Berman (of all people), had, praise God, begun to do battle with the natural order of the universe.

Now, facts are facts, and I, who was there, if not for the beginning, then at least for the end—if indeed it was the end—can state this fact: no one in his right mind would have thought that Berman, with his bad back and nearly seven decades of life, would be the one to go on a personal mission for the Jews. After all, this is the same Berman who, ever since he lost the Hasid in Poland—and this was nearly fifty years ago—tried to forget about Jews and their constant troubles; the same Berman who fell into safety during the terrible forties and fifties because the Kirov Ballet, not the Master of the Universe or His Chosen Ones, needed his skills; and the same Berman who, as an old man, had no wish to pack up his thoughts and language and leave for Israel (where David was once a king!) with the other Jews. It takes my breath away even to suggest this, but it is whispered that this Berman, who was no refusenik and couldn't care less about God's holidays, is even now being driven about in an old black Lada sedan between the Baltic and Kiev and, whenever the mood strikes him, finds another old Jew who knows how to tell a good story about what used to be. "A hem for a tale," he yells as he drags his sewing machine from its case. "A dress for an epic!"

In Kiev, close to the entrance of the Hotel Dneiper, he caused a commotion because he was tape-recording a Yiddish tune sung by a blind Ukrainian Jew. In Novgorod, Holy Russian Novgorod, he rearranged a few exhibits in state museums "so people shouldn't forget." Recently in our new St. Petersburg, he expertly turned himself into a living exhibit and became, at least for thirty minutes, a ragged Jewish tailor from the Pale and actually drove a horse and small cart into the courtyard of the Hermitage—frightening several dozen Finnish tourists—because sometimes a good story has to be lived as well as recorded. "Fix a coat, fix a blouse," he yelled from his seat above an old nag three clops away from the slaughterhouse. "Give a poor Jew a tale." And now in Moscow, with the Communists disappearing faster than traveling salesmen with shoddy wares in their suitcases, Berman-as-Hasid from the eighteenth century, with his fancy black hat trimmed in fur, does a sweet Jewish dance within sight of the Orthodox patriarch himself!

You might say: what a senile old Jew! Such a meshuggener! Does he think he's in a movie? What's this business with horses, carts, costumes, and silly playacting? What are these stories he's collecting? Can't this old man take his Victrola and his tape recorder and get on an El Al flight for Tel Aviv like everyone else who ever spoke a Yiddish word? Why doesn't he just go to a place where Jews have a chance? Can't he let a quickly dying world be? Or, turning another corner of possibility, you might, just like those Russian patriots with their meat-red faces and fascist-brown shirts, want to squash this annoying kike and turn him into nothing before the international press finds him and his photograph appears in London or New York. Or maybe, like the few ancient souls who've been waiting for Berman to show up in Ostrov or Vitebsk, you, too, might want a blessing on your head, or a tightly mended pair of trousers, from this strangely costumed Jew who knows how to listen so well. Or maybe, like a certain former militia officer close to the KGB—please, even in our new Russia, don't believe that his type has vanished like the snow in May!—you know that this half-witted Jew Berman is an embarrassing boil on the ass. Let's be honest: the many recent appearances of our tailor Alexandr Davidowich Berman are causing a lot of trouble!

Mind you, none of this has been easy for Berman to accomplish. He's come unexpectedly and somewhat hurriedly to this strange new calling. And, truth to tell, as the stories go, he doesn't seem to have too much time left: he is a few days short of seventy, his back is getting worse, his teeth hurt, the Lada is falling apart, his elderly driver—more about this unfortunate man later—is getting nervous (if anyone knows, I should!). And rumor has it that one of those devoted KGB types in a bad suit is on his way to drug Berman into real insignificance with a good dose of sulphazine.

But nothing is settled yet. Nothing. The old women swear that Berman is still out there—either pissing behind a linden tree in Gorky Park, stalled on some forsaken road outside Moscow (probably lost without a good map), or eating a stale sandwich in Odessa while thinking about where to find his next story, where to drop another shard of memory. Maybe he laughs when he thinks about how he started in this business? Maybe, as some think, he feels a stone pressing in on his heart, or, above the Lada's racket, hears the insistent buzz of talking gnats in his ear? Maybe he has his eye on his own Messiah? Maybe he is close to the edge of nothing because "about some people you shouldn't forget?" Maybe, God willing, he got out of the way of that speeding sedan?

Who can say? Who knows anything about a blessed meshuggener's fate but to hold one's breath, juggle a dozen possibilities in the air, and recall how everything began.

2

In the beginning, not too long after the great Gorbachev himself had begun to bury the cockroaches of a terrible past, Alexandr Davidowich Berman, sixty-nine, once the best costume tailor at the Kirov Opera and Ballet Theater, wanted nothing more for his last years than to be left in peace. His legs were always stiff in the morning, he had terrible backaches in cold weather, he suffered from nightmares, and flatulence was a problem. However, during better moments—from late morning until the evening meal—Berman knew he had enough strength left to carry heavy weights in an emergency and a tailor's skill that would allow him to sew anything, even in the dark. Because he was such an excellent tailor, his old trousers and shirts, which he had made himself, would last until the end of time. He owned two very well made woolen caps and a decent pair of fur-lined boots. He had two extra pairs of spectacles—enough, he knew, to serve him until his eyes fell out from rereading the same books—a good portable Victrola, and a large collection of Melodia records.

On the positive side, his habits were decent enough. He didn't drink too much, nor did he curse or spit at every third person he saw. Unlike the other pensioners he met in the village whenever he took his daily walks, he didn't slobber over himself or mumble dim thoughts. To keep himself from going crazy, he had a small leatherbound notebook in which he drew crude sketches of the many costumes he had sewn, along with a few notes to himself—for what practical purpose, only Alexandr Davidowich knew—about this or that dancer's measurements, habits, and abilities. And, while Alexandr Davidowich still thought about women, he usually fell asleep before his brain played too many tricks and his body reacted with a cruel attempt at an erection. He still received small gifts of money—though most of it, foolishly sent through the post, was stolen before it ever reached him—from grateful dancers, many of them now living in the West, who had never found a suitable replacement for their gifted Jewish costume tailor. "Just say the word and I'll bring you to New York," Baryshnikov once wrote. "And you'll be set for life."

"Tailors don't travel well, Misha," Berman replied in the only letter he ever sent abroad. "Their needles require the local atmosphere."

But best of all, as a reward for his forty years of costume-making service for the Kirov Ballet, Berman, now retired, was allotted two rooms (twenty square meters!) and four windows in a pleasant village not far from what was then Leningrad, where, many years before, the great and blessed Pushkin himself had once attended school and written sweet boyish verses about birch trees and snow. After so many years wasted in airless Leningrad flats, sharing communal toilets and kitchens that always reeked of someone else's problems, Berman, who sometimes thought he was in heaven, now had the use of a garden in which he grew tomatoes, beans, onions, and sunflowers. Since he liked to eat nothing more complicated than vegetable soup, along with flatbread that he baked for himself sprinkled with coarse salt and bits of onion, he never had to face the meat lines or the humiliating reality that rubles were now worth less than dog's spit.

Berman rose at the same time every morning, before four, just as he had once done in the camps. Despite the passing of a half century, he still listened for the wheeze of his own breathing and the possibility of a shriek on the other side of the wall. To be certain he had another day, he bit his tongue and slapped his cheeks. "Make the pain rush to your head," a Greek Jew from Salonika had told him in broken Yiddish during the winter of forty-four, "and then you'll feel a bit of life." Even though his tongue was always sore, the pain usually riding atop every sound he made, Berman never forgot the valuable lesson, or the Greek.

But the days went by, and Alexandr Davidowich—who, with his broken nose (a Latvian guard's gift during that same tongue-biting winter), could still pass, unnoticed, through any anonymous Russian crowd—only wanted to live out his time listening to his portable Victrola or sitting in his garden with the one-eared cat he'd adopted, reading the same books over and over, or taking long walks by himself through the lovely grounds of the nearby Catherine Palace Museum. He rarely spoke to anyone, except the schoolchildren who came to visit the palace museum and stood open-mouthed while one or two pigeons sat on his shoulder or balanced on the tip of his long finger, snatching stale crumbs of flatbread. "Never hurt them," he would say, when one of the filthy birds landed on his head, "or they'll tell their sisters about you."

But nothing is as it should be—no one is allowed such relative peace—especially a tailor like Berman, whose fingers once glided skillfully over silk and lace for the Kirov's best dancers—Zhdanov, Ulanova, Osipenko, and the amazing Makarova. A retired engineer might be able to fall into obscurity, leaving little behind him other than a name on a set of blueprints or instructions—who cares about the bridge he once built or the highway that crumbled after three years?—but a tailor protects the world because he really makes something useful and beautiful out of nothing. This was only common sense.

Simply put, Berman, who out of habit still walked everywhere with one or two straight pins dangling from his mouth, plus a few inches of extra thread and a swatch or two of material attached to his lapel, couldn't refuse to help his neighbors' wives or daughters when they pleaded for a straightened hem or the repair of a blouse. Every morning, someone hiding an embarrassing tear or rip was waiting for him when he came out for his walk. "How long will it take to make an old woman happy, Alexandr Davidowich?" he would hear, as the garment was displayed for his inspection. And one time, a mother and her soon-to-be-married daughter stood beneath his window. The girl's mother was sobbing as she tried to fix an impossible tear along the front of the daughter's wedding dress. "Excuse me for disturbing you," she cried when the tailor appeared with his bag of stale salted flatbread. "But I think my life is over!"

For his help—Berman never asked for money—he was paid in sticky cakes, bags of strong, dark tea, and cigarettes. "Why not?" he always said, removing his glasses. "But please, tell no one else," he begged the women who kept coming to him holding stained and tattered dresses made by the state's industrial machines. "I can't do this forever."

Still, word about a good tailor traveled quickly—"This Jew is a magician," the women gossiped. "He works for the price of a cake!"—and Berman was besieged by requests and rewarded with useless sweets he left outside for the birds, cigarettes that fell apart after two puffs, and, from the grateful mother of the bride, a supply of pungent dried fish he fed to his cat.

"Berman lives here in Pushkin?" the new chief curator at the Catherine Palace asked one of his assistants, recalling how the tailor's insignificant name was always listed on the bottom of innumerable Kirov Ballet programs. "The Alexandr Davidowich Berman from the Kirov? Is he healthy? Can he walk? Would he want to do a little extra work for us?"

"This would be difficult, Vasilly Petrovich," the young man answered.

"And why is that?" the curator, a man of liberal sentiments, asked. "Is he an invalid? Is he senile?"

"No, his health is satisfactory."

"What is it, then? Is he a Zionist with one foot in the Holy Land? Is he a thief?"

The assistant smiled. He looked at his director as if the eminent art historian had been asleep for seventy years of good Soviet rule.

"This Berman is a Jew, Vasilly Petrovich. No doubt about it. If word ever got out to the wrong people that he was working with our royal collection . . . "

The curator rolled his eyes, then he took his assistant's soft hand and patted it.

"Ahah, I see your concern. Berman's a Jew, you say? Tell me, my dutiful friend, do I want him to cut cloth or foreskins?"

"But . . . "

"Find him," the curator ordered in a deep voice. "Bring him to me, Grigori. We must have a decent tailor!"

The next afternoon, Berman, like an expensive piece of pottery, was carefully transported to the palace museum. He was met and embraced under the arch of the Gatchina Gates by the smiling chief curator himself, who quickly took the tailor's hand in his own. "Come closer, Alexandr Davidowich, so I, a lifelong devotee of the ballet, can tell you how much I've admired your stunning work for our country's dancers. Come and do me the great honor of sharing a cigarette with me in the gardens."

Times being what they were, it didn't take Vasilly Petrovich longer than three puffs and a long sigh to make his case. "Everything is going to ruin, Alexandr Davido-wich. Our exhibits are falling apart by the day. The ministry has no money and doesn't give a damn about us. If you only knew what a state we're in! Please, if you could just see fit to spare us some of your time."

No fool despite his age, Berman saw looming ahead in the curator's request the end of what was left of his precious garden time. Unless you're half dead or blind, he thought, they'll never let you be. So he bent over, pleaded the constant pains of his bad back, insomnia, and an embarrassing stomach condition that made it impossible for him to work alongside others without giving offense. He even curled his fingers to feign arthritis.

But the curator flattered, begged, and very gently uncurled the tailor's hand. "We are without dignity," he said, his voice choking. "Everything is turning into dust."

Before Berman had a chance to refuse, Vasilly Petro-

vich appealed to Berman's patriotism and his war record—
"I've made a few inquiries, Alexandr Davidowich. Certain
facts can't be hidden, and I know how you've suffered, my
friend," he said, pointing to the tiny blue numbers he knew
were covered up on the tailor's wrist. "Believe me, I know.
But facts are facts. Your country needs you more than ever.
I feel you can work wonders here, so just listen to my
offer."

The curator offered the tailor a monthly stipend to sup-
plement his pension, as well as easy access to the museum's
special store. "We have good cheese, cigarettes, even stereo
equipment from Germany," he said, lowering his voice.
"And as for your medical problems, I will personally
arrange an appointment with the best internist. No waiting,
I promise. Anything, you see, is possible."

Berman tried to make himself look small.

"I have no needs, Comrade Director," Berman
answered—saying "comrade" because, since he didn't pay
much attention to recent revolutionary developments, he
wasn't sure how to address officials anymore. "Forgive me,
Vasilly Petrovich, but I am retired."

Tears formed in the deep wells of the curator's eyes. He
blew his nose and slumped over, a man on the verge of de-
feat. Berman was about to leave when Vasilly Petrovich,
who had advanced in life because he had always known the
value of a decent bribe or a dramatic gesture at just the right
moment, stepped back a few paces and tore open his suit
jacket as if to free a pounding heart. "But can you leave
these alone, Alexandr Davidowich?" he cried, taking an envelope from his shirt pocket. "Have you no conscience
about anything? Look!"

In this melancholy and despairing mood, the curator

unsealed the envelope and handed Berman some color photographs that showed the ruinous state of the Catherine Palace Museum's renowned collection of royal clothing: silver gowns falling apart at the seams, bejeweled vests with moth holes, satin pantaloons with stitching as thin as cobwebs, silk shawls with jagged runs, and—here the curator, choking back his emotion, had to turn away—a pair of Peter the Great's favorite riding breeches with a gaping hole in the center of that giant Romanov czar's once seamless crotch.

"Such freedom you will have here, Alexandr Davidovich," the curator said. "Your own key and separate workroom. Set your own schedule. A decent supper. Coffee and fresh rolls. Please, there is no one else I can turn to."

Berman smiled. He inhaled the garden's fragrant air while he studied the photographs, the miserable proof of so much criminal neglect. "Ayy!"

"Now you see what we are facing without your intervention. I beg you, Alexandr Davidowich," the curator said, falling to his knees like an old Leningrad babushka at prayer. "Do this for your poor country. Do this for my Russian children. What is a nation without a preserved and living past?"

Berman stared at the photographs and, because it was in his blood, considered the possibilities. He asked for another cigarette, did a little counting on his callused fingers—was there ever a good tailor who didn't figure out everything on his hands?—and made his decision. Then he put his arm around the curator's shoulders.

"But you must let me work alone," he said. "And I get to bring my cat."

"Anything!"

"For three months, Vasilly Petrovich. No longer. Agreed?"

"Done."

"Only three months, yes? Through the winter."

"On my mother's sweet and precious memory, Alexandr Davidowich. Not a second more, I swear it!"

Berman nodded. "Then everything will be better than new," he promised, helping the curator to his feet. "I know my trade."

For the first time in his distinguished life, and without the slightest worry about form or the possibility of being seen by anyone, the curator kissed an old Jew's hand. Then he slapped Berman's back so hard that the tailor spat out his cigarette.

Only a few minutes after agreeing to save Russian culture, Berman, arm in arm with the curator, was rushed across the wide green lawn to the palace and, once through the great parquet hall and a dozen marbled Romanov bed-chambers, through a back wing into his new workroom. "Look, look!" the curator sobbed. "Can you believe it?"

Berman was surrounded by enough timeworn royal garments to provide a lifetime's devotion—so much for a peaceful retirement with the Victrola!—but after he made his initial survey, the tailor's stomach no longer heaved and swayed under the sharp pressure of so much gas, his back was free of pain, and he suddenly forgot about his garden. Say what you will, miracles occur when a tailor who knows what's what spots a sharp pair of German scissors and a well-made prewar Singer sewing machine with three bobbins and a solid, wrought-iron treadle.

The curator stood nervously next to a pile of gowns, lace underclothing, and velvet codpiece covers neglected by generations of his inept and careless predecessors, party hacks and sycophants who knew nothing about the delicate and sublime art of aesthetic preservation. He watched as Berman carefully inspected the clothing, doing a kind of tailor's triage—"useless for now, so-so, can be fixed," he mumbled through a mouthful of pins. Vasilly Petrovich held his breath.

"Is this all you have for me?" Berman asked. "Nothing more?"

The curator nodded.

"Then don't worry, Vasilly Petrovich," he finally said, when one large pile became three. "Just go away and let me work in peace."

"Bless you, Alexander Davidowich," the curator said, as his prize turned away and began to thread the Singer. "Bless your gifted hands!"

But Berman, who had just declared himself an independent country separated from the rest of the world by a border of straight pins and split hems, was soon lost in the repair of a hole, and therefore took no notice of Vasilly Petrovich's bowing exit.

A few minutes later, a euphoric Vasilly Petrovich met his suspicious assistant in the hall. The curator's instructions were clear. "See to it that he gets tea and an afternoon meal—and if you value your career and my support, Grigori, keep my little Jew tailor happy."

Vasilly Petrovich was so overjoyed with capturing Berman for almost nothing that he was already making plans for a traveling exhibit of Berman-refurbished clothing—"The Romanov Adornment from the Age of Peter the Great to Nicholas II," it would be called on the posters—to go to Paris, maybe even London or New York. He saw his future international reputation being created by a Jewish tailor who had once worked, unseen and almost unknown, for one of the world's best ballet companies. "His skill makes the years vanish," he later told his wife, "and I got the old man to accept only three hundred a month!"

Ignoring her approving smile, the curator ordered that a keg of cherry brandy and a kilo of better-grade garlic sausage be immediately delivered to Berman's flat in the village. "To celebrate the return of Alexandr Davidovich to his rightful place," he wrote in a personal note to the tailor. "Here's to the repair of our history!"

Later that evening, with an old Melodia recording of the score of *Giselle* playing on his Victrola, Berman—who had never before seen so much brandy in one container—offered several toasts: to his beloved and still-unnamed cat, to the beautiful ballerina Natalia Makarova—who had once told him that she would be buried in the white swan costume he had made for her—to his soon-to-be-neglected garden, to his mama and papa of distant and blessed memory, to the Greek Jew, to the seamstress Maximova, and to whatever fate gave him a steady hand and the ability to mend a czar's trousers.

Enough said.

3

While the world outside Berman's workroom door was changing—with Armenians being killed by Azerbaijanis, Lithuanians preparing to move into another universe, and a brave soul in the new People's Congress having the chutz-pah to suggest that Lenin be taken out of his marble mausoleum in Red Square and reburied—"as God intended him to be," he said, "next to his mother"—Berman the tailor was too busy to take notice. Instead, he had his new and important work, his cat for company, the ever-grateful cu-rator's daily blessings, the cherry brandy, his portable Vic-trola, and, as luck would soon have it, the adoring company and rapt attention of Yelena Gailova.

Yelena Gailova, a cleaning woman of indeterminate age, was one of fifty or so ancient babushkas who swept and washed the Catherine Palace's parquet floors. Her nose was bulbous, her face sagged on all sides, and her body was a burden she carried from one spot to another with great sighs and moans. "I've been assigned to clean your room, sir," she told Berman a few hours after his arrival at the palace. Balancing herself on wrapped ankles swollen to the size of small green melons in August, Yelena Gailova took her first trembling look at the tailor's delicate hands, and was absolutely certain that the loving Mother of God had sent her a precious gift.

"Here's a hot something for your lunch, sir," she said when she waddled into Berman's workroom, sliding on old felt slippers that made her look like a Neva tugboat finding a dock. "They told me you was to get the day's soup from the bottom of the pot, but I still had to skim the fat off and add a few fresh beets and onions of my own. Good health to you, sir. May the sweet Savior keep you from choking."

Berman was to discover that, despite the Orthodox crucifix that hung from her neck, Yelena Gailova cursed like an Odessa whore, especially at the schoolchildren who tried to rub their snot on a czarina's silk divan or spit into one of the priceless Chinese vases—"I tell 'em I'll take their necks for my supper," she reported to Berman, "and their pricks will soon follow." But she never raised her voice at the Jewish tailor over the messes he left every evening when he went home, and never, miracle of miracles, scratched the ancient sore of Christ's unfortunate demise. Instead, there were only gentle, teasing reprimands as Yelena hovered above the tailor, occasionally brushing her breasts against the busy man's neck or shoulder. "Don't eat so fast, Alexandr Davidowich," she told him when, after he spilled broth over his trousers, she sopped up the mess with her handkerchief. "Your life is too precious."

In the weeks that followed, while most of Russia stood in long lines for invisible margarine or cheese, Berman was overwhelmed by Yelena's generosity and kindness. Gifts of fresh-baked honey bread accompanied his midday meal; gooey marzipan cookies, wrapped in old issues of *Pravda*, were placed on his worktable; the cat received bits of sausage rind. She always brought flowers—Berman knew she picked them from the palace gardens—and set them next to the tailor's sewing machine. "Say my name and it sounds the beginning of a song, Alexander Davidowich. 'Yeee . . . lenna,' " she sang when she delivered his soup or polished his records. " 'Daughter of old Ma . . . ree . . . na and hand . . . some. . . .' " Yelena usually cried before she finished the verse, and Alexandr Davidowich, her sweet gentleman recently delivered to her from God's throne, kissed her chapped hand and clapped.

Even when she was nowhere in sight, Berman sensed her presence. Maybe it was the aroma of sweet almond paste reaching his workroom that warned of her approach, or it might have been the way his cat, kneading his paws against a pile of cotton scraps like a nursing kitten, began purring in anticipation of a treat. Whatever it was, Yelena, her cheeks on fire with cheap rouge, would push open his door, balancing a samovar and some delicate china cups on a silver tray. "Time for tea, Alexandr Davidowich. Time for tea from your Yee . . . lenna. . . ."

"Join me," Berman always said, pointing to a chair next to the Singer. "Please."

"No, no, it gives me bubbles, but with your permission, I'll rest and listen to the music for a few minutes. I promise, not a word will disturb you."

Berman smiled and played his best Melodia recording of *Swan Lake*—the old woman's favorite record, the one she always polished—while Yelena swooned, stroked the cat's one ear, and coughed into a torn handkerchief.

"How's your little Moses?" the other palace babushkas teased Yelena when they saw her trundling down three flights of steps with a borrowed samovar and some antique teacups from one of the storerooms. "Does he let you twist his devil's tail?"

"Screw your mother," Yelena mumbled, without breaking stride or looking back. "And let your brothers stand in line for seconds."

But, truth to tell, what could happen between Yelena Gailova and an old tailor at this stage of their tired lives? Not much, really, except the constants of food, tea, a purring cat, and brief conversations about sewing or the ballet. "Tell me about the fine ladies and dancers in Leningrad," Yelena always asked. "Did they smell like flowers?" If Berman was busy ripping apart some mismatched seams or oiling some hidden gear inside the machine, she told him about the mystery of the Orthodox saints ("You should give them a chance to work for you, Alexandr Davidowich"), the new priest's sermons, or the ikon of St. Stephen she knelt in front of and kissed every freezing morning in the village church. But she never said anything about her past or her losses. Berman suspected a husband, taken away during the fifties; if there were children, he was afraid to ask. And she never complained about her labored breathing or coughing, which he suspected might be the result of her once having had to live in the East. To Yelena Gailova, who always kept one callused hand on her precious crucifix, the world now rolled by on tiny wheels of personal concern for her tailor's simple needs and incredible accomplishments—anything else, it seemed, was beyond possibility.

"Ah, I see your fingers are getting pricked," she would say. "Use some of this honey cream I've made for you." Or, after adjusting the lamp above his sewing machine: "You must not work under such a strong light, Alexander Davidowich. You want to strain yourself?" Or the question Berman never responded to: "What kind of a Jew are you, Alexandr Davidowich? Do you ever pray?" Or, when she saw Berman skillfully work a string of tiny pearls into the sleeve of a czarevich's sailor suit: "Ahhh!"

On the morning after All Souls Day, however, Yelena angrily spat on the floor and threw her newspaper across the room. Unlike this tailor, who always made something beautiful out of nothing because little else mattered, she, with both feet on the ground of life's more obvious agonies, had to say a few words about the world beyond his work-room—where "nothing comes from nothing."

"I know what the life here is, Alexandr Davidowich. Those new bastards in Moscow are the same as all the oth-ers. Thieving bedbugs living off our bodies, that's all. Give me a small taste of that brandy of yours and let me tell you what I think about 'em!"

Which was exactly what she did, day after day, soup after soup, well into Berman's first winter at the palace—the promised three months soon became four, but Berman lost count—well past the time the tailor completely over-hauled the sky-blue cavalry uniform of one of Catherine the Great's young lovers—"that hussy must have loved to wrap her legs around this thin boy," Yelena speculated, in-specting the finished work like an envious laundry char—and the czarina's four silk nightgowns, each one dotted by a ring of tiny bloodstains that made the old woman blush for the tailor's sake. Berman smiled and sewed, and he always saved the royals' scraps beneath his worktable for Yelena Gailova, who promised to sew all of them together into a warm sleeping cushion for the cat.

But one freezing, snow-heavy February afternoon, when Yelena nervously reported how Mikhail Sergeyevich, sitting on a Kremlin dais above the rest of Russia, heard his foreign minister—"the honest Georgian with the beautiful hair like a white cloud," as she described him—tell the Soviet world that Stalin's heirs were in good health and planning terrible things—for the first time, Berman began to stare at Yelena's body and pay little attention to her words. Like a leering beer house drunk, he took in every inch of her hips and breasts, carefully sizing the various details of her bulk. "Stay, stay," he pleaded when she told him she still had two floors left to scrub and polish. "Make more tea."

Over the next few days, Berman asked for dozens of marzipan cookies and forced down a river of Yelena's dark tea—anything to keep her sitting in his workroom. He pretended to work on a satin robe, but actually kept his eye on his real work: memorizing the details of her heavy breasts and the probable dimensions of her buttocks and hips. Although his tortured bladder became a bayonet pushing against his side, he never left his chair or took his eyes off Yelena Gailova. "Let me see you in the light," he said. "Hold still." "Ahh," Yelena cooed when she saw how he concentrated on this important and promising work. "Ahh."

It didn't take a gypsy to unravel the tailor's plans. With all of his staring at breasts and hips, Yelena knew that, in the view he enjoyed between three large bobbins atop the Singer, Alexandr Davidowich, now her "Sasha," was mentally rubbing against her as no man had since the summer of 1952. "Thank you, Mother of God," she muttered when the tailor, swaying like a bloated drunk, had to find a toilet. "I bless your belated gift!"

In the ten minutes it took Berman to relieve himself of so much tea, Yelena pushed her thinning hair back into place beneath her scarf. She smoothed her wrinkled dress and willed herself not to cough or lose her erotic position. Since Berman was interested in her chest, she tightened her undershirt—Yelena had long ago given up on anything fancier—and held her breath to keep her breasts from sagging too far below her waist. And for the sweet good luck that had apparently brought her this far into the tailor's heart and brain, she milked the fragrant oil from a fat marzipan cookie and, like any woman who knows the power of a good smell, daubed the sticky almond oil around her neck and ears. She also undid the top two buttons of her dress. This tailor was finally hers, she told herself. No doubt about it. She even kissed Berman's cat.

When she finally heard his footsteps, Yelena sat up as straight as the excited cat's quivering tail. She slapped her cheeks to raise a bit more color and sucked in her breath to make her chest rise a good three inches. She hoped he could smell the marzipan and sense what the future might be like. "I'll let our little Sasha offer himself," she whispered to the cat. "A man needs to make the first move toward the sheets. It's Yee . . . lee . . . na," she giggled when the tailor returned. "Daughter of old. . . ."

Before she had a chance to finish her song or deflate her sorely tried lungs, Berman lunged at the sewing machine like a madman grabbing for a young girl in a back alley. He completely ignored Yelena's scent and posture. She blew out the air that couldn't be held in any longer. She felt her breasts, and her heart, sink toward her knees.

"I need some time for myself," Berman said coldly, as if nothing else mattered. Impossible as it may be to believe, he ignored the trap set by the almond perfume and a body painfully held together by force of will. He told her to leave. "And no more tea, please."

You must understand what poor Yelena was feeling! Thrown out without a nod or a word of explanation, her dreams of waking up next to the tailor beneath her heavy down comforter little more than a worthless memory. No matter what she said or promised in the way of more sweet cakes or dark tea—"They'll taste like heaven itself, Sasha"— he rejected her pleas with a curt hand wave, though he eventually looked up from his worktable to bid her a belated "healthy day." Then, without so much as a glance, he locked the door and began pushing hard against the Singer's treadle.

In the two or three weeks that followed her forced exile from the tailor's world, the old woman, scorned, became a tyrant with anyone she met. She kicked at her wash bucket when the guides were trying to explain the wonders of the palace to tourists. She yelled at the other maids, cursing their families and their worthless menfolk's undersized virility. She was careless about washing herself. She didn't change her socks or underwear. "Move aside, you little slut," she screamed at any woman under the age of sixty who stood next to a man. "Aren't you ashamed!"

Yelena became desperate. No matter what the weather, she went outside to catch a glimpse of Berman. Coatless in the freezing air, she scratched her legs climbing over thorny hedges to get close to his workroom window. But aside from the muffled music and shaft of yellow light that penetrated the Chinese screen in front of his window, Berman was little more than a shadow hunched over a prewar Singer. He was there and not there. And this was when Yelena Gailova's weight began to drop faster than the doctor had told her it would, when she began coughing up thick, dark globs, and when her hair, falling out in clumps from the drugs she took, was picked at by ravens, which then discarded the stuff as too coarse for a good nest.

Berman, however, only thought about his unfinished project. Work, as always, was everything, and his attention to details erased time. Without the benefit of Yelena's presence, he deferred to memory and the crude sketches he had drawn of her form and entered in his journal. "A woman needs warmth," he said to the cat, running his hands up and down the pencil lines of Yelena's thighs. "Nothing should be left to chance or later alteration."

Setting aside the royal capes of some minor prince, Berman worked on his surprise gift for Yelena, until his eyes ached and his spectacles felt like small iron weights cutting into the bridge of his nose. With all the skill that once made grateful dancers send him flowers and imported cigarettes, the tailor carefully sewed together several pieces of silk he'd removed from the undergarment of some long-deceased Romanov. He used a special needle, thin as a horsehair, to embroider with alternating blue and silver thread the outline of a saint's face. Then he filled in the space with red and brown threads that turned the saint into a true likeness of the sepia-colored ikon of St. Stephen that Yelena always described. With some rich thread taken from an unknown naval officer's uniform, Berman set a golden halo above the saint's innocent head. For a final touch, he even cut off one of his cat's whiskers and used it to create the embroidered saint's eyelashes. "Good, good, good," he said when he was just a few eyelashes short of the saint's completed image. "She will never forget this. It will be something to see."

Berman put the final eyelash in its proper saintly place sometime after midnight. He was badly in need of a bath and a shave, but he was too tired to walk home at this hour, shlepping a snoring cat in a box. Since it was so late and his legs were stiff, he folded his good wool coat along the length of his cutting table to make a bedroll. He spat out the remaining pins and stacked several records on the Victrola's changer—Shostakovich, Bach, Mozart—and a certain clarinet recording, a bittersweet lament by the great, long-dead Hasidic musician Fishbein. Music in his ears, he quickly fell into a dead sleep and never felt the cat gently knead and suck on the material of his trousers.

Just before dawn, with the wind yowling like a beaten dog, Berman was startled awake by some loud gagging noises in the corridor. The cat hissed and moaned, and its tail grew to twice normal size. Frightened when the noise became louder, the animal dug its claws into Berman's thighs and jumped, hissing, into a corner. "Shit," a wounded Berman yelled. "Shit!"

In anticipation of the worst—thieves, a fire—the tailor grabbed a pair of long scissors. Shivering from the draft and his fear of whatever it was that made such an awful noise, he threw a satin dress over his shoulders and waited by the door. The fear he felt running through his body was like a hammer pounding at his tense muscles. He kept a very weak hand on the latch.

When a foul smell made its way under the door and grabbed onto his nose, Berman yanked the old copper latch before he fell against a rack filled with gowns and lace slips. "Who is it? Who is it?" he yelled, wrapped like a mummy. "I . . . I . . . have a weapon!"

In a square of purple morning light, her head hanging over a metal pail, was Yelena—sprawled on the floor, her legs buckled in a growing island of vomit. Berman's nose sent the message to his brain and he, too, gagged. Then he threw off the dress and crawled next to her.

"What?" he managed to say. "What's happened?"

Yelena, whose body shrank with every dry heave, weakly pushed him away. She couldn't stop shivering. Her crucifix stuck to a chest that had retreated inward. The scarf on her head had fallen off. Most of her hair was gone.

"Zher's a ringing in my ears, Zhandr Vidvish," she lisped. "The medishun waz too strong."

"Shh," he answered. "Shh."

He used the end of the satin dress to wipe her lips and forehead. He opened her mouth so she could breathe, then put his mouth over hers and blew in some air. She spat up over both of them. He covered her with the once-lovely gown and lowered her bald head onto his lap. He was afraid to move.

"Shh."

It was the assistant curator who found the old Jew next to the babushka in the rank hallway, and it was he who called the ambulance. It took two attendants several minutes to pry Berman from Yelena's shaking body. "Get a blanket, Valeri," one of the men yelled at the other. "This is the one who was in for the chemo today." "Damned if I care," said the other attendant, still reeling from the home-made vodka he'd drunk on the way over. "All I know is that I'm freezing my balls off out here."

Alexandr Davidowich ran back to his workroom and grabbed the best covering he could—the white-and-gold nightgown adorned with an ikon, his perfect replica of a czarina's French import, his belated gift to repay so much of Yelena's kindness. The old woman opened her eyes when she felt the silk rub against her face. She clutched the hand of the tailor, who walked alongside the stretcher. Before she could speak, she coughed up another dark mass of phlegm.

"Zhasha."

The tailor bent next to Yelena's face. He tucked the nightgown under her chin until the embroidered saint's head cushioned her throat. Yelena's eyes followed his hands. Berman slowly wrapped her fingers around her precious crucifix.

Yelena Gailova pointed to her mouth, which Berman wiped with his hand. "Zhander Vidovish," she said, rising a bit on the canvas stretcher so only he could hear.

"Let's go," one of the attendants yelled when the ambulance door finally opened. "Now!"

Berman tried to crawl in back with Yelena, but he was blocked by the drunken attendant. "Piss off, old man!" he yelled. "Find another ride." Berman patted Yelena's head and said he would find some other way to be with her. Just as he was backing away, Yelena yanked on his sleeve.

"Zhasha, Zhasha, you have to tell me," she said, pulling the tailor toward her. "Please, are you the kind of Jew who could say a Kaddish for me?"

4

Within two weeks, Yelena Gailova had shrunk to the size of a large doll that shuddered and occasionally moaned. Her breathing drifted away, and her eyes, now little more than dark sockets, were usually closed. It was understood by everyone in the ward that her bed would soon be available for someone else. "They go quickly at this stage," the nurse told Berman. "Even your little princess here in her fancy silk gown."

But the tailor—her sole visitor during the time it took Yelena Gailova to vanish—was always with her. The small packets of coffee he gave the nurse assured him a few extra evening hours by Yelena's bedside, and a three-hundred-ruble bribe to the clinic pharmacist bought a bit more morphine than was generally given to hopeless patients like Yelena. And even with the other ward visitors watching him and holding their noses, Alexandr Davidowich was never ashamed to empty her bedpan or massage her thin legs, or, no matter who listened and laughed, to sing: "Yee . . . lee . . . na, daughter of old Ma . . . ree . . . na and hand . . . some. . . ."

"There won't be any surprises with this one," a young medical student told Berman. "Just moisten her lips and keep her warm. She understands nothing now."

This advice marked, Berman knew, the end of any

further clinical care. Still, to hide the awful noise in the crowded ward, in which young mothers in labor were only a few meters away from poor Yelena Gailova, he continued to sing and, from time to time when she stirred or her fingers began moving, put his mouth next to Yelena's ears so she could hear him promise a final ceremony—he never mentioned a Kaddish—with "some flowers and the music from the Victrola." He also said that he would arrange everything with the village priest. "I swear this to you," he said. "Everything will be the best."

Twelve hours before she died, Yelena Gailova suddenly opened her eyes in the middle of the night. Her back stiffened and she straightened her legs. She fluttered like a spring insect in a cocoon. "Lift me up," Yelena cried to the surprised nurse, in a remarkably clear voice. "It's worth a lot of money if you do what I say." The nurse, who was always frightened whenever the nearly dead made a sudden reappearance on this earth, shrieked and fell to her knees.

But the promise of extra rubles—"maybe even a little gold when my Sasha comes"—worked a miracle of care for what was left of Yelena. The nurse, who now ignored the other complaining patients in the ward, propped Yelena up and combed the old crone's matted hair. "Put some nice red color on my lips and some blue under my eyes," Yelena ordered. "Do you have any marzipan around?"

Having stood for hours on the only available bus to the suburban Leningrad clinic where the village physician had sent Yelena to die, Berman was numb and out of breath when he arrived at the hospital. He slowly made his way up three flights of stairs that smelled like disinfectant, sour cabbage, and stale cigarette smoke. The closer he got to Yelena's floor, the more he dreaded tumbling into a dim hole.

He tried to hum the song, but his throat was blocked as soon as he stepped into the ward.

When Berman saw Yelena in a corner of the ward, propped up against a pillow, her eyes were clear and bright, like bits of jade with small candles in front of them, her mouth was smeared over with cheap pink lipstick, and her cheeks were as rose red as a Moscow Circus clown's. The nurse had had the wit to cover the old woman's bald head with a clean scarf, over which she dribbled a few drops of her own perfume.

"Sasha!"

As soon as he saw her, the tailor lost his breath. She'll get over this, he thought when he saw her sitting up. Maybe a miracle? A belated gift from her beloved St. Stephen?

Berman ran to her bed, stumbled, and fell against an iron railing. Someone cursed his life for making so much noise. "You stupid old shit!"

Berman ignored the moans coming from either side of the floor, where two veterans from the Afghan war, both young enough to be the grandsons he never had, struggled with their ill-fitting restraints and artificial limbs. For Alexandr Davidowich, however, there was no one else but Yelena—Yelena who had come back to life!

Yelena watched the tailor limp closer and fall into the chair by her bed. He was sweating so much that the front of his cap was soaked. She stroked his shaking hand until he calmed down.

"Listen to me, Sasha."

He bent low enough to hear what he knew must be some message about her startling overnight redemption— "They've given me a new drug, Sasha. Look at my color, already I'm stronger," or even a miraculous laying on of hands by some wonder-working priest—but the syllable-by-syllable rasp that came out in waves of rancid breath brought him back to a present that offered no recovery, and never would. "Don't worry about the priest and the old women," she said. "Bury me with a Kaddish, Sasha. Wear a Jew's prayer shawl and don't forget to cover your head."

Yelena was soon out of breath and fell back onto her pillow. Berman's back began to ache. His head was pounding, his chest on fire.

Before he could tell her to rest, Yelena sucked in a little more air and managed a half smile. Then she pulled his sleeve. She pointed to her mouth. Another request. "Listen, Sasha, I've got an ending for you. "Yee . . . lee . . . na," she sang, cupping her hands over the old man's ears, "daughter of old Ma . . . ree . . . na and hand . . . some. . . ."

"I know, I know," Berman answered.

" . . . and handsome Yitzhok!"

Yelena squeezed Berman's hand.

"Now you have to say Kaddish for me. Say the prayer. I think I have a Jewish soul. I know I had a Jewish father."

Job done, she sank back into her rough linen pillow. She belched and closed her eyes.

Berman groaned and cursed. He staggered to the window and looked outside. An early spring snow began to drift over the broken concrete in the hospital courtyard, covering the dustbins and mounds of refuse. A few patients were frantically calling for absent attendants to wheel them back inside. Berman couldn't believe what he had just heard—such information was too much to understand—and so he smoked to quiet his nerves. "Yitzhok," he kept mumbling. "She came from a Yitzhok!" What could he now say to this old woman who weighed less than a child, whose lungs had turned into tissue paper covered by a black grime? What could an old man like Berman do for the sake of some recently announced Jewish father? A Kaddish for Yelena Gailova who never knew that a claim for the old faith came only through a mother's milk? A Kaddish for a woman with an embroidered silk ikon over her breast?

Berman returned to her bedside. He smoothed over her wrinkled gown and covered her with his own long coat. He pulled the blanket up to her chin. He was certain she was sleeping and wouldn't understand anything.

"When the time comes, I'll take you to a quiet place and bring the Victrola," he whispered. "I'll wait until the priest finishes his work and talks all about your lovely saint, then, after he leaves, we'll hear some real music . . . maybe something from *Giselle*. And flowers, Yelena. No matter what time of year, plenty of beautiful flowers that I'll pick myself from the palace gardens."

With these words riding on his shoulders like a ghost, Berman, cursing his cowardice, said, "But no Kaddish, please." Yelena, floating back from somewhere, maybe at the mention of some word or other, caught his sleeve and coughed. Berman wiped her mouth. Then, because he was such an idiot and never said the right thing, she opened her eyes, shook her tiny gnarled fist at him, and pulled off her head-covering.

"No! Do you hear me. No! There's no one else, Sasha. You're the only one left. Promise you'll do this one blessed favor for me, or I swear I'll come back as a summer gnat and burrow into your brain forever and never stop talking!"

The tailor felt Yelena's pulse race. She was now panting, and her dry tongue lay on one side of her sunken cheek. This had been too much for her. Yet she never stopped staring at Berman-who-said-such-stupid-things. There was only one way out of this nonsense. "How can I say such a prayer without nine other Jews?" he said—he dared not mention that poor old Yitzhok couldn't do much to make Yelena a sudden Jew. "It wouldn't be right. It's not permitted. Why take a chance on insulting the sky?" he said, pointing upward (Berman couldn't bring himself to say "heaven" or "God"). "It's the sacred law."

Yelena swayed as if she'd just been struck across the face. She pulled off her blanket and clawed at her stubbly scalp. Berman thought he'd won. The law did it. He was saved. A victory for music and flowers. When he heard the nurse snicker, he put his hat on Yelena's head.

"So stand in ten different places!" she shouted, turning on her side, causing the other visitors in the room to stare. "You think our Lord on high cares? If he can raise a bleeding Christ from the dead, he can tolerate ten chanting Bermans!"

"But what about the flowers? The music? They're much better than any prayer."

The daughter of Yitzhok closed her eyes and shook her head. She breathed deeply. Berman knew she never heard his last offer until another small explosion of bad air swept across his face. She crossed herself.

"Fuck the flowers and the music, Alexandr Davidowich," she said, after a third loud belch. "Say this Kaddish for me or the gnats will come into your head. Swear it!"

Berman nodded.

"Swear!"

Berman swore on what was left of his own life.

"And don't forget to cover your head," Yelena cried. "Like my father who was. . . ."

"Shh. A promise is a promise," Berman interrupted. Then he began to sing, putting Yitzhok's name in its proper place.

Two hours later, just after Yelena Gailova, her head now buried within his coat, puffed out her last breath, Berman fell on the floor. Cursing like a madman who has suddenly been forced to leave the safety of his attic, he began to wrestle with the air—maybe he saw demons?—because, as you know, he'd just promised to be a public Jew again, a one-man minyan, available to say Kaddish.

5

If a good tailor is given a job, and the fee is sufficient (it might even be a promise), he works without stopping. A czar's pantaloons, a czarevich's sailor suit, a czarina's coronation gown, a silk nightgown for a maid, even a Jew's tallith—all require his attention and devotion. A good tailor, they say, works to ensure a tight stitch that will last forever. Nothing less.

And so Alexandr Davidowich Berman, whose sides and back were still aching from his tumble to the hospital floor during his cosmic battle with some gnats, returned to Pushkin and made—he didn't need a pattern—a tallith. For twenty hours he cut, sewed, and embroidered, leaving his chair only to drink tea and smoke. He also remembered to attach the ritual knotted fringes to each of the shawl's corners. "Just as she wished," he told the cat, now thin from lack of sausage rind and attention. "A tailor's word is worth more than gold."

It was just after five in the morning when Berman, tallith tucked under his heavy coat, began to rehearse, imagining the scene at the village cemetery. He cleared a space in his sitting room and concentrated on the required steps. Move this way, slide a little that way, he thought as he marked places for himself on the floor with pieces of bread, just as he'd once seen so many Kirov choreographers do for the nervous young dancers. First measuring space in his journal, then moving to the floor, Berman envisioned the scene: The priest will stand there; Berman the idiot-who-should-know-better will be here, tallith tucked under his shirt, mumbling in quick-time Hebrew behind the old women hired to mourn for the partly Christian soul of Yelena Gailova. He rehearsed his five hops to the left, the remainder to the right. With each hop a Kaddish would follow. His shuffling practice made him certain that, once the priest's incense cleared and the babushkas' wailing stopped, Yelena's gnats would vanish and, as promised, she would be well on her way to somewhere, armed with all of the blessings of the western world.

Then he felt his bare head and slapped his face.

"Ahhh."

Once again, he practiced what had to be done, keeping a careful prayer count—but this time, head covered by his best winter hat, he did his ten moves to the accompaniment of a beautiful Borodin concerto.

The next day, tallith safely hidden beneath his coat, the well-rehearsed words of the quick-Kaddish hardly making his lips move, each mourner's actions committed to memory, the ten Bermans waited in the village church while Yelena's remains were attended to by the priest. He leaned against a pillar and watched the babushkas circle around Yelena's shrunken corpse like blackbirds. One of the old women led the others in singing by raising and lowering her hand to mark the high and low notes, while the priest kissed a small ikon he held over the open coffin.

"Please, I'm not well," Berman said when they stared at him. "A little air will help." So he left them to their ceremony and went outdoors.

Neither the wind nor the cold bothered him when he walked into the old cemetery next to the church. He found Yelena's freshly dug grave, still smelling from the fire that had to be burned above it to thaw the earth. He was too nervous to smoke, so he walked around in circles like an idiot.

With no one to confide in, Berman spoke to himself. "Here, fool, this is a good place," he said, spotting the merciful cover of some low-hanging branches just behind Yelena's mound of black dirt and pebbles. "You turn this way and then. . . ."

A wobbly figure wearing an enormous fur hat and filthy trousers emerged from the caretaker's shed outside the cemetery fence. A few meters before Berman recognized the gravedigger, Kolokhov, he smelled the vodka fumes that preceded the caretaker's arrival like a bad omen. Berman waved—"Be careful, Sasha," Yelena would have said, "take your time"—but he was ignored. "Nothing comes out of this shit job," Kolokhov said to Berman, suspiciously eyeing the old Jew who wore such a nice long coat. "How much you think an honest man makes these days digging holes and freezing his prick off?"

Berman shrugged. He tossed Kolokhov two packages of smokes and a box of matches. "They won't be here for a few minutes, brother," Berman said. "Here, comrade, take these and step out of the wind."

"Comrade my ass, just don't take too long with this business," Kolokhov whined as he fondled the packages and considered how he could scare some more fags away from the old man. Order given, the gravedigger pulled himself back along the fence to his shed and his vodka.

Despite the cold, Berman began to perspire after he calculated that ten moves could be made within inches of one another. As for what it would look like if the priest saw him swaying, he knew nothing would come of it. This is how we are, he told himself. Old men move like this. Like half-dead birds.

After so many years of avoiding any prayers—Alexandr Davidovich hadn't been in a synagogue since he was a boy—and with only a few years left before Kolokhov would have to dig another hole, for him—he, Berman, who should have known better, was about to do something absolutely stupid for the sake of a decently kind woman who, in a moment of pain, promised a curse of gnats or some such on his head. His wobbly legs bowed like rubber sticks, while his spectacles, fogged over by his hard breathing, slid down his wet nose and fell into the dirt.

In the shed, safe within a haze of blue smoke from the Jew's imported cigarettes, Kolokhov tore off a piece of stale, dark bread and quickly washed it down with a drink of homemade pepper vodka. He wiped his greasy hand across a small window and watched Berman shuffling and talking to himself. He suspected that the old Yid must be planning to steal one of the ceramic photos of the dead or maybe a small iron cross attached to a grave marker. Look how he points to the ground and counts. But what did he care? He already had the bastard's expensive smokes, so let him grab whatever he wants until he croaks.

If a medieval Italian astronomer could have transformed everything taking place around Alexandr Davidowich into a map of the heavens, here is what he would have included: a young Orthodox priest, silver-and-gold vestments trailing behind him, would become a planet making a slow and deliberate revolution toward the bright sun of Yelena Gailova's grave, while a few old babushkas, dark, misshapen, and insignificant moons, would revolve around this fearful priest-planet, unwilling to get too close; and Berman the tailor, the colors of his own handmade tallith tucked in a black corner of space, would be a blazing comet from some strange and unknown place that requires a dark hat.

And so it was to be—so this odd universe appeared—as soon as the simple pine coffin, carried by four pallbearers hired by Berman, arrived. The universe now had its center, and, within minutes, its planet and moons. Comet Berman, working his hands under his coat as he backed away behind the branches, waited until everything was in place. "Ten times," he mumbled. "Only ten."

The priest, shivering within his layering of vestments and sweaters, began chanting even before the coffin rested on the crude wooden supports across the grave. He swung the polished gold censer in a wide arc over the coffin until the incense wafted back into his face and hovered just below his thick beard. Berman heard names with every swing of the beautiful censer: Christ's, Yelena's, the blessed St. Stephen's, her parents'—Yelena had lied to the priest about Yitzhok, who, may he rest in peace, had become the good and faithful Russian, Leonid. The priest bowed in several directions; the babushkas wailed in turn and crossed themselves at the mention of every holy word. "He is with her, always," one cried. "The saints abide in the precious blood," the others answered. The priest raised the Orthodox cross over everyone present. He brought his hands together and lifted the cross toward the sky. Then he closed his eyes and dropped his chin into the full beard, which would have been the pride of any good Hasid.

The babushkas huddled together against the wind and moved closer to the priest. Their discomfort, spiritual and earthly, was almost over. "It's time to send her to her reward," the priest told the pallbearers. "But try to do it right this time."

Slowly and without skill, unable to arrange the rope in the correct spots beneath the coffin, the pallbearers stumbled and twice dropped the coffin. They finally managed to lower one end, then the other, into the unevenly dug hole. The priest shook his head and made the sign of the cross over the men, one of whom nearly fell backward. Each one of the babushkas dropped a handful of dirt on top of the coffin. "To Christ, in all things," the priest said, keeping one eye on the clumsy pallbearers. "In all things, to Christ."

Vey iz mir, thought Berman, feeling the prayer shawl's fringes burning into his sides. I can't do this.

But the tailor's feet and hands, long experienced in defying common sense, acted on their own. After all, a comet is always in motion toward its own end. Besides, nothing comes easily or works well when a soul is involved. And this is when Berman began to move, far more than he had ever rehearsed or thought possible on those bread markers in the safety of his own room.

At first, the babushkas thought he was cold, so they took no notice of his mumbling and the way he kept bumping into the branches and tripping over some stones. What was this old man to them, especially one who staggered to the left and right like a common drunkard? Father Pavel will chastise him later, they thought. Look how this old man acts like a pig running in all directions!

The required wailing grew louder as the service was about to end. One of the old women tore at her breast and pounded on her chest.

Berman saw what was happening. He wiped his forehead, took a deep breath, and, even though he had not planned it this way, somewhere before the seventh Kaddish, he finally remembered to pull a beautiful scarf over his head until its silver fringe—made from as fine a fabric as the priest's ornate vestment—hung over his woolly eyebrows like thin icicles.

First, the tailor closed his eyes. Next, because he knew he was so stupid and there was now nowhere else to go, he said, "Vey iz mir." Then, with his tongue as rough as a piece of heavy leather, he began the eighth Kaddish, the words of which, extolling God's blessings, blended in with the priest's chanting.

"Yitgadel, veyit kadash," Berman began, forgetting to make his voice a low murmur, "shemai raba. . . ."

The babushkas hushed and backed away from Berman. The pallbearers laughed and poked one another. The priest's censer came to full stop against his robe. Kolokhov, watching this commotion, came out of his warm shed to witness something he'd never seen before at the burial rites of old believers or repentant party members.

"He looked like a roach chasing crumbs around a table," Kolokhov would later tell his friends. "Ask any of the boys who was there. This old Yid does this 'uzza, uzza, uzza' shit of his. He thinks he was real quiet with it, but I knew what he was doin' cause I seen him practicin' before the priest got there. Then, somethin' happens . . . he starts movin' more after he wraps himself in a fancy Arab towel. Hoppin' he was. Just like a roach, I swear it. He moves one way, does the 'uzza, uzza, uzza' stuff, then goes a few paces to the side. The more he moves, the more he scares the others. He wouldn't stop. When the priest finally figures it out and holds the cross over the Jew, the old Yid yells out 'Ten,' real loud, and falls back into the snow with this towel pasted over his big nose."

True, all true. The many Bermans did get a little excited. Who knows? Maybe he was battling against those buzzing gnats and they got the better of him? Maybe the tallith with the silver fringe clouded his senses as well as his eyes? Maybe he was looking for bread crumbs in the snow? Maybe he did believe Yelena Gailova's threats—or maybe he just kept a promise, because what else is there to believe in on this earth but promised words? Eleven times he said Kaddish—he lost count at the end—and after the final one he fell into the snow, just as the gravedigger said, looking as worn out as the old babushkas and the horrified priest.

"Others will hear about this," said the priest, now as red faced as a raw sausage. "You should be ashamed."

Berman struggled to get his feet working again. He finally righted himself and found his spectacles. He felt he'd gained a year, and as many pains, for every Kaddish he had recited. His back hurt, his boots leaked, and the tallith was pasted against his sweaty forehead like a strip of mismatched wallpaper. All he could think about was a smoke and a little peace.

"A hundred apologies, Father," Berman said. "I didn't think you'd notice."

Father Pavel held the cross in front of Berman. "Desecration cannot be forgiven in God's world!" the priest yelled when Berman started to walk away. He pointed a trembling finger at the grave. Frothy spittle stuck to his beard. "Was . . . was . . . was this one a Jewess?"

Berman was either too tired or too nervous to remove the tallith before he answered. What's done is done, he thought. Everything comes to an end. After all of this, what could happen now?

"Truth to tell, Father," Alexandr Davidowich Berman said through the curtain of holy fringe draped over his blue lips, "she was and she wasn't. No offense, but I personally would have preferred a little music and some nice flowers."

Later that night, not too long after Yelena Gailova, peace be with her, was offered the comfort of several prayers, Berman was still wrapped in his stained tallith. Guarded by a skinny cat, Berman-the-defiler drank, wept, cursed his aching back, and batted at the air behind him. "It's you, Gelbat, isn't it?" he yelled as if the Hasid himself were weighing him down, his weak legs jabbed into Berman's ribs. "Gelbat!"

"So you weren't such a goy after all, comrade," a hollow, distant voice answered in bad Russian. "Is it such a crime to do a good deed when there's no one else left?"

Reaching for his back, Berman tripped over his howling cat, cursed, threw up some cherry brandy, and counted his days.

"Gelbat!" he yelled, when he could manage a sound through a clogged throat. "Gelbat!"

6

In the blessed spring of 1945, only a few days after his liberation from a camp in Germany, Alexandr Davidowich Berman, a Red Army prisoner of war, refused to let a skinny, typhus-ridden Polish Hasid be mistaken for dead and left to the spiked open mouth of a British bulldozer.

They say it was very hot that day in April, and the stench from the camp, which kept even the birds away, made everyone retch. An order had been issued by the pale British medical officers whose faces were covered by army issue handkerchiefs: corpses had to be buried before the infections they contained spread throughout the rest of the continent. But after two years in a number of camps, prisoner Berman knew how to survive the odor of the dead and the nearly dead.

Still, Berman wasn't feeling well himself. His stomach burned, and he had trouble holding down the many tins of British army pork he'd eaten on his third exhilarating day of freedom. To calm his nausea, he collapsed on a lumpy pile of discarded SS uniforms, near an electrified wire fence, to smoke his first whole cigarette since 1943. The smoke, which he inhaled in huge gulps, made him feel dizzy and secure. He lay down across the musty-smelling jackets and trousers, unaware of the lump that began to move beneath his hips.

As the Polish Hasid, Leo Gelbat, promised to repeat to the end of his numbered days, the sharp pain that was about to strike Berman was a blessing from the Master of the Universe—for who else but He Who Made Everything could, for only a few seconds, turn the unseen lump beneath an *Unterscharfuhrer*'s coat that was Leo Gelbat into a rat that bit hard into Alexandr Davidowich's bony and pockmarked rump.

When the rat found its mark with a chomp that tore away a tiny bit of Berman's loose flesh, the former tailor from Leningrad yelled, jumped up, and lost his holy cigarette. He kicked and swore at the pest, only to smack, instead, the side of Leo Gelbat's now partially visible head. Covered by the foul uniforms, gasping for a little air, Leo rose to the surface like a red bubble. His nose was bloodied, and only a few black teeth dangled from his rotten gums. The remains of Berman's cigarette smoldered next to the Hasid's hollow cheek.

Although he probably didn't realize he was part of some unfolding scheme to save a Polish Hasid in the dead heart of Europe, a British private, who had just been ordered to push everything that didn't move into a huge, freshly dug grave, drove his bulldozer straight toward the same offensive hill of lousy uniforms where Alexandr Davidowich was frantically extracting the rest of a dazed and weeping Leo Gelbat. To be fair, with all of the smoke, and with fumes from his powerful machine rising on both sides of his face, the British soldier, his mouth covered by a strip of canvas, couldn't possibly have noticed a half-dead Russian Jew trying to free a bloody head and torso from a pile of the devil's waste.

How Berman managed the strength to do what he did

next is, given the circumstances, beyond logical explana-tion, but only a moment before the bulldozer's shovel ar-rived, Berman grabbed what was left of the Hasid's scrawny neck. "Up, you bastard," he cursed, and tossed Leo Gelbat's seventy or so pounds into an abandoned wheelbarrow filled with smelly chicken feathers, a timely gift that gave Leo Gelbat another few minutes to enjoy God's world.

Even with greasy feathers pasted over his eyes and lips, a rush of fetid air still found its way into Leo Gelbat's mouth. He sucked in the air, now mixed with the bull-dozer's exhaust, removed the film from his better eye, and finally recognized his savior, this Russian Jew who always kept to himself and never prayed, even on the holiest of days. "Leave me be," he croaked in Yiddish. "Enough!"

"*There* is better?" Berman yelled, pointing the lopsided barrow and its whining passenger toward the clouds of lime dust hovering over the open grave. "You want to be lying with them?"

"Let me out, goy!" Gelbat cried. "For this ride I'd rather be dead."

But Gelbat, once the strongest boy in his yeshiva, was now draped like a filthy dishrag over the side of the barrow, in no position to escape from this Bolshevik pig. With his legs as weak as twigs, all he could do was pray that Berman had enough of a Jewish soul left not to let him suffer too long. So he took in a bit more air and repeated his last demand.

"For this ride, Comrade Goy, I'd rather be dead."

"For this ride," Berman answered, wincing at the bite on his sore ass as he pushed the barrow next to the electri-fied wire, "you'll have to shut up."

* * *

Even after ten kilometers, the odor of decomposing animals and garbage hung over the two Jews like a used shroud. The roads leading away from the camp were clogged with hundreds of refugees and liberated prisoners blubbering requests in a dozen languages, but no one ever offered the Jew pushing a barrow a ride on a cart or truck.

Helpless to be rid of this Russian who had suddenly decided to leave all graves to the British, Leo Gelbat had no idea he was being pushed in the general direction of the Red Army's occupation line in Poland. He sank into his cockpit of feathers, and, though he couldn't stop shitting, he still managed enough strength to irritate Berman by weakly singing a few psalms. But when the flies began to stick to his face and dance in place on his forehead, he begged Berman to bathe him in a clear stream of cold water. Sick as he was, who was Leo Gelbat to celebrate the Master of the Universe's mysterious plans with flies over his eyes and mouth? "Please, Berman," he begged in Yiddish and Russian.

"Please."

Berman pushed the barrow off the road toward a low embankment by a cow pond. He tore off a piece of his rotten striped shirt, dipped it in the cold water, and roughly scrubbed a layer of dirt and blood from Gelbat's face. But when Berman dunked his own head under the water and drank until he thought his chest would burst, Gelbat began rocking back and forth, chanting. He threw his arms toward the sky after each mention of a lost brother or grandparent, and when he reached the names of his wife and three children—and here, specific mention must be made; they were: Sophie, Lev, Eva, and the baby, Roza—he leaned so far to the right, still praying and crying, that the barrow broke loose and rolled down the embankment into the pond. It took Berman a long time to pull the old barrow and a sodden, crying Hasid from the mud. He pounded Gelbat's chest until he coughed up dark water and opened his eyes. "Let me swim to the Holy Land," Gelbat said after spitting a mouthful of water in Berman's face. "Only a devil would stop me."

Berman's hands were cut across both palms from pulling the barrow up the slippery embankment, and his legs were cut down both sides from the rocks embedded alongside it. He wanted to cry, then to choke the Hasid's skinny, worthless neck. "The next time you start to pray for all the Gelbats and tip over," he hissed through chattering teeth, "I'll let you drown."

"Goy!"

"Rat!"

"Red!"

"Fool!"

"Torah hater!"

After this incident, a cool breeze comforted both of them. Berman fell asleep for hours, and, when he awoke, vowed to make sure to get a grip on the barrow whenever Leo Gelbat began chanting and sobbing. Even though Berman wished the doomed believer a quick death and re-union with his beloved family, he never again let Gelbat sink under the water or roll too far away, though the Hasid upset the barrow a dozen more times in various ditches and mudholes in Germany and, finally, Poland.

Of the several camps each had survived, and about the low numbers tattooed on their forearms—proof enough that here were two Jews who had outlived everyone who once knew them as children—they said nothing to one another. Berman heard enough about the Gelbats from listening to Leo's endless prayers. What good would it serve to tell the Hasid about the end of the Bermans when there were so many present needs to think about: preventing the skin on his own hands from splitting open (he ignored Leo's suggestion to use a balm made from spiders' webs and birch leaves), finding small apples and clean water, avoiding Jew-hating peasants and thieves.

Like the other refugees who were everywhere, Berman and the weakening Hasid slept under any available shelter. But after they saw some young Czech Jews openly copulating in front of them in a field—the tailor had memories of such he would prefer not to reawaken—Berman avoided the main road and chose, instead, to follow the worst paths, which only a peasant or a one-time Red Army scout like himself would remember and be capable of navigating. Day after day, they ate what they could find and, whenever it was necessary, insulted one another in three languages. For the Hasid, a ride was still a ride—even if it came from the diminished strength of an apostate Russian Jew who spent his life trampling on the Holy Word.

Days passed.

When Berman was finally close enough to the outskirts of Stettin to see a few famished Polish seagulls hovering above them, he, exhausted beyond immediate recovery after pushing Gelbat uphill for an hour, collapsed next to a roadside shrine and hit his shorn head on a decapitated saint's chipped ceramic robe. The pain took away his speech for ten minutes. When his vision and senses returned, his head was carefully bandaged with a strip torn from Leo's prisoner's jacket. Out of necessity, Berman asked the Hasid to walk for at least part of this one day. "I can't push you forever, rabbi," he said.

"God forbid, comrade," Leo answered as he steadied Berman's arm and also held onto the barrow's handle. "God forbid."

On a road that was covered with discarded uniforms and horse droppings, the Hasid and the tailor were less than three kilometers from a chunk of recently liberated Poland. As soon as Leo Gelbat saw the first hand-lettered sign in Polish, his face began to turn the color of thin gruel. He threw himself on top of the barrow and dug one foot into the ground. He spoke in senseless Yiddish and beat himself on the chest with a stone. He began to eat dirt. "It's over, goy!" Leo shrieked. "No more for me!"

Try to understand the complicated situation here: as they came closer to the city where so many Gelbats had once worked as devout tanners and shopkeepers, Berman, still dizzy from his injury, had enough wit left to see that Gelbat was going mad. He'd seen it before in the camps: eyes that didn't focus, crazy laughter followed by weeping, hands that tore at faces or beat on chests. But what were the choices? Wait by the road until Gelbat choked on handfuls of dirt or found the will to roll beneath some truck's tires? Beg a ride from a Polish peasant who might kill both of them? Hope Gelbat's Master of the Universe appeared with first aid and a clean canvas stretcher? Or maybe conjure a lie to save a life?

"Look, Gelbat," Berman yelled, turning the Hasid's head toward the open door of a ruined farmhouse. "Shul!"

As you've guessed, Leo Gelbat stopped sobbing. He spat out a mouthful of dirt and teetered on the edge of the barrow. He even grabbed the goy's arm and happily took the skullcap (it was a Red Army cap with a singed bullet hole in the middle) that Berman scooped off the ground and put on his head. But when Leo weakly adjusted the cap and sang out some prayer or other, Berman clenched his own raw hands together and gave him a good clop on the side of the head. Gelbat whimpered like a baby and slumped down.

Berman righted the unconscious Hasid in the barrow, which, with its off-balance cargo now shifting from side to side, soon lost its wheel just before the undercarriage, pushed far beyond the endurance of its maker, split in two. Berman's voice must have been heard in Berlin itself as he cursed every bone in Leo Gelbat's inert body. But what Berman started had to be finished—the Russian would not leave the Hasid to die by himself—and he waited one hour until he recovered enough strength to do what must now be done.

"Up, Gelbat," he ordered. "And don't let go!" After several failed attempts, Berman hoisted Leo onto his back. He wrapped his arms around Gelbat's legs and felt the Hasid's dry, swollen tongue against his neck. Dazed, Leo kept muttering fragments of psalms or other praises to a God Berman knew was either a fool or a murderer. However, for the sake of his aching back and the few remaining kilometers, Alexandr Davidowich Berman never let go of Leo Gelbat— all of this done, perhaps, to give poor Gelbat some peace and rest before the end.

"Hold tight, rabbi," Berman yelled between the Hasid's mumbled praises to dead prophets. "Now you're on a tailor's back."

When the first Soviet trucks were within sight, Berman and Gelbat, fastened together into a dirty, striped lump, joined a column of refugees on a road that hadn't been completely cleared of bloated horses and overturned *Wehrmacht* wagons. The road was jammed with Poles, Czechs, Lithuanians, Gypsies, Hungarians and many others who couldn't be easily identified. Everyone was dazed and hungry; children screamed and hit one another; several women were in labor; and so the sight of one sick Jew carrying another made no impression on anyone.

With each labored step, however, Berman fell behind the crowd. He rested by leaning against piles of rubble, somehow managing to hold onto the snoring load that felt like an iron weight pushing him into the ground. He yelled at anyone who came too close to Gelbat. He even painfully stooped down to retrieve Gelbat's cap-become-yarmulke. After several years, Alexandr Davidowich Berman—whose shorn and bruised head was bandaged with the remains of a slave's jacket—was returning home with the bony ankles of a delirious true believer pressed into his sides. "Get out of my way," he yelled in pidgin versions of several languages. "Out of my way."

With so much confusion and noise all around him, how could Berman have noticed the hundreds of flags or the searchlights that suddenly illuminated the road ahead? And, within this light that became brighter as he followed the backs in front of him, how could Berman be expected to see the Red Army newsreel photographers perched atop some old Ford trucks, capturing for Comrade Stalin this amazing scene of earthly redemption?

Somewhere—Berman was afraid to look—a band played from another beam of light. Confused, blinded, burdened with Gelbat's inert body, he fell even farther behind the others, hunched over so far he felt he could touch the ground with his nose. Scores of Soviet soldiers ran alongside the liberated prisoners and refugees and planted tiny red flags in their ropebelts or hands. "Wave these for our victory, comrades!" one shouted when he reached the Jew wearing the cap. "The fascist beast is dead." The soldier wedged one flag between Leo's hand and Berman's chest; a second one he slipped into the bullet hole of the emergency skullcap that still covered the Hasid's head.

Berman, too exhausted to greet his comrade in Russian, quickly stepped to one side to avoid a truck filled with cheering soldiers that pushed its way into the crowd. Great clouds of diesel fumes from the truck mixed with dust from the road and covered everyone. People coughed and choked on the fumes. Berman, now a human barrow without direction or support, fell against several others and, together, they collapsed into a wheezing pile of stick legs and hips.

This sudden turn of events was enough to jolt the Hasid. He awoke with his arms wrapped around Berman, his head suddenly, amazingly, clear. "Lord Jesus, help me!" an old woman on the bottom of the pile cried. "Mother of God, I can't breathe!" "Not now," Gelbat said in Polish in answer to this call for Christ and his mother. He pulled himself closer to Berman's trunk. "Up, up," he pleaded with someone he thought was Berman. "Get up, goy, before their Jesus comes!"

Berman pulled against anything he could find—an arm, a broken wagon wheel, maybe the leg of the one waiting for Jesus—until he steadied himself on his cut knees. The Hasid, screaming in Polish, was now a permanent part of the tailor's body, and he kicked against Berman's sides like a tinker urging on a lame horse. "Up, Mr. Goy, please. Help a Jew."

Berman grunted and rose to his feet. He could hardly see through the swirling, choking dust. His mouth bled. Someone kicked him in the groin. He swatted at the Hasid, pulled the Jew's legs toward him until he had a firm hold, and began to hobble like a drunk toward the center of a road that was now even brighter than before.

In a cloud of illuminated dust, a reborn Gelbat, his Red Army skullcap still securely riding his dented head, gave thanks for the vision he now saw in front of him. His arms flapped at Berman's sides as the dazed mass of bodies stumbled, fell, and were blinded by the intense lights. "Mr. Goy!" Gelbat shouted above the din. "Ayy!"

What Leo Gelbat saw at that precise second—lost to the Russian cameraman but understood by other, clearer eyes—was as important to him as the second when Abraham, knife poised above his naive and trusting son, heard the voice of the Master of the Universe atop Mt. Moriah. For, not far from where Berman and Gelbat staggered and choked, the Hasid saw an old woman and a girl. The woman, her back so bent it looked like the entrance to a tunnel, was carefully guarding a child with black hair and dark eyes. Given the horrible dreams he had had astride the goy Berman, the sight of the woman and girl in their babushkas made Gelbat pull up straight against Berman's back—Abraham went up Mt. Moriah; Gelbat scaled Mt. Berman—and shriek because he wanted the whole world to hear that, after so many years, he, Leo Gelbat, had just seen a healthy, living Jewish child. Toothless though he was, throat burning and raw, Gelbat still planned to celebrate the absolute holiness of this moment.

Surrounded by enormous banners and Russians throwing flowers, the Hasid with the bright red star on his head sang a few weak verses of "David, King of Israel" in Hebrew because his recent life had confirmed—or so he had thought—the end of all children. And since he wasn't sure if the girl remembered the ancient language, he also sang in Russian, Polish, German, and Slovak. "A Jewish child," he rasped, kicking Berman's flanks. "Look, Mr. Goy. Sing . . . sing!"

For no other reason than to keep the Hasid alive and himself on his feet, Berman, lurching from one side of the road to the other, sang—about a Jew, he screamed in Russian after hearing part of Gelbat's song, who should be king of Leningrad.

The great Eisenstein himself couldn't have devised a better scene for the lucky Russian newsreel cameraman who, at that very second, spotted Alexandr Davidowich and his burden. "Move closer, closer," the Russian told his driver, "or we'll lose them." Here, he knew, was a shot that would be celebrated throughout the world—two striped victims of the fascist dogs, one astride the other, awash in red flags, their freedom and safety provided by a victorious Soviet army. This was a shot that Stalin himself would treasure forever! This was the beginning of everything!

And so it would be, especially the part when—in the tight focus afforded by a good Zeiss lens—the Poles and God knows who else surrounded the two Jews and pressed them up against a low brick wall. "Here's to your fucking communist Jew-king," someone screamed as he brought a rock down on the Hasid's head. "Enjoy!"

Berman was trapped beneath the Hasid, his flag signaling his place and a cry for help. Like small spears thrown by wild men, bone chips from the blow that split Gelbat's head cut into Berman's cheek. Gelbat's fingers, which somehow worked for a few minutes beyond the end of his brain's commands, were dug so deeply into Berman's neck that they had to be cut away.

The tailor's eyes had doubled in size, or so it would later appear in the film. When the soldiers dragged him away from the angry crowd, his right hand somehow clutched the arm of Gelbat's attacker. Like the Jew he'd lost, Berman kept shrieking in Russian about some damn king—"King? Did he say king?" a soldier asked—who was bound to come back to Leningrad. One of the soldiers put a blanket over Alexandr Davidowich, another poured water and tied a soiled bandage over his face, and a third finally broke his handhold on the sleeve of the terrified Pole who had made an end of Leo Gelbat. The newsreel photographer, and many others, had already lost interest in what was left of the world's last Gelbat and turned, instead, to help the poor brave comrade who fended off a reactionary nationalist pogrom—brief though it was—with a small Soviet flag, his iron will, and his proletarian grip.

The God who hovered above Moscow in 1946 was quiet, but his Georgian servant in the Kremlin—who was choking with laughter, drinking until dawn, even dancing a few waltzes with poor, frightened Molotov—was not. Stalin, the one dancing in the Kremlin and dipping his foreign minister in a mock tango, watched films, sucked on his pipe, and ordered his projectionist to replay countless scenes captured by his devoted cameramen.

In clearly focused black and white, Josef Vissarionovich, Man of Steel, the generalissimo himself, watched the defeated and humiliated Nazi shits flail in front of him, their death's head battle flags burning in great piles in Red

Square. Once, tiring of Beria's incessant chatter, he even summoned Eisenstein from the Mosfilm studio to sit with him and applaud the tremendous cosmic victory, and to watch the impressive final end of Leo Gelbat and the courage of a liberated Soviet soldier.

The great director, abruptly snatched from the editing room where he was working on a final cut of the second part of *Ivan the Terrible*, was driven to the Kremlin in the middle of the night—imagine what must have passed through his mind!—to drink goblets of brandy, eat from mounds of smoked fish and plates of Black Sea caviar, and listen to the Georgian's ideas about film, culture, and the depravity of the cosmopolite intelligentsia. "Consider yourself lucky, Sergei, all he wants from you is a good movie," Molotov whispered to Eisenstein when the lights were turned off. "So for your own sake, agree with anything he says. He's worried about the Jews."

Lucky for the Jew Eisenstein, who died in his sleep in 1948; but for many, many others there was something else waiting. For this was the moment when the Soviet curtain, so to say, began to drop on the heads of those who had once had Jewish mothers or fathers: on poets and doctors, officers who spoke Yiddish too often, actors, librarians, linguists, engineers, students, artists, archivists and historians, teachers, musicians, chemists, rabbis, cantors, children, tinkerers, and locksmiths. These were the Yids—rootless cosmopolites all!—that Stalin, a onetime seminary boy from Georgia, had always hated and envied. These were the same Yids, he knew in the good marrow of his soul, that all Russians hated. "Plots have been uncovered," Beria said, keeping his killer's beak close to the paranoid Georgian's ass. "The snakes are to be found everywhere, Koba."

And so it began. "We'll hunt them down," Molotov said he overheard crazy Beria telling Stalin; the NKVD boss was eager to take this work in hand. "Where do they think they can hide?"

Indeed, there were, in fact, few places—unless, of course, one was very careful, mute, or lucky. Or unless one chose to become invisible, like an underweight Alexandr Davidowich Berman, recently returned to a devastated Leningrad with a tiny bone fragment from a Polish Jew permanently embedded inside his lower jaw.

"I know how to sew for men or women," Berman told Vera Maximova, a skinny seamstress at the Kirov Theater, "and I don't need any help or training. Please, anything you have. I need as much work as you can give me."

"Then fix this as a test," she said, picking an impossibly torn pair of tight leggings from the scrap pile. "You may take the afternoon to finish. I'll check your papers."

The seamstress stared at the emaciated figure before her, who had been, his internal passport noted, released only two weeks ago from a military hospital in Minsk. A Jew from Leningrad; occupation: tailor. Party membership: none. Service record: member of General Pyadyshev's 177th Rifle Division, captured and held since 1942, a former "uncontaminated" prisoner of war, even a hero of sorts (Stalin Commendation, Third Class) for his actions in Poland just after the war. "Treat with respect," an army physician had written on the bottom of the Jew's transit papers, and, stamped in red next to the doctor's name: "Bearer to be allowed a seat on any crowded public transport."

Vera Maximova stared at the Jew hunched over his test. His eyes bulged, and his nose was so thin that his cheap wire-rim glasses kept slipping down onto his colorless lips. His legs trembled. There were sores along the side of his neck; a half-inch bluish scar marked his cheek. His suit, with a small medal attached to a frayed lapel, was too large for him; his shoes didn't match. Vera Maximova could see that his hair, however, was beginning to grow back. She knew where he'd come from. For safety's sake—she was no fool—Vera Maximova was about to send this Jew away. Medal or no medal, there were enough of them in the Kirov.

But when Berman required only twenty minutes to make such an intricate repair, the seamstress smiled, and her heart softened, professionally speaking. "Come back to-morrow," she said, amazed at what she had just witnessed. "We have a small room in the basement where you can sleep."

Overcome by exhaustion and relief, Berman dropped to his knees and kissed Vera Maximova's hand. From an old rack of clothes left over from before the war, she gave him a suit, some clean underwear, a pair of used shoes. And because Vera Maximova could see that the tailor shifted un-comfortably on his buttocks, she also gave him a pillow to sit on. Pity drove her to add three cigarettes and part of her stale sandwich.

"Leonid," she yelled down the hall. "Bring in the stuff for *Giselle*." A boy wheeled in several racks of costumes, saved for years during the great and heroic siege of beloved Leningrad. The city's party leadership had already ordered the Kirov's staff to prepare for a full season ahead. "Can you help with these?" she asked, pointing to the costumes. "They're in no shape to be worn."

Berman nodded.

"Then work, work, Alexandr Davidowich," the seam-stress said, as she offered the Jew a fresh cucumber and some salt. "But a word of caution. Say nothing to anyone about where you've been. Keep everything to yourself. For-get about your losses. Don't read anything. Become invis-ible and stay away from the other Jews. And always, always, be careful who you speak to."

"I'm a tailor," Berman answered. "Nothing else matters."

"Then cover your wrist," she whispered, pointing to the tiny blue digits that rode atop a large, purple vein on the tailor's wrist. "Something is in the air."

Master tailor Berman—and who in his right mind could deny him this distinction?—wore, from that day on, long sleeves, winter or summer. If anyone asked, Alexandr Davidowich said that the scar on his chin came from a childhood accident. "I fell," he said. "The doctor was a lousy seamstress."

Over the next three or four years, Berman kept to him-self, eventually finding his own room in a communal build-ing within walking distance of Theatre Square, always taking his afternoon meal and tea with Vera Maximova in the costume shop. He came to the Kirov early in the morn-ing to finish his fittings and alterations for the Kirov's dancers and never left until after performance time, though he always stopped to kiss Vera Maximova's hand. He never forgot to give her a small gift—a jar of honey, some flowers, ribbons tied into a bouquet—on her nameday or the New Year. Once, only once—this may have been in the winter of 1950—when Berman suddenly began to cry over some memory or other, chief seamstress Vera Maximova, whose own husband was a useless drunk with a liver the size of a blackened fish, slept with the Jew, more out of pity than longing.

And this was how the dark years passed. If Alexandr Davidowich Berman ever said a Hebrew prayer or foolishly played the Jew in any other way, no one heard about it in Moscow, or in other places closer to home.

Or so it was thought.

7

Several days after Yelena Gailova's funeral and the circumstances surrounding Berman's many Kaddish prayers and vivid dreams, the tailor had no reason to stay away from his unfinished work at the Catherine Palace. Even though his head was stuffed full of ancient memories of a bite on the ass and an aching back, a good tailor like Berman knew what was right to do: You give your word to mend everything in front of you. This is simply the way it has to be.

Sweating under his stiff black hat—the same one he'd worn to Yelena's funeral—Berman stood in the curator's large office. He hadn't bathed in at least a week, and he looked as gaunt as a hungry raven. "With your permission, Vasilly Petrovich, I'm coming back to work on the old clothing. What else is there for me to do?"

Vasilly Petrovich extended his hand. As a sympathetic man who knew all about the Jew's lengthy death watch over the old cleaning woman, he was prepared to do anything to keep Berman. To lose such a tailor now would be a disaster for the other palace storeroom, still loaded with exquisite gowns, jackets, and uniforms from three of Czar Peter's prized regiments.

"But you should take some time off, Alexandr Davidowich," the curator said, anxious to seem concerned over the old man's grief and bedraggled appearance. "We know that you've been through a difficult period. Please, take a week's holiday and rest. I'll even arrange some decent meals for you. Be my guest at the administrative commissary; eat all you like."

The curator's words were lost in the fog swirling inside Berman's head. No, the tailor said, special food and drink were unimportant. No offense intended, but he could always bring along some mushroom soup and maybe a little fruit compote from his flat. He did ask permission, however, to stay in his workroom beyond closing. "Just to finish what I start in the mornings. I've lost so much time."

Vasilly Petrovich couldn't mask the joy he felt. Getting Berman in the first place was a victory, and this current return was an additional gift, a tonic for the curator's sagging spirits during awful times. His hands trembled as his mind raced over the increasing possibility of an even grander exhibition. The country might be falling apart at its dialectical roots—there was thunderous grumbling everywhere—but he, Vasilly Petrovich, always a brilliant survivor, would find his way out, straddling crates of magnificently restored Romanov clothing bound for the West.

"Then have a drink with me, Sasha," he said as he poured two large glasses of his best Armenian brandy. "You have no idea what it means to have you back with us."

Berman sat down on a leather chair. Without thinking, he brushed at his forehead, oblivious to how he might look to someone like Vasilly Petrovich. He accepted the drink, which burned his stomach, and one of the curator's British cigarettes, which did a similar job on his throat. Vasilly Petrovich towered over him, his head obscured by smoke, his thoughts racing, until he noticed Berman, who was also somewhere else, finish his cigarette and replace it with a few straight pins.

"As long as you are here, Sasha, there is just one small matter . . . a minor detail of form."

The curator put his drink on the table. Berman looked up. Before he could wipe his dripping brow, Vasilly Petrovich removed the tallith from the tailor's head—where Alexandr Davidowich, perhaps without feeling its presence, had left it for so many days—and, just as quickly, folded the stained prayer shawl inside a sheet of newspaper. "Go home, Sasha," he said. "Wash up, shave, throw some rose water over your face, have a long sleep. It's all over. Put this package in your drawer. You're in a different kind of sanctuary now."

In the weeks that followed, Berman, freshly bathed and hatless, attacked his work like the dutiful Soviet soldier he once was. With his retirement now a distant memory and his garden ignored beyond hope, he left for the palace before first light, carrying a jar of fruit compote, some bread, and his extra pair of good spectacles. So as not to be too distracted by memories of Yelena Gailova, he left the cat in the care of his neighbor, Yevgeniya Vasilevna—he didn't want to hear the creature's pathetic mewing every time someone walked by his workroom door—and selected records for his Victrola that Yitzhok's daughter, may she rest in peace, never listened to.

Even on the most beautiful spring mornings, when the gardens and parks of the Catherine Palace were in full bloom, he never took advantage of these splendid surroundings for a restful walk or a half hour's rest by the great Pushkin's statue. Instead, feeling the press of each wasted minute, he worked ferociously until late at night, stopping his sewing only to eat his compote or heat water in the old samovar he used for his weak, unsugared tea.

There was, you see, so much to be done. He oiled and repaired each overworked gear and spring of his sewing machines; he rebuilt an old electric sharpening stone so that he could fashion his own special needles for embroidery work; he drew intricate patterns for blouses and jackets; he selected special thread and organized scraps of usable Chinese silk or satin by texture and weight. Left completely to himself by direct order of Vasilly Petrovich, he listened to the same records over and over—what could be better for a tailor's concentration than Rubinstein playing Chopin or Mozart?—and often politely refused entry to the new cleaning woman assigned to sweep up his ashes or scrub his floor. "I'll do it myself," he'd say to the poor woman over the sound of the Singer. "Don't worry about me." When a few of the woman's comrades decided to peek through his outside window just to see the old Jew's mischief in the making—by now, everyone who worked at the palace knew about the ill-fated nightgown decorated with a beautiful ikon—Berman, remembering Yelena Gailova's futile attempts to watch him, covered the windows with black felt and arranged for a brighter lamp.

And such work he had to finish! Not only did the curator's apologetic assistant suddenly appear behind two porters carrying heavy armloads of tattered silk ballgowns from the German and French mistresses of Prince Menshikov—"He's even sewing up some whores' dresses," the porters told the cleaning women—but he was also asked to see if he could save Menshikov's own floor-length satin and ermine coat. "This is a priceless artifact," Vasilly Petrovich said, winking. "I have it on the best authority that this was a gift to Menshikov from Peter after a two-week debauch in an Amsterdam brothel. See what you can do with this beauty."

Berman accepted the robe without protest, only requesting the curator to provide him with any drawings or books that might help him "be true to the original spirit." Ever obliging, Vasilly Petrovich sent two huge volumes from the palace library—Petrovian court artist Gretchkovsky's original watercolors of period dress and costumes and a seventeenth-century handwritten notebook with "simple chemical solutions for the astute silversmith and handler of precious objects," composed in ungrammatical Russian by some homesick Dutch craftsman who followed Peter to the czar's new Venice on the Neva.

Working as hard as a young apprentice, Berman, following his best instincts, first read everything he could about the project at hand. He studied Gretchkovsky's notes about the "wondrous quality of ermine" and the specific care one must use in "attaching the delicate sections of pelt to manmade materials." He even discovered the old master's large watercolor sketch of Menshikov himself wearing the same gown that was now draped over a wire form in his workroom. "Work slowly as a Hebrew counting his money," Gretchkovsky wrote beneath the prince's measurements, "and all glory shall be yours." Berman winced, but kept true to his trade. He sharpened several long needles to cut through the torn pelts, separated each strand of fur with a fine-toothed comb he made just for this purpose, and reattached the dark brown hides to a layering of brushed wool. Obeying the precise instructions the Dutchman offered in his pidgin-Russian for cleaning and polishing

Menshikov's tarnished pearl and silver filigree initials and buttons, he brought out the original luster of each jewel and stylized letter by soaking and resoaking them in a solution of vinegar and lemon juice with a rag "squashed in the juice of a young pig's daughter."

After two more weeks of intricate repair, Menshikov's restored gown was finally finished and hanging next to the several dresses of his amply proportioned lovers from Rotterdam and Berlin. "Easier than I thought," Berman said when he presented his work to the curator and his staff. "Not too different from the costumes I did for *The Nutcracker* in '57."

Vasilly Petrovich ran his hands over the rich fur, shook his head, and stood back a few paces to take in the full splendor of Berman's work before he hugged and kissed the tailor. "Look at this, look at this!" he shouted to his staff. "I'm in heaven." He immediately sent for two bottles of good Georgian champagne. "From this moment on, my friends," Vasilly Petrovich said when he was able to be heard above the clapping, "our Alexandr Davidowich Berman, our restorer and teacher, will be part of us forever."

That night, the first he had spent in his own garden in several months—"A two-day holiday for you, friend," the curator had said—Berman put away his books, special needles, and his tired thoughts about fur and satin. He sat on a wooden lounge chair he positioned next to a patch of giant sunflowers that blossomed despite his criminal neglect, put a cool, wet cloth over his eyes, and gulped in great mouthfuls of fresh air like a cosmonaut given his first taste of sweet earthly aromas. He covered his legs with a thin quilt. Before he fell into a dead sleep that would last until dawn, he let his affection-starved cat sleep on his stomach and knead his paws while Berman hummed Yelena's song, adding his own name now and then because it seemed to fit the rhythm. Then, a wink before he dropped off, he made plans for his free day.

The next morning, while all of Pushkin was asleep before the day's struggle, Alexandr Davidowich selected two of Yelena Gailova's favorite Melodia records, the ones she had listened to so many times while he worked. He walked to the cemetery and, along the way, picked some rooted clumps of blue and yellow wildflowers. While a Kaddish is always important, he still felt something was missing. "Forgive me, Yelena," he said when he found her untended grave. "There are ways and ways to do things."

Bending down, he pulled weeds and stones from the grave and cleaned away the grime from her simple marker and the Orthodox cross embedded next to her name. Then, crazy as it sounds, he dug a shallow hole and buried the records. The wildflowers he planted on top of the freshly dug dirt.

Although he'd already scraped his shins and was slightly nervous about being seen by someone, he decided to stay a bit longer. Fearing he might cry, he lit a cigarette and sat down.

"Ah, Yelena, you should have seen Vyroubova flying across the stage in *Giselle*," he said, pointing to an imaginary stage where amazing leaps into the air were taking place. "The light passed through her skin for hours, and she flew . . . ."

Before the air became too chilled, Alexandr Davidowich covered his head. With an attack of gnats always a distant possibility, he said a Kaddish for Yelena Gailova, for her father, and, because it couldn't hurt, for Leo Gelbat.

8

In the coming months, the work being done by Alexandr Davidowich was talked about even in the curatorial staff offices of the Hermitage itself. Word leaked out—how long could such a secret be kept by Vasilly Petrovich or his assistants?—that, week by week, a tailor and craftsman "of the highest order" was, without instruction or much money, refurbishing the old Romanov wardrobes in the Catherine Palace. "We wish to see the great man for ourselves," an old colleague of Vasilly Petrovich said before their miserable telephone connection was lost to static. "Expect us at any time."

When the visitors arrived, Vasilly Petrovich immediately took them into Berman's workroom, where the tailor, surrounded by stunning gowns and uniforms, overflowing ashtrays and a stack of old records, was using a magnifying glass to find a hidden seam in the uniform of a court page. Despite the late summer heat and the room's stuffiness, the tailor was wearing a heavy black hat.

"It takes one's breath away, doesn't it," Vasilly Petrovich whispered to his awed former comrades from Leningrad. "Can you imagine what the Americans will pay to see all of this?"

"Quiet, please," Berman said when the distinguished visitors came too close to his work. "This is a difficult piece."

The curators and professors backed away to a respectable distance while Berman used a small iron to press a section of velvet into place, fold one edge over another at the proper angle, and insert a long needle into a jagged run. They watched him pull a strong light so close to his face that his cheeks turned red and his spectacles glowed.

The tailor held up the material when the hole was faultlessly mended. Several important people clapped. One even yelled, "Bravo!" Berman sucked on a sugar cube and adjusted his hat. He might have bowed.

Beaming, Vasilly Petrovich quickly motioned for the others to follow him into the hall.

"He's worth his weight in diamonds, Vasilly," one of the Hermitage curators said. "The finished work is magnificent."

Vasilly Petrovich nodded thoughtfully. "I think he'll stay in this room until we have to carry him out, and all of this for only a few hundred a month and an occasional carton of British cigarettes."

"Ah!" the others agreed, already thinking of various ways—a very good flat on Gogol Street, say, or maybe a piecework contract paid in precious hard currency—to get this Jew to return to Leningrad and help them with their own aspirations. "Ah!"

Despite the annoying violations of his sanctuary—with countless unannounced visits by art historians and other well-connected experts from institutes in Moscow and Gorki, one of whom, a curator of a small, provincial museum in Volkhov, managed to slip her calling card and private telephone number inside Berman's pocket ("Please, call me. We have things you wouldn't believe")—Alexandr Davidowich worked without giving a thought to his future possibilities.

To protect his privacy, he began to work at night, often for long hours, saving the days for minor repairs, reading Gretchkovsky's wonderful book, or brief visits to place flowers on Yelena Gailova's grave. Sometimes, just to help the babushkas, he fixed their dresses or replaced a zipper on one of the guards' baggy trousers. For these favors, no one minded if he strolled unaccompanied at night through the vast palace to stare at the huge Flemish tapestries or the portraits of the royal retainers whose rich clothing now passed through his hands.

It was on such a late August night that Berman, taking a break for a smoke, wandered off for a brief inspection of the last bin of clothing left in a corner of the basement storeroom. He had just put the finishing touches on the Empress Catherine's lace stockings, a job that strained his eyes and his hands. Removing his hat to air his brain, he thought to relax by searching for the most beautiful item. Berman knew that a tailor's best thoughts occurred during such solitary moments.

The storeroom was in a pitiful state after being riffled through by lazy, incompetent porters who piled wooden boxes atop one another and left priceless items uncovered. Lit by one weak light bulb fit only for a small closet, the room was a mess: papers were strewn about, dust swirled in the air, and Berman smelled mouse droppings. Thin hangers lay scattered around like barbed wire on a battlefield. Still, a job was a job, even though the fetid air made Berman dizzy.

Using a flashlight, he stepped over cartons, tripped, fell, and banged his knee against a rotting wooden chest that split open. He immediately dropped the flashlight and swore at every son of a bitch responsible for this horror. As

74

he reached for his bruised and throbbing knee, he felt, inside the broken chest, something as rough as any vicious rodent's back. Frozen in place, he slowly wiggled one finger, sensed a slight movement, and realized he was trapped. Berman cried out, then stopped like a soprano interrupted in the middle of an aria. He gave a hard yank, fell on his backside, and pulled from the wreckage of the chest a musty-smelling, padded coat.

He was furious, not so much over the injury to his knee or the ache in his chest—these afflictions were bad enough—but about this disgraceful shithouse of a storeroom where everything was being ruined and left to rot. Do something about this or I quit, he would tell Vasilly Petrovich first thing in the morning. Look at the crap I nearly crippled myself over, he would say. This is no joke. Do something today, comrade curator. Do something or I leave. And, holding out the coat as evidence, he would say: This must stop!

Limping through the darkened hallway, rehearsing one hot curse after another, Berman brought the rag back to his workroom and threw it over Menshikov's robe. His kneecap was already swollen. He was drenched with sweat.

Those who will forever care about Alexandr Davidowich Berman (even those who will damn him for his stupidity and incredible naiveté) will someday say that the real story of the tailor's "redemption" begins here—for this was when Berman, pain moving like a lift from his knee to his buttocks, found a carafe of cherry brandy and drank one glass after another. After all, it was late at night; he was alone and needed immediate relief. Pointing his lamp toward the black rag, the source of his current misery, how could he have known what would happen next?

Berman touched the black coat—a peasant's Sunday best? a porter's rotten jacket?—as carefully as one would test a soiled diaper. The grease-stained material smelled of garlic. His fingers moved slowly from top to bottom, probing a torn pocket filled with dirt, a lapel that had been cut away. When he was a second away from throwing the coat into the trash pile, the tailor's fingers accidentally slipped into a hole by a section of lining, which dropped away like a thick cobweb. Then, there was a flutter in the coat's sleeve, and a yellow cylinder flew out and broke open, just like a cocoon or, worse, a spider's silk nest.

Berman yelled and dropped the coat. He nearly lost his balance. He squeezed his hands together to stop them from trembling. Just as he was about to step on whatever it was that was rolling toward him on the floor, the cylinder came to a full stop in a patch of bright light. No larger than a cheap cigarette, the cylinder unwound like a liberated watch spring. Or maybe like the world's smallest Torah.

Which, in a manner of speaking, it was. And this was when Alexandr Davidowich gave out a good, loud moan and knelt down on his better knee to pick up the scroll.

"I write in Russian because if I used Yiddish no one would understand this," he read, bringing the first inch of paper with the tiny script close to his eyes. "Today, may He weep along with me, they came and took Isaak, who is only ten. We may never see him again."

Berman's good knee collapsed. He was now on his side. He unrolled a bit more of the Jew's scroll, and brittle sections of paper broke off in his hands. He reached on top of the table, found his magnifying glass, and held the scroll up to the light. Under the glass, the letters and words spoke more loudly.

"Please, such good will to the Excellency who might find this. Wherever you are give a look for our Isaak who does not know how to care for himself. He has, our Isaak does, brown hair and a mark in the center of his cheek. This mark is our kiss. And his hair is long, as we must keep it. He is one meter and half high. He knows a bit of Russian so you can speak to him. Praise the Almighty, but bring Isaak back to his mother and father," the scroll's author wrote, "because his shoes will never last through the winter."

His heart racing, Berman struggled through a sentence that was written at least twenty times until, by the last word, the ink had faded into a dim impression.

"I, a man of no importance, only want my son to come back."

Berman finished the last of the cherry brandy. This was some night!

Sometime after three in the morning, Alexandr Davido-wich, his legs stiff from his night's work, got up from the floor and dunked his head in a basin of cold water. The chill sent signals through his body which made him shudder and choke. He took off his shirt and splashed water under his armpits. Without drying himself with a towel or putting on his smelly shirt—such comfort would work against his con-centration—he massaged his legs and breathed deeply. Just to be safe, he also bit his tongue, winced from the pain, and thanked the Greek who knew how a man could remind himself he was still alive. Then he read everything again.

Hours ago, Berman had carefully pinned the scroll to a large scrap of felt he had nailed to the floor. Stretched out end to end, the fragile scroll looked like a strip of cheap paper from a telegram or a message retrieved from the twig legs of a hungry carrier pigeon. A few drops of water rolling down his sides, he found his place and thought about every word he would say to Vasilly Petrovich about this amazing discovery.

Bend down, comrade curator, look at this! Come closer. Take my magnifying lens and read this scroll written by an unknown scribe who hid his work inside a Jew's black coat still rank with a soup's garlic and covered by grease spots. Notice how each word was written with a quill that must have been sharpened into a point thinner than a baby's first hair.

Leaning over the scroll, Berman anticipated the curator's reactions. With his higher education and years of training, Vasilly Petrovich would not be fooled in any way. Naturally, he would ask good questions. A scholar's questions.

And how old is this strip of paper? You found a date?

Who knows, comrade curator?

The name of the writer? From which place?

By a Jew from somewhere who is nowhere.

Not much of an answer, friend. Well, then, what is this great find about, Alexandr Davidowich? Why are you wasting your time and mine?

Ah, comrade curator, I'm no intellectual, but I do read and I know this is about names and parts of stories. Tiny scraps of this and that. Written quickly, you understand. Then hidden and left behind.

How long is it?

Berman will be ready for this one.

Five times I've read through this. Five times I've counted sentences—four hundred and ten, exactly, Vasilly Petrovich—and come across names: Isaak, the missing boy with crappy shoes; his father (unnamed) who lost sight of everything because he banged his head against a horse trough and went blind and stupid for a year; a certain Pavel Jacobovich who beat up his brother because he couldn't stand the boy's violin playing; or the girl, Esther, who got thrown into the mud after kissing a Shabbes goy, "her tongue slipping inside" the peasant's mouth; or maybe the six sentences about the rabbi's wife (unnamed) who grew such long hair when she shouldn't have done so; or the Jewish actor who walked through the village and said he was a long-lost cousin of the czar! And even a deaf tailor, dear Vasilly Petrovich—maybe the one who made this coat, though he never knew how to sew a straight seam—who, you will please forgive the language, thought the czar (unnamed) was "worth less than a goat's runny turd." Our scribe had a very good ear and sense of humor, Vasilly Petrovich, so let me tell you about a few other events. . . .

Berman sees the curator holding the scroll as he scrapes away some of the dirt and inspects the paper. He reads a little, stops, laughs—"such grammar"—at the sentences about the tongue. All very amusing.

Sasha, Sasha, of what possible use is this stuff? he finally says, his attention withering away. It may be a forgery, a trick, more likely some foolish writer's notes, or simply a bad joke. (Are you playing a joke, Alexandr Davidowich? Have you been working too hard? Have you been drinking?) Real history is more serious, you see. And it always has dates. Believe me, our gowns are better, my dear Sasha. Beautiful garments we will display in an exhibit that will make a fortune for us (don't think you won't get paid!). Who cares about this other business? You should be thinking about large glass cases edged in fine mahogany that will hold your work. Aren't I talking sense?

Then, just then, an idea burst inside Berman's head with as much force as one of those god-awful explosive blasts he remembered from the war. Only this time, the world wasn't dying and shrieking. It was all so clear that his ears rang from the pounding.

Listen, Vasilly Petrovich, trust me, we'll find the dates you require. We'll find everything, because. . . .

Sasha?

Berman was off the floor, dancing, sort of (remember his bad knee). This was a sweet moment. Yelena's gnats, which he thought he had laid to rest, were buzzing—yet could they become a blessing? He saw everything as it would be: the czar's gowns in one case, the stories from the scroll (maybe there were others?) enlarged (a technician would surely understand how to do this bit of magic) and framed within glass. "The Romanovs and Their Jewish Subjects"—nothing less would do. Side by side: a gown, the story of Isaak; a hussar's uniform, Isaak's sightless father; Menshikov's ermine-trimmed robe, the hapless, bloodied violinist; Peter's own riding breeches, the story of the rebbetzim's long hair. And so on. Case after case. A world of history! Don't you see, Vasilly Petrovich—they will be our mutual Dead Sea Scrolls—but unlike those poor scraps found in a cave, these will be something whole for us to enjoy. Who knows where it will end if we search every corner of every museum. Think of the stories we will uncover! Think about the coats we haven't even found, and a thousand Isaaks hidden away.

A moment passed. Berman became dizzy. Whatever happens, he thought, don't twirl like a fool in front of

Vasilly Petrovich. Be calm. Don't pant. Catch his eyes. Then make your best plea: Vasilly Petrovich, please, don't you see that about some people we need to remember!

It was in such a state of mind—his head filled with mock conversations, images of the scribe's stories being given equal billing with their earthly rulers—that Berman returned to the storeroom with his best lamp and searched through every box, inside the lining of every garment. Maybe there was another coat? A hat? A pair of trousers? A lined blouse or a pair of gloves with a few more scrolls? Maybe dates and a scholar's proof? He moved boxes, felt each dress and vest, ran his hands over every inch of the floor, sucked in dust and cobwebs. Nothing.

An hour before dawn, he finally gave up the search. His eyes were red and burning, and the storeroom's dust clung like heavy snow to his eyebrows. For now, if nothing else, he had what he had nailed on the floor of his workroom.

Later, when questions were being asked, an old babushka who saw Berman that early morning would give Vasilly Petrovich a real earful. "There was no call for what he did, sir," she would say. "Here I was, doing my job. Cleaning his sewing room, right, sir? Doing my job, that's all. So here comes the old man covered by dirt and droppings, kind of limping and running at the same time, and scaring me when he throws open the door. His face, sir . . . well, all I can say is that it was just like a drunk's. Here I think he's the polite one who might appreciate a clean floor, washed nice. So why did he scream at me? What did I do but sweep and wash?

" 'Paper,' he shouts at me. 'Where's the paper?'

" 'What paper?' I asked him. 'What are you babbling on about?' And before I can do anything, his face goes all white. It scared me, Vasilly Petrovich . . . more than I can say with words, because then he starts looking through my wastepail where I dropped everything I picked up. Sure, all the stuff was wet. What did he expect when he leaves mounds of wet tea and messy compote everywhere? So why did he yell at me? Why? It's not fair, Vasilly Petrovich. No one should treat me like this over some trash. It's not right, I tell you!"

9

About several recent events, Alexandr Davidowich Berman would always be as certain as a physicist: the last free day he spent sitting in his small garden before he first saw a czarina's underwear; the afternoon Yitzhok's dying daughter asked him to wear a tallith that later enraged a priest; a vivid dream about a rat and the Hasid in the barrow; the magnificence of Menshikov's ermine gown; the criminally stupid loss of his amazing scroll; his aching knee; and the slow walk back to the village in a cold, driving rain. Everything after happened in a fever that made him shiver and lose time for one, maybe two whole days.

"Alexandr Davidowich," an official voice beloved by policemen and clerks intoned after an initial pounding on the tailor's door. "Alex . . . andr . . . Davi . . . do . . . wich . . . Ber . . . man, are you in there?"

Berman pulled a quilt over his face. They've all heard about me, he thought, as the thumping on the door grew louder and the neighbors in the flat beneath Berman's began to scream for some quiet. One Kaddish for a half-Jew and the world explodes! The pounding continued. At once he felt sick. And frightened.

The cat growled and spat a warning from its safe place atop Berman's stomach.

Squinting about the room, Berman knew he'd finally run out of luck and time. They had found him. "No Yids here!" they must be chanting about the Pushkin desecrator of ceremonies and graves. Perhaps burglars looking for his money from abroad? Or his Victrola? Some finale.

"Ber . . . man!" the voice repeated, this time with more impatience. "Ber . . . man! We are waiting."

"Berman's dead!" he shouted, throwing out his last words before the pogromists or thieves—he imagined the old babushka mourners from Yelena's funeral goading the others on, or maybe, he suddenly remembered, it was the charwoman he'd yelled at—broke down the door or threw a torch through the window. They must be drunk.

"There's no one here!" he shouted. "Or if there is, he's too sick. Go away!"

When the door latch turned, the presently deceased tailor covered his eyes with the stained quilt and hugged his knees. This was it. He held his stale and rancid breath.

"Alexandr Davidowich, what's wrong?" a familiar voice said, no more than a few inches away from the tailor's shrouded face. "Are you ill?"

"Is this to be my trial?" Berman asked, too nervous to open his eyes or peek through the quilt.

The voices laughed.

A hand removed the quilt from Berman's head. Someone placed a cool cloth over his eyes. No one tried to choke him. No axe fell.

"A glass of mineral water for our star," the soothing voice of Vasilly Petrovich urged. "Open a window, Misha. Give us some fresh air. Make some tea. Feed this damn cat."

A glass was gently held next to Berman's parched lips, a hand was cupped beneath his chin. With the mineral water

dribbling down his neck, he quickly fell into the safety afforded by Vasilly Petrovich and his two assistants. Then he
began to cry. The curator offered a handkerchief as well as
his concern over Berman's illness. There was no mention of
any yelling at an old woman. No one remembered. No one
cared.

"Sasha," the curator said when Berman finally composed himself and sat up, "a very great honor has fallen on
your shoulders."

Still dazed, Berman had a sudden image of a crucifix-
ion, and this horror made the gaseous mineral water
bubbles reach his nose, and he snorted explosively. He
apologized.

"No thank you, Vasilly Petrovich. I did what I could.
Honors I don't need. The three hundred a month is more
than enough."

Berman gratefully accepted a cigarette and closed his
eyes. Vasilly Petrovich stepped away from the bed. He
cleared his throat as if to make a speech. Berman, half-
awake, the throbbing in his bad knee beginning to hurt,
was very confused. He opened one eye and bit his tongue.

"This is the man," the curator solemnly announced,
"who is going to fix Vladimir Ilyich's trousers!"

Berman, who had probably burned too many bridges to
allow any immediate escape, asked for a second glass of
water.

"Lenin? *The* Vladimir Ilyich? He's still got some
trousers?"

"Ahhh!"

The tailor considered a quick Kaddish for himself, just
in case, but his tongue ached and he'd suddenly forgotten
the first few words.

"Yes, it's Lenin, Sasha. Our Comrade Lenin needs your help. His trousers are falling apart!"

Berman winced. Some dreams, he thought, are too real. "Please," he asked. "Say that again."

"Vladimir Ilyich."

"The one who's dead?"

"Who else, Sasha?"

Berman squeaked out a high-pitched "Oy." He said, "This is a bad joke to tell a man who isn't feeling well, Vasilly Petrovich. Very bad, I must say. Enough already."

The curator sat on a wooden chair at his bedside. "Come, prepare yourself."

Although his tongue was still heavy and his thoughts a bit confused—the black coat? Isaak's bad shoes? no babushkas leading a pogrom? Lenin's trousers? a waxy Vladimir Ilyich, his pants falling to pieces like a ragdoll's inside a granite tomb?—Berman, now swallowing hard, had enough sense to keep quiet until reason returned and the pain in his knee subsided into a dull ache.

"Sasha, my good friend," the curator said as he took Berman's hand in his own. "We've only a little time to get ready. Drink your water. You will need some strength. Shall I call a doctor?"

Berman asked for another smoke. Vasilly Petrovich smiled and tapped the tailor's arm.

"Misha," the curator then told his assistant. "Ask Academician Pudenkin to come in now."

A few minutes later, the curator rose and stood at attention like a new army recruit. Even in the bad air of his sick room, Berman's nose caught a whiff of formaldehyde and—some memories you never forget—the sweet odor of decomposition.

Vasilly Petrovich bowed and cleared his throat. "Academician Pudenkin, may I present Master Tailor Alexandr Davidowich Berman."

"No need for such courtesies, comrade," Berman heard from the doorway. "Absolutely no need at all."

Shuffling from behind the curator's assistant, an elderly man approached the bed and offered Berman his thin hand. He studied Berman as if the tailor were a mysterious specimen on a museum table.

"I won't waste time or words, Alexandr Davidowich. Now that you seem to have regained your color, will you help us?" the academician asked, sliding onto the chair next to Berman's bed. "The situation is very grave."

Pudenkin was no more than a few inches away from Berman's face, close enough for Berman to see the details on each of the academician's many medals. He counted five tiny Lenin faces and eleven Red Stars. Then caught a good whiff: formaldehyde. Definitely.

"Maybe hopeless, unless we intervene," the curator added, waving his hands. "The end of everything."

Of course, a man can think of anything in such circumstances, and Berman was no exception. He listened as Pudenkin—"a great pathologist," the curator had said, bobbing back and forth in front of the ancient doctor, "and the last living member of the original Immortalization Commission to assist Professor Zbarsky with the secrets of eternal preservation!"—explained exactly what had happened to the revolution's beloved deity.

The academician stretched out his legs. "Look at Comrade Lenin's pants, Alexandr Davidowich."

Berman leaned over. "Where?" he asked.

Pudenkin's voice rose.

"Here, here, in this place . . . just above the knees. Holes have appeared. And also here, running alongside the shoulder, a small tear that reveals the process by the armpit. Unfortunately, you see, Krupskaya herself insisted we use the suit he wore during his last great year."

The academician continued to stroke the trousers and coat of his own expensive suit. He insisted that Berman do the same, directing the tailor's hand to this place and that. For illustrative purposes, the great academician, whose good suit was now Lenin's, was stroking an open wound, an affront to the glorious past. Pudenkin's face turned red. Berman saw the old man's eyes mist over as his voice choked. He spoke slowly, carefully, like someone approaching the heart of a terrible sin.

"And now . . . and now, Comrade Berman, the scum even want to change the name of Lenin's great city. Yes, real scum!"

Berman withdrew his hand when the old man began to shout.

"Look, comrade, you must know the party is under attack from all sides."

Berman shook his head. "I don't pay attention to politics."

Academician Pudenkin stood up, exhaled loudly, looked at Vasilly Petrovich, then stood directly above this pathetic Jew he was forced to deal with.

"Look, Berman, it's enough for you to know that memories are being assaulted, lies told, and history revised to suit the purposes of those fools who have no idea about the struggles we endured. They equivocate like lawyers. The swine have taken over, why . . . even in Moscow they hold public debates about fundamental truths. They. . . ."

The academician coughed and lost his breath. He wheezed and flapped his arms. Vasilly Petrovich jumped to his side with a glass of mineral water, but the old doctor waved him away.

"Who knows what will happen to Vladimir Ilyich's remains when everything falls apart? The jackals are out, Alexandr Davidowich! What the party cherished is being thrown away. They even say we should remove Ilyich and throw him next to his mother! We must act, dear comrade and friend! As a veteran of the Great Patriotic War, surely you can understand what I'm saying."

The academician squeezed Berman's bad knee. Vasilly Petrovich offered a glass of water. Comrade Pudenkin trembled, shook his head, then asked for something stronger.

"You must understand me, Alexandr Davidowich Berman—your mending must be perfect! We can no longer trust anyone. We used to employ special tailors supplied by Interior Ministry, but the cretins they sent us must have been blind when they learned their trade. Terrible work! Terrible! Slipshod and beneath contempt. Real shit. We must act on our own to rectify past mistakes. And now we are left with the one and only suit Vladimir Ilyich himself wore in 1917—*the* suit, comrade"—Pudenkin slowly cleared his throat—"the *very* suit he wore when he arrived at the Finland Station in his moment of glory!"

Pudenkin's chin was shaking. Vasilly Petrovich gave his arm to steady the old man. Vodka was offered.

There was a long pause.

"Vasilly Petrovich has shown me your work at the palace," Pudenkin said after he drank. "He speaks of your skills in glowing ways. 'The best,' he told me. 'He works like an old craftsman.' And so we—and here I speak for many others who are too busy with events to be here—but let me mention the name of Comrade Ligachev, for one—expect you to provide the same quality workmanship for Vladimir Ilyich's last suit that you have already given to a czar's underwear."

"Perfect," the curator echoed. "Nothing less."

Berman cautiously sucked on a cigarette. His head was spinning, a small lump of three-day-old food stuck in his throat. Finally, he understood. One last bit of sewing and they'll be ready to hear about the lost scroll.

"So where is the suit?" the tailor asked. "I can do the work here. How long could it take? A suit is a suit."

The curator tittered like a schoolgirl. He patted Berman's hand, then lowered his voice. "You don't understand. All of us go to Moscow. The suit, you see, stays on Vladimir Ilyich's own person—to remove it would be a disaster for the remains, which, I tell you in strict confidence, are in a precarious state. All work must be done quickly and quietly in the mausoleum itself, under controlled conditions. Naturally, we will offer a generous stipend for your time and effort."

"Please," begged the tailor, who considered falling to his better knee. "Isn't there a choice in this matter?"

But no one, it seemed, paid any attention.

Berman fingered another cigarette. He closed his eyes; he thought he'd also done the same with his mouth. "Yelena promised if I did the Kaddish there would be no gnats."

"Is there a problem?" the academician asked. "Speak up, comrade. What did you say? Why do you need a vat?"

"My cat, sir. I said, 'Will someone promise to feed my cat?'"

"It's time," the curator announced as he offered Pudenkin his arm. "We have a car outside, Sasha. Change your clothes."

Berman snuffed out his smoke and stroked his cat's one ear. "He likes dried fish, comrades, and also small pieces of bread soaked in milk."

The curator's assistant made a note.

"Yes, yes, don't worry. Misha will see to everything."

Further discussion about a scroll's stories, the tailor knew, would not be permitted in a world that lumbered along without hope, or logic, or even the chance to object.

Vey iz mir.

Hoping against hope that he was in the middle of the most vivid dream of his life, Alexandr Davidowich was still far too nervous to bite his tongue and return to reason. There was so much happening around him: the bath Vasilly Petrovich insisted he take in his own home; the ride from Pushkin to the Leningrad airport after midnight, the quick takeoff, and the battering his eardrums received from the air pressure; the academician's endless instructions; the cold, greasy chicken an Aeroflot attendant dropped on his tray; and the promise he heard himself repeating and signing three times because, being nervous, he kept misspelling his name: "Never will I, A. D. Berman, under penalty of law, including the possible forfeiture of all state pensions and benefits, reveal the purpose of my journey on behalf of the Soviet people."

"It must be perfect work," the academician shouted above the whine of the jet's engines. "Remember, this is the original suit. You won't be working on a tailor's form, Alexandr Davidowich, so you will please, at all times, keep a steady hand."

The Aeroflot jet dropped into a bumpy cloud, bounced, dipped through a pocket of air, and finally settled into a quick descent. Berman's stomach separated itself from its tether. He lurched forward and hit his head on the plastic tray, praying that the pain would help him awaken in his Pushkin garden alongside his cat and the Victrola. "This business no one needs," he kept saying, until he heard the loud screech of hard rubber tires hitting concrete. "No one."

"Then do me a favor," a distant voice said from somewhere on the other side of the pain batting against his head. "Try to be a mensch."

It was in such a condition—with dead voices inside his head, blood tingling through his gums, and air-pressure deaf to everything else—that Alexandr Davidowich Berman, along with the signed pledge he had hastily wrapped around his half-eaten chicken, arrived safely back on good Soviet earth.

So much for dreams. This was Moscow.

10

"Listen carefully, comrade," the academician told Berman when they were seated in the Zil limousine. "There is no excuse for being unprepared, and no time to waste once we are inside. This is what you need to know."

The plan was explained: the academician's special group would wait until the mausoleum was cleared of all regular personnel, save a few security officers ("for our own protection, I assure you") and two "preservation and refrigeration" technicians from Pudenkin's own Institute of Anatomy and Pathology who would remove the Plexiglas cover over the chilled remains; next, the tailor would be allotted five minutes—"only five, comrade,"—to study Vladimir Ilyich's suit before beginning his repairs. "Please remember that you have a moral obligation," Pudenkin stressed, "to do nothing that will disturb Ilyich's peaceful repose. Do not press too hard against his chest or remove anything. Above all, do not touch any exposed areas on the face or hands. There are, you see, certain problems beyond your understanding."

Berman nodded. He had some idea about corpses.

"And my tools? Scissors, needles, thread, a swatch or two of extra material? What am I to use?"

"Everything will be waiting for you."

The academician opened his leather briefcase and gently withdrew a neatly drawn sketch of a suited torso. He switched on a small reading light above Berman's head and drew the heavy purple curtain that hid the Zil's important passengers from the half dozen or so drunks staggering around Moscow's deserted streets.

"Here are the trouble spots," he said, pointing to several marks below the figure's lapel, above the right knee, and along a leg seam. "Study these specific areas. As you can see, the wool is pulling apart or is too frayed to hold together. The idiots we've employed to take care of this business were never up to the demands of such detailed work. Their sewing was hastily done. I suggest you use the time we have left to make yourself ready. Memorize everything."

The tailor took the paper and adjusted his glasses, which Academician Pudenkin suggested he "make spotless" lest any dust interfere with his vision and concentration.

Berman obediently cleaned his glasses, then looked at the sketch of a headless torso that was drawn as precisely as an architect's blueprint. Minus his balding head, Lenin, measured in exact centimeters, seemed to be floating between here and there. "V. I. Lenin," he read. "A cross-sectional view."

Beads of sweat formed on the tailor's forehead. His back began to ache as he felt himself sinking into the soft plush of the Zil's overstuffed seat. His ears were buzzing. "Give me more light and a sharpened pencil," he said, huddled over the drawing like an artist protecting his work from the world. "Trust me, I'll fix everything."

Someday, ladies and gentlemen, when a dozen historians try to piece together the changing fragments of Alexandr Davidowich's incredible life—or when a certain aging militia officer named Viktor Semyonovich Kostov, late of the KGB, searches for the causes of a Jew tailor's madness—much will be made of this particular episode in the Zil. There will be facts to sift through, testimonies to judge, chronologies to establish, mysterious actions to evaluate. As part of this process, a nervous academician, Dr. Pudenkin, will describe in detail the visit to Berman's room in Pushkin—"I thought he might be a bit disturbed from his flu," the doctor will say, "but understand how time was pressing in on us!"—the flight from Leningrad, and the exacting protocol he explained to Berman. He will then present the tailor's signed pledge with its several rewritten signatures. Curator Vasilly Petrovich Arkov, who will also be called to account for his obvious errors of judgment, will, after much probing from interrogator Kostov, undoubtedly reveal the manner in which, during the darkened ride from Shremetyevo airport to the hub of the quickly diminishing Soviet universe in Red Square, the old Jew bent over the sketch of the headless, levitating Lenin and studied it as thoughtfully as any rabbi engrossed in the Talmud. "He was paying attention to what needed to be done," the curator will say. "How was I to know what else he was planning?" And the Zil's driver, a young KGB private who stood to be reprimanded for not being more vigilant about his vehicle and passengers, will say, "I thought I heard the Jew whimper when the motor died."

Not a whimper, exactly; and certainly not a moan born of a moment's panic. No, it was more of a high-pitched, "Ayyy"—the sound, you might suspect, made by an excellent costume tailor just before he inserts a first carefully considered stitch into a choice piece of aging, expensive cloth. Or, perhaps closer to the truth, the sound a Jew makes after feeling, once again, a bite on the ass from a dead Polish Hasid. Or, resting in the heart of another truth, the audible response Berman had once he understood the implications of a tremendous idea that had been burning inside his head like a thick tallow candle on a nameday cake ever since he'd read that incredible scroll. Remember, as Alexandr Davidowich was surely understanding at this point: "About some people you shouldn't forget."

"Dear Vladimir Ilyich," Berman quickly wrote in the open space just beneath the diagram of Comrade Lenin's floating body, in letters so small they fit under half of Ilyich's foot. "The revolution is over. This is your last chance. Pay attention to what I write."

"Berman," the academician asked, somewhat worried when he saw the manic way the pale Jew was scribbling his tailor's instructions, "do you want a cigarette?"

But Berman was somewhere else. Cigarettes meant nothing; nor did he hear the tongue-lashing Comrade Doctor Pudenkin delivered to the driver when, somewhere along Kutuzov Avenue, the magnificent black Zil came to a sputtering stop.

"Idiot, idiot!" the academician yelled at the nervous private. "Give me your name!"

The driver promised on his mother's sweet life that all would be set right within twenty minutes, maybe even fifteen.

"Twenty minutes until you fix this thing? You can't deal with a simple matter in less time? Who is your commanding officer, idiot? Who? Who?"

Berman, who couldn't be touched by anything, just kept writing, forcing his hand to keep up with the images and voices that swirled around him. After so many years of hiding like some sort of phantom, throwing himself behind walls because there was no choice, he now knew what was possible when he sensed a long, collective past chasing after the Zil's enormous red taillights. "Ah," he moaned. "Ahhh!"

"Berman? Berman?" Pudenkin was calling from somewhere far away.

"My mother's name was Sophie," he wrote on the diagram in the space above Lenin's vest. "She knew Hebrew and gave me my first needle; we made a suit for a doll. She could dance and sing. My father was David Aaronovich, a locksmith who could fix anything made from metal or wood. He believed in you, comrade. He thought that even a Jew could pray for your revolution's success, Ilyich; even one who wrapped himself in a tallith. 'It will be a better world for us, Sasha,' he'd say to me. 'This Lenin has good eyes!' Me, he gave up on—'Talmud is lost on this one!'—because I didn't care.

"But I learned to sew, better than anyone else. Others talked; I made with my hands. This was enough for me. I was saved by needles and cloth. My mother smiled. 'Talented kike,' they called me in school. 'No,' said others, who studied my thick, dark hair, black eyes. 'A Gypsy.' But I said I knew Stalin; they let me be because there was a war before the war—millions vanished. (Have you added up the numbers yet, Ilyich? You should, you bastard!) The Georgian who came after you went crazy, Ilyich; you should have known better than to trust that murderous shit; you should have done something about him when you had the chance (your wife, she should rest in more peace than you, was right about him)."

"Only fifteen minutes, I swear," promised the Zil's

driver when he finally ignited the monster's engine. "Rest easy, comrades."

"Berman?"

"And then, Ilyich, the Georgian made war on all of us. Everyone vanished like a late spring snow. This I will tell, Ilyich: In '38, David Aaronovich, my papa, fixed a lock on the wrong door, the door of a state enemy. He should have left the building earlier, but he did good work, a job was a job . . . so he stayed. Was it his fault to be there when the thugs showed up to take some general away and, not to be messy, also took the Jew locksmith who was inside? 'He must have done something!' people said. Everyone did something in those days.

"My mother loved her husband. After he was taken, she had nothing. I was living away, old enough to care for myself, she must have thought. Then why hold back? 'I'm also an enemy, take me, the revolution is crap! Stalin is a pig!' she screamed until the neighbors informed. 'I'm just like David Aaronovich.'

"So she was taken, too. And I, barely twenty, pissing my pants every hour, lost my head for two years in an asylum in your prize city by the Neva, Ilyich—until the beautiful summer of '41, when even the crazy ones like me, at least the ones who could still walk, had to fight another war for the socialist motherland, to help the Georgian who was asleep or drunk when the real Yid-killers from Berlin came running east like wolves to do what the Georgian couldn't do for himself."

"Along the embankment. Take us by way of the embankment road," the academician ordered the driver. "They have a space for us."

The flashing red light of a militia patrol car reflected inside the Zil, and Berman dropped his pencil. He hid the paper in his sleeve.

The Zil's driver followed the militia escort along the Moskva side of the Kremlin. Within minutes, the tailor saw the illuminated onion-shaped cupolas of St. Basil's Cathedral hanging in the air like great colored clouds. When both cars stopped, he thought about what was left to write on the diagram-become-letter.

"If it's not too much trouble," the tailor said to the militia lieutenant who opened the door, "I need to urinate."

But who listens to a tailor's concerns when he is caught amid a knot of busy men? "Now we're ready," the academician announced, pushing Berman into the cold air. "We're late."

Although Berman wished for this night to pass quickly, he still needed a bit more time. Clutching his midsection, wincing from some imagined pressure, he feigned a good Kirov theatrical grimace. "Comrades," he moaned, doubling over. "I beg of you, give me a moment to do my business."

"Yes, yes, anything he likes," Academician Pudenkin said, throwing his hands up. "Take him behind the barricade."

The lieutenant saluted Pudenkin, then escorted Berman to a small tree by the embankment. He used his flashlight to point out a spot. "I'll wait here. Don't take long."

Working his way up to the second act, the tailor held his hands in front of his face. "Forgive me, but I don't need a light to pass water. But with my tricky bladder I need to take my time."

The officer swore and shut off the flashlight. He walked over to the others. Everyone smoked and laughed. A very nervous Academician Pudenkin put his arm around Vasilly Petrovich and stared at the Moskva.

("And so, my dear comrade," the elderly Kostov, looking a bit like a Jewish patriarch himself, will one day flip open his notebook and ask the militia lieutenant. "What did Berman do when you escorted him away from the Zil?" "He found a tree, sir. He did what he had to do." "For how long?" "A few minutes." "So much time?" "It was just an old man's piss." "And?" "Sir?" "Speak up, then what?" "He bent over." "And?" "He made sounds and talked to his prick.")

Or maybe, as you must have guessed, what the young officer heard was actually the scratching of a pencil, withdrawn from a sleeve and directed across a sheet of paper held crotch high by a tailor who had a few more thoughts to add to an important letter.

"Ah, Ilyich," Berman muttered, then scrawled, "about some people you should remember."

"Quickly, you!" the officer called from the darkness. "We need to leave."

Berman, who had always been good with his hands, made a smooth shift from pencil to his member to his zipper, but not before he added a few more lines—filled with names—for Vladimir Ilyich, dressed in his best wool suit, to consider until the end of time.

"Enough! We're waiting, Alexandr Davidowich."

"I, A. D. Berman, present these thoughts for the sake of his mama and papa and. . . ."

"Sasha!"

" . . . Isaak with his bad shoes and for all the others whose lives were twisted like rags."

"Hurry up!"

And then Berman, a former goy who had been hiding away for so long, a tailor who knew what he must do before there weren't any Jews left to remember what used to be, dropped his pencil and forced out a thin stream of water that washed over his good shoes and the Kremlin's cobbled stones.

"Ahh."

Flanked by bored technicians who fiddled this way and that as they worked to lift the heavy cover of the sarcophagus, the tailor, wearing the required surgical mask, waited until the air conditioning that chilled the preserved remains was set on high and sent a sickly sweet odor of preservative chemicals throughout the chamber. Two guards in face masks stood at attention on either side of the technicians, automatic weapons resting against their chests. A dim light shone on Lenin's face, brighter lights on what needed to be repaired. The cool breeze parted several wispy strands of Ilyich's trimmed and beloved goatee.

"To work," the academician ordered his special tailor. "The cover must not be removed for more than ten minutes."

("So you never took your eyes off the Jew, is that correct?" the academician will be asked. "No, he just did his mending." "And the diagram, dear comrade academician?" "I destroyed it," Pudenkin will lie, suddenly realizing his terrible mistake. "Nothing remains." "You say there was no talking or slip of the hand?" "No, he just sewed, from top to bottom, as instructed. Nothing more." "How long did he work?" "By my watch, no more than six minutes. He was very well prepared after my specific instructions. He never said a word.")

A half truth: there was no talking, but there was a bit of whispering behind a muslin face mask. "Like so," Berman said to himself as he quickly repaired three frayed edges along Ilyich's lapels, working a long needle into the rough wool. "And like so." He tried not to touch what was beneath the material; Ilyich felt like a badly dressed mannequin.

Berman then worked on the torn seam that ran along Ilyich's left thigh. Easy enough for Alexandr Davidowich: pinch the wool, trim away the bad parts, tuck and fold the material under, draw the matching thread through in three spots. Then snip. Done, done, done.

Academician Pudenkin stood next to Berman like an assisting nurse in an operating theater. The old pathologist held the precious material and the tailor's implements. "Such an artiste," he cooed when Berman closed the final cloth wound over Lenin's knee. "You're a true believer, Alexandr Davidowich."

Berman turned toward Pudenkin's voice. Then it happened.

It might have been the result of an itch inside the tailor's nostrils—Berman's nosehairs were tickled by the irritating chemical smell and the constant rush of cold air—or it's possible that, with the final penetration of his "artiste's" needle into Lenin's bourgeois suit (bought, as everyone knew, from a banker's tailor in Zurich), Berman sensed that he had less than a minute left.

And so, as he tied off the last stitch just above Lenin's skinny mummified knee, Alexandr Davidowich gave off a monumental sneeze. This phenomenon of nature began in three, maybe four seismic rumblings somewhere deep inside his lungs, and culminated in a blast of moist air with enough force to send his muslin mask flying across the room.

Three horrified technicians, two guards, and Academician Pudenkin dropped to the floor—a bomb? a pistol report? another revolution? the end of Ilyich's socialist utopia coming sooner than anyone had predicted? During the ten seconds' worth of nervous excitement (in which Pudenkin scrambled beneath the sarcophagus), no one saw Alexandr Davidowich Berman insert his letter inside Lenin's silk shirt and—this is absolutely astounding to imagine—quickly squeeze the great Bolshevik's waxy nose so that, to be honest, it looked a bit like the late David Aaronovich Berman's thin Jewish beak. And certainly, just before the aged Academician Pudenkin recovered enough presence of mind to reclamp the muslin face mask over Berman's mouth, no one saw the tailor inspect his sculpting or hear him tell Vladimir Ilyich Lenin, the unquestioned father of the revolution, to "fuck off, now and forever."

When order returned—and it required but a few seconds to realize that a sick old Jew's sneeze was not a bomb—the sarcophagus cover was immediately replaced and fastened. Arm in arm with the academician, Alexandr Davidowich was hurried from the chamber, through the underground passageway, into a control room filled with operators sitting in front of computer monitors, past more uniformed guards, up a stairway, through a large door that led into another narrow catacomb, down a few red steps and, finally, with the rearranged and newly informed Lenin now somewhere behind him, into the cold Moscow air of Red Square, where the black Zil waited in front of a fir tree.

Berman clutched his coat lapels against the chill. His nose still dripping, a thick sliver of mortician's wax wedged beneath his fingernail, the tailor was congratulated and kissed by both Vasilly Petrovich and Academician Pudenkin.

"You gave us a fright in there, comrade. Still, a true hero will always enjoy the undying gratitude of the Soviet people," Pudenkin said. "But he will also remember his solemn promise never to reveal what he has done."

That said, Pudenkin stuffed an envelope into Berman's pocket. "With our gratitude," he said, making his way toward the car. "There may be other work for you in the future."

Berman refused the offer of a quick return to Leningrad, saying that, given his nervous stomach, he preferred a later flight and could find his own way to the airport. "A long walk will help."

Before he left with Pudenkin, Vasilly Petrovich again embraced his tailor. "Do you realize how you are bound to history, Sasha? My debt to you is enormous. And you have my promise that when I return from England in three weeks, we will discuss the future."

"England?"

"Of course, you don't know, do you? I've arranged for our great work to be displayed in London. This is just the beginning, Sasha. If the Louvre is interested, Milan can't be far behind. I leave this evening."

Vasilly Petrovich gave Berman a fresh package of Marlboros before he kissed him, as one must under such circumstances. He also promised that Alexandr Davidowich's name would be "prominently displayed" in the coming exhibitions. "But about this arrangement," he said, motioning toward the mausoleum, "nothing will ever be said, yes? No matter what happens."

Just before the curator walked away, Berman asked Vasilly Petrovich how many museums there were in the country.

"Enough for a thousand tailors and twice as many curators, Sasha," he laughed. "Enough to keep us busy for three lifetimes."

Berman smiled and clapped his hands. His cheeks were burning, as if on fire. Vasilly Petrovich thought Berman looked like a clown from the Moscow Circus.

When the Zil pulled away and the guards resumed their vigil at the entrance, a toothless old woman rounded the far corner of the mausoleum. She pointed to the mess of cigarette ashes Berman had dropped next to this holy place. Cursing his ignorance, she swept clean the ashes at the Jew's feet. The tailor apologized and slowly walked across the wide expanse of Red Square just as a fresh contingent of young guards marched toward the mausoleum from the Kremlin's Savior Tower. Even though the tomb would not open to the public for another few hours, a long queue was already beginning to form.

When he was finally alone beneath St. Basil's Cathedral, Alexandr Davidowich faced the mausoleum in the distance, into whose polished red granite Lenin's huge golden name was engraved. His back now ached from so much writing and the ancient memory of a devout passenger. He thought that he could hear Leo Gelbat's chanting, Yelena Gailova's singing, and the voice of a scribe telling the story of Isaak, and some others. Given what he had already done, he knew that anything was possible for a skillful tailor with a revived memory and the beginnings of a crazy idea.

Suddenly short of breath, and moved by some pressure surrounding his heart, Berman had a startling vision. Some say that *this* was the precise moment when Alexandr Davidowich Berman—tailor, one-time revolutionary sculptor, and collector of buzzing gnats that now hovered inside a scroll—became convinced he had nothing left to lose by going on his own personal tour, dressed appropriately in a black coat, to collect more stories from any Jew who had something to offer in exchange for a fixed sleeve or a repaired zipper. But this time, he promised himself, no one would ever throw their lives in the rubbish bin; this time, working to preserve anything he found, Berman finally knew how an old tailor could give history a real kick in the ass.

"Ahh!"

So, without fear—who, after all, would notice an old Jewish tailor acting like any other drunk hobbling about from one loss to another across Red Square?—he cupped his hands over his mouth and shouted out names, his mama's and papa's, among many others you already know, in time with the cathedral's great clanging bells. With his vision and head clear, he saw all of them walking past him, these victims of so many different czars: Sophie laughing, his father holding up a broken lock as if nothing else mattered, Gelbat covered by Polish river mud, the Greek from Salonika, the scribe's violinist, and even a poorly shod boy in a thin coat next to the longhaired rebbetzim.

Then, knowing he had nothing left to lose, Alexandr Davidowich Berman pointed a steady hand toward Lenin's mausoleum and waved at the old babushka sweeper, who, with her birch-twig broom, appeared at this distance to be the size of an insect.

"Hey, Ilyich, I want *them* to know that you're still an asshole," he shouted so that the ghosts could hear him before they vanished again, "but at least now you've got a decent suit and a much finer nose!"

That said, Berman smiled and finally removed his dirty spectacles. He lit another precious cigarette. After a few comforting puffs, he closed his eyes and felt the sliver of mortician's wax jammed beneath his fingernail.

And this was only, you might say, the opening act. . . .

Vey iz mir.

PART TWO

I

There used to be a central point of wisdom in my family, a maxim as good and direct as any rabbinical saying: Deal from the heart with a stranger and you risk pissing away your life in someone else's pot! Not bad, eh? Makes wonderful sense, especially for the Jews in Mama Russia. "Keep everything locked away at home," my papa, may he rest in blessed peace, always told me before he pulled the shutters on a Friday evening. "Because once the door is open, who knows who'll walk in and bother a Jew." At the end of our miserable century, who can deny that the evidence of history, you might say, has always been on my father's side?

Well, it's too bad that I, Simon Moskovich Zorin—currently running quickly toward the end of my narrow road—turned out to be such a deaf schmuck! A real violator of common sense. So be it. What could I do if the Master of the Universe, All Praises Due, wished everything to work out in a certain way? To some, He gave a good brain and the ability to put one foot in front of the other; to me, He allotted a double measure of soft foolishness—and an opportunity to indulge it in the case of this notorious Alexandr Davidowich Berman.

Still, what happened, happened, and so I include the more important mistakes in my life's story only because they are necessary for your complete understanding.

Mistake number one (which includes many parts): Many years ago, when I could have better spent my free time reading books or trying to improve my proletarian self, I learned to play the bugle like a true master, was always one to pass on a good joke or dirty song to others, and— here, you should forgive my vanity—I could make the tears well up in the eyes of any audience. But I don't want to rush past too many events without the proper introduction, so I'll begin . . .

I was born in Moscow, a great city, more beautiful to those who know it than any other. My parents greeted my arrival, which came, luckily for me, on Lenin's birthday, with tremendous joy. After so many years of yearning for a child, they finally had me in the middle of their lives—and on such a joyous day for all of the oppressed workers of the world. This was in 1920, a revolutionary time, before everyone in Moscow—and especially the poor Yidn—had to think twice before saying a prayer or visiting a shul. "There were fireworks everywhere," my father told me about the day I, "slippery as a pickle," popped out, "so don't ever let me hear you say all of Russia wasn't ready to celebrate for you!"

My father, an engineer and a good Jew who kept to the faith despite everything, was already fifty when I was born, my mother two years younger. I only mention this because, given life expectancy in those hungry times—even in great Moscow—they didn't think they would have too many years left to watch their only child grow and prosper. So my mother sold a pearl necklace, a wedding gift from her sister, and had my photograph taken every single month of my early life. "Bury me with these," she said to my father. "I never want to forget what my Simon looked like." But my father, who thought the photographs were a waste of good rubles, decided instead to devote his time to my education—mathematics, geography, principles of chemistry, and Hebrew (taught only at night, both of us chanting beneath a bedcover he held up with a stick)—all of which seeped out of my head as fast as he could turn a page, explain a problem, or conjugate a verb. "It's no use with him," he said, slapping his cheeks in frustration. "He better learn to make something with his hands, not his brain."

By the age of sixteen, having demonstrated to my Soviet teachers that not every Jew was born with a head for numbers or complicated abstractions, I left school, bade farewell to my parents, and went to work and live in the Potemkin Incandescent Decorative Bulb Factory in the Tushino District ("We Light Up the Revolution for Comrade Stalin," our huge banner declared), where I learned to blow glass as well as anyone else, and earned, after only five months on the job, three commendations for my willingness to labor for the Soviet Union for fifteen hours every day. "Our little Jew has good lips and strong lungs," my foreman told our political director. "He'll do whatever he's asked." And, with that comment, my life changed forever—for it was on that day, a Tuesday, I think, that Comrade Political Director Bulkovsky, a real shithead, called me to his office and spent a full five minutes staring in silence at my glassblower's mouth.

"Simon Moskovich, do you know anything about music? Can you carry a tune?" he asked as he studied my papers.

"Nothing much, comrade, except for a few songs."

"Good, that's enough," Bulkovsky said, handing me a black case. "Then practice on this. Take two weeks off and, by Comrade Lenin's birthday, learn how to play 'The Red Flag Over Moscow.' I want everyone in the factory to hear it twice a day, morning and evening shifts. Take this job very seriously, Simon Moskovich. That's all, comrade."

I was so nervous—in those days, few workers ever emerged from Bulkovsky's office unescorted by one or two NKVD officers—that I immediately agreed. "Anything for Vladimir Ilyich's birthday!" I shouted, adding, of course, that this glorious day also marked my own entry into life. But I didn't know what I had agreed to until I returned to the workers' dormitory, opened the case, and found a dented bugle and two tarnished mouthpieces that, when I blew through them, tasted like blood. I nearly wet my trousers. "I'm really fucked this time," I shouted. "It couldn't be worse for me!" My roommate, Damchuk, an elderly Ukrainian from Odessa who wished me and mine to vanish from this earth, couldn't have been happier to see me wallow in self-pity. "And if you try and blow that thing in here I'll kick your skinny Jew ass, Zorin," he said. "You've finally stepped into a real pile!"

I waited for Damchuk to leave for his shift, changed my trousers, locked the door, and gave a good glassblower's try. Nothing. I tried again. Worse than nothing. I blew into that mouthpiece with its taste of death until my chest felt as if it had been trampled by a horse. Again, nothing more than a few pathetic squeaks emerged from my snot-covered instrument. But my fear of Comrade Bulkowsky's probable telephone call to the NKVD should I fail—"an unreliable worker, comrades, possible case of sabotage here!"—gave me all the incentive I needed.

After two days of blowing my lungs into soft cheese, my lips finally cracked open and bled. I could hardly force a breath out without shooting pains stabbing me here and there. Even holding the bugle up became torture. And while my pathetic efforts never resulted in more than a few squeals and trills that made me sound like a bitch in heat, I kept working. Five minutes of blowing, ten minutes of burning from one end of my head to the other. By the third day I knew I was lost, probably doomed. I wrote a farewell note to my elderly parents. I considered suicide. Damchuk offered his knife.

But a brain deprived of enough air and food is capable of fantastic visions and incredible feats. With only ten days left, I packed the bugle in its case, bathed, gathered together my life savings—enough to buy three bottles of vodka!—and walked from the workers' dormitory to the Tchaikovsky Concert Hall. "Save me," I would beg any horn player I could find. "My life is in your hands!"

So you must know what happened, yes? I stood in the snow for six hours by the hall's rear door, cradling the bugle case like a baby, my blue lips now broken open like a piece of split liver. In that damn cold, I was an hour away from oblivion. "Put some oil on your mouth," a large man in a heavy coat said. "Or you'll never play again." Say what you might about musicians, a horn player can never pass a colleague whose mouth is split three ways toward hell. "Comrade artist," I whispered, falling at his feet in the filthy snow. "I don't think I can play at all."

To make a long story short, I was rescued, though it cost me dearly. Third trumpet player Nikolai Leonivich Belikov, a former bugler himself for one of Comrade Marshall Tukachevsky's cavalry regiments, became my savior for the price of sixty rubles (instantly converted into three bottles of the best vodka) and two dozen new light bulbs, which I had to steal from the factory, risking execution in those mean days. "You bring me the bulbs so I can see my music at home under decent light," he said, "and I'll teach you how to play like an angel."

And so the deal was struck: I got lessons and a reprieve from hell, Belikov got his light bulbs and vodka, and I told a disappointed Damchuk to cut his own balls off.

Then the miraculous happened. I learned to play the bugle! Not only that, but I, Simon Moskovich Zorin, even with my newly greased lips sliding over the mouthpiece, worked through the pain to discover one of my two blessed gifts from God: I had, Belikov realized during our first "lesson" together, perfect pitch and, all thanks due to Him, an ability to imitate any tune. Don't ask me how. It just happened in a lucky whoosh of air I forced through the bent mouthpiece at three in the morning. "Amazing," Belikov drunkenly exclaimed. "This calls for a toast."

For ten days, living on sour tea, boiled cabbage, and little sleep, aglow in the blazing light of Belikov's six revived lamps, I did nothing but play. Once Belikov taught me how to purse my lips in twenty different ways in order to control breath, tone, and pitch, I could repeat any tune after hearing it only once. My teacher, half-soused on vodka, would play a piece on the trumpet and order me to repeat what I'd just heard, note for note. Belikov stood a few inches away from my face and smiled, close to tears when I managed my perfect sounds. After two weeks, "The Red Flag Over Moscow" was only one of many songs I had mastered. On our last day together, we played "The Hussar's Charge" and embraced like brothers, after which I collapsed and slept for fifteen hours in the trumpeter's very bright room.

If, after all these years, that bastard Bulkovsky is still

alive somewhere, oatmeal dribbling down his criminal's chin, I would wager my soul that he still thinks about the day in 1937 when two hundred glassblowers and fifty-three electricians from the Potemkin Incandescent Decorative Bulb Factory cried after hearing my rendition of "The Red Flag Over Moscow." The Soviet Union may have been deprived of a few dozen light bulbs—I stole another dozen as a parting gift for Belikov—but the workers had gained the great Zorin. "You've earned a new life," Bulkovsky, who also wept, told me that day. "We're giving your lips to the revolution."

And so he did, saving my ass as well.

In the twelve months after my fateful Moscow debut, I traveled everywhere. Assigned to a group of musicians and actors too frightened to refuse the honor of entertaining workers and peasants, I visited factories, meat packing plants, shipyards, and collective farms throughout our magnificent socialist paradise. I blew my way from Moscow through the Ukraine, Armenia, Georgia, Byelorussia and even as far east as Irkutsk and Vladivostok. Our show, a collection of rousing proletarian songs and patriotic plays about the incredible accomplishments of our motherland under the wise guidance of Comrade Stalin, played for audiences in dirty factory halls and on makeshift platforms beside huge diesel combines and threshers on the collective farms. There were ten of us—six actors and singers, two violinists, Artur Bodikian, an Armenian juggler with a clubfoot who could also blow smoke through his eyes, and one supremely gifted Jewish bugle player who, when the need arose, offered a few innocent jokes in the appropriate language when everyone was too drunk to stand or object. "Do you know the one about the honest worker whose fly froze over?" I asked countless times, standing atop stages next to milling machines or red-hot iron cauldrons. "Or how about the thresher whose wife looked like a goat?" After enjoying such acclaim, I forgot, God should forgive me, about praying or writing letters to my parents.

The first of September 1939 is as memorable to me as the date of my own honored birth. On that day, while my comrades and I played for a group of piss-drunk, blackened Siberian miners in Novosibirsk, one of the political commissars who accompanied our troupe burst onto the stage in the middle of the performance and announced that the Germans—"Our trusty allies in the fight against the English and French imperialists"—had begun that very morning to beat the shit out of the Poles. "It's started, comrades," he said, expecting applause. "There's no turning back from our duty."

That's how it began: the Poles got trampled into jelly by tanks and bombers, while our glorious army drove west to the Bug River and took what was rightly ours. "Psst, Simon," Gardakov the violinist whispered to me while the commissar spoke, "your Jews in Poland are fucked!" One hour later, held up by Gardakov and Bodikian, I threw up a day's worth of barley soup over the juggler's good foot.

You know the rest of the story. You know that Gardakov was right. By 1941, a beautiful summer, the balmiest I'd ever known, those Nazi pigs had turned on us. The poor Jews, may they all be in paradise, got covered by quicklime in a thousand ditches, while I, Simon Moskovich, was posted to the medical corps, saved from the front by bad eyesight and my gifted and well-trained lips. "You're one lucky Yid," Gardakov told me before he reported for service to his tank battalion. "You've been saved by those filthy jokes you tell in three languages . . . so don't screw up and embarrass us."

For four years, accompanied by the Armenian, I made my way in the back of Ford trucks from one field hospital to another. I played sweet Gypsy tunes for crippled Ukrainians or Russians, getting a laugh when I could; Bodikian blew smoke through his eye sockets and juggled bayonets and practice grenades. We even improvised little plays, including a two-man version of *The Cherry Orchard*, in which I played three roles while Bodikian hobbled through the others. Our specialty, however, was a fifteen-minute dramatization of *War and Peace*, with Bodikian bewigged and beskirted as the important female characters, while I, a master of the quick-change, was Pierre and the entire Russian army! When I wasn't performing, which happened more and more, I sat in stench-filled tents and wrote letters to the mothers and wives of the wounded and the almost dead. It's enough to say that my hair turned completely white, but to tell you more about those days might make me cry, and lose whatever sanity I have left.

So, ladies and gentlemen, after years away, after the fascist beast had been beaten into nothing, I returned to Moscow in the last stinking car of a long hospital train, carrying my nightmares and my precious bugle. Mama and Papa had died—God only knows how or when—and I was alone. True, I could always make a few rubles playing my horn in the best restaurants, but I was content to take up my old trade and create a million decorative light bulbs and earn dozens of commendations for my contributions to socialism. Again, my good lungs saw me through the dark years, and I kept my bugle in the closet next to a photograph of Bodikian taken in Minsk in 1944, his eyes billowing smoke while he juggled seven brass balls and balanced on his one good foot. Only once—one hour after I heard of Stalin's death—did I remove my bugle from its case, back in a corner of the closet, to blow a joyous tune to celebrate that Georgian son of a bitch's deserved end.

As the great and real Soviet world changed, so, too, did my life. My glassblowing skills improved, and I was soon making intricate creations shaped like tiny animals—I specialized in unicorns— and crystal chandeliers for the splendid dachas of the Central Committee members and the party elite. "Get Zorin," they said, whenever a new building or block of flats was renovated for one of those numerous shits. "He'll make the room sparkle." Artistically speaking, I was still one lucky Yid! I had some money, a fairly decent flat on Perovskaya, and, playing my connections for what they were worth, enjoyed frequent trips to Black Sea resorts. Early in 1955, I married my beautiful red-haired Tatyana, who, before she passed away from a weak heart, gave me great joy and three daughters, and who made me promise to "find my bugle and play some music for the girls."

"They'll be lonely for me, Simon," she said before her heart gave out, "and your music will be like a tonic for them."

So it was, in every way. I played: lullabies, the Jewish songs I remembered from my childhood, Gypsy melodies I learned during the war, Ukrainian love songs. That first awful spring after Tatyana left us, I took my music to the playground in our courtyard. As it happened, my bugle's sounds carried everywhere, echoing off the concrete and steel. Other children from the building swarmed outside to listen: if some were sick, my own or others, I played for them or told a few simple jokes about the goat-faced woman and the crippled dog who pissed while standing on two legs. Imitating Bodikian, I put on funny hats and juggled a few apples. I even did our *War and Peace*, but this time I played every character and made excellent horse sounds! "Take him to the white-haired Jew in 347," my good Russian neighbors cried whenever a child was sick or couldn't get to sleep. "He knows what to do."

Distracted beyond their grief by my promise to Tatyana, my daughters survived and grew: Sonya, thin as a straw, eyes and hair dark as my mother's; Miriam, her mother's face and voice layered upon her own; and my youngest, my precious Ida, with a gift for music and an ability to invent fantastic stories. How was I to know that the simple Jewish songs I played would penetrate their hearts and make them dance and swirl around me on Friday evenings? And though I told them stories about the Jews, they wanted more than I, with my poor grasp of things, could offer. "Let's keep all of this at home," I said, wrapping my arms around all three of them. "Better to listen to the bugle and sing." "No, Papa," Sonya, my eldest, said. "Take us to the synagogue."

Some things can't be fought, and so we went. That's how it was at the beginning of the end for us: walks to the great synagogue on Arkhipova, looking this way and that for the drunk hooligans whose comfort in life came from yelling at kikes or pushing them into the snow. Sometimes we saw them, and one time I was ready to turn around and return home, but Ida, then eleven, simply grabbed her sisters' hands and marched past those shit-faced bastards without a glance. "Cover your ears and hum as loudly as you can," she told Miriam and Sonya. "We're going inside." Her sisters did as they were told, even when they were splattered with mudballs or called "Zionist spiders." Wiping the mud from her face, little Ida laughed just as if she had heard one of my better jokes, faced her tormentors, and said, "So long, comrades. It's been fine to know you!" Another Jew, a visitor from Latvia who was leaning against the door, clapped and hugged her.

Once inside the synagogue, buried under a tallith with my little Ida repeating perfectly the Hebrew she heard while she spun a silver fringe around her small finger, I knew I had lost my girls. "Forgive me, Tatyana," I said after reciting Kaddish. "I just didn't know how to stop them."

Whoosh!

All of which led to the moment when my lousy heart, pumping like an engine about to run out of petrol, was ready to quit. Surely you understand that my daughters, my best audience ever, had to leave. Why? Those Jewish songs I played with too much skill? The hours we spent wiping mud off our faces on Shabbes and holidays? My surname pissing off our Russian brothers? Sonya the pediatrician marrying Herschel the scholar of Middle Eastern languages? Miriam and Ida, graduating from the Pedagogical Institute and coming together with Ginzburg the physicist and Siegel the botanist? Their mutual dreams about settling in Israel with their children? "So we can sing with a clean face, Papa," Ida laughed, "whenever we want." Because, schmuck that I declare myself forever to be, I never followed my father's rule and kept our shutters locked? "It's too much for us here, Papa," Miriam, the last to marry, said. "We'll all go to Israel." And I, the day after Tatyana's gravestone was defaced ("Good rest, Jewish bitch"), knowing that I would never leave her alone in Moscow to wallow in such filth. Never.

So it happened. Airport tears for Sonya, who left with Herschel and their one-year-old son in the first wave in 1976. ("You've applied for a visa, yes?" Sonya asked me. "You'll be coming soon?" "Of course," I lied, "but you know how long it takes.") For pregnant Miriam, six days after they buried that bushy-eyebrowed cretin Brezhnev (do you remember how they dropped his enormous casket at the tomb?), another terrible departure in 1982. And finally, toward the end of Mikhail Sergeyivich's more benevolent reign, when the Jew-haters in Moscow, those Pamyat scum, dressed like Nazis in black T-shirts and thick belts, Ida, laughing Ida, fell apart while I waited with her family—she, too, had the blessing of three girls—in the crowded departure lounge at Shremetyevo airport. Ida, who knew the truth about me from those first moments when she hid beneath my tallith so many years ago—"This is your place, Papa, isn't it?"—understood that I could never bring myself to leave Tatyana's small square of earth. "Do something, Simon," Ginzburg begged, frantic to keep his daughters from seeing their mother weeping as if she were already facing the Holy Wall in Jerusalem. "She doesn't want to leave you like this. Promise her that you'll come."

Ginzburg was right. Ida was beside herself. Twenty minutes before the first boarding announcement, an El Al attendant and two militiamen shot nervous looks at Ida, who had fallen on the floor next to my legs. Soon, my little granddaughters did the same, and, as the line began to form and the Moscow market flowers everyone carried were dropped because every Russian Jew had to kiss someone's mouth and to hold on with both hands, I did the only thing I knew how to do. I, too, sat on the floor, brought the children and Ida close to me, and took out my bugle's mouthpiece. "Shh, listen, my lovelies," I cried. "Do you remember this one?" But for the first time since I was a boy with split lips and aching lungs, I just couldn't make the sounds come.

Given my emotional state, how could I have seen the old man who was about to enter my life? Walking as quickly as a two-year-old set free from his mother—or maybe like someone who had recently teetered along the cusp of obsession in Red Square with a few straight pins in his mouth—a Jew in a black hat pushed through the crowd until he found us. Without an introduction, he sat next to Ida, spat out a pin, and began to sing. Then, scooping up little Sophie so fast she didn't have time to pull away, he showed her how the "great ballerinas" used to dance for him. "Up and down, up and down and twirl," he said, pointing his toes. "Touch the sky with your hands!"

God be praised, He who made the world and sometimes quiets frightened children also gave me some air and a tune. I got up, kissed Ida and my granddaughters, and then began to squeak out some sound from the brass mouthpiece. "Faster, faster," the stranger shouted, begging everyone close to him to join the circle as he forced it to move closer to the departure gate. "Up and down. Twirl!"

Somehow, I found myself next to the old man. When the final boarding call was made, Ginzburg, who was also dancing until the last second, suddenly herded his family toward the queue at the gate. "Come soon, Papa," Ida screamed as her husband pushed her along. "Come soon!" A militia officer at his wits' end told them, "Quickly, you need to leave. No looking back, move ahead."

Surrounded by the remains of trampled bouquets and uneaten sandwiches, afraid to stop playing, I blew away until Ida and the girls disappeared. This was how it ended, more or less, until an awful pressure grabbed hold of my chest and, breathless, I had to lean against a chair. "Hold on, bugler," the old man said as he held me up and caught my mouthpiece before it hit the floor. "I'm Berman, Alexandr Davidowich."

"Yes, yes, I'm grateful," I said, taking his steady arm. "And I . . ."

"No need for that now," he whispered in Yiddish, motioning toward the closed gate. "They may all be leaving this place, but I promise you, friend, about these people we won't forget."

On the balcony above us, someone took a flash photograph of this latest exodus. Those attending the departure of Jews fleeing mother Russia were not to be trusted—or else why would they still be here?

So much for the safety of a locked home.

2

It's true, why lie about the past? Without even a thought for what it would mean for the rest of us, too many Jews have dropped their meshuggener ideas on a hungry world's plate. There were those holy men in Spain who refused to bless Jesus and got the worst of it from black-robed priests in pointed hats; wandering Hasids in forsaken Polish villages who danced around God's trees even when the Cossacks, a curse upon their rotten souls, rode over their heads; and in great Russia during my own time, poets—good ones, I hear—who recited their Yiddish verses when all they were expected to do was to freeze their balls off east of the Urals in Stalin's camps; or a little girl, like my Ida, who once stood next to a synagogue and told a group of soused comrades to fuck off and let her sisters be! I won't even mention a bugler and joke teller who performed in front of Ukrainians. "Some of us have had our feet above the earth," my engineer father used to tell me when I was a stupid boy. "Take pity on their floating, Simka, but never go along for the trip."

If only I had paid attention. If only I had been a better son and not, in my white-haired old age, forgotten everything and turned into a balloon whose thin string was held by a tailor wearing a black hat. Still, for his recent help— "Hold my hand, little one," this Berman said to my granddaughter, "up and down and twirl"—I owed him a little time and a glass of tea. How could it hurt?

The Jew unfolded a small scrap of newspaper and picked something out of it, holding it in front of me like a jeweler displaying a rare gem. "Do you know what this is?" he asked me in the airport lounge after the latest chapter in my family's diaspora. "Take a good look."

Some trips begin with an idea—"How 'bout a drive to the lakes and a little fishing for carp?" Simple, yes? A good idea for anyone. But my trip, so to say, began over a glass of rancid tea when—can you believe it?— I was asked to believe that what I was looking at was nothing less than a tiny sliver of Lenin's nose, pinched by a Jewish tailor who said he had recently mended the old Bolshevik's trousers! Some joke.

"I swear, Simon Moskovich, everything I've told is true," he said, as I examined the yellow wax that might have come from a candle. "This is what I say it is."

Then and there, ladies and gentlemen, before I was trapped into this mishegass, I should have walked away. No more for me, thank you. Just a polite goodbye. But I couldn't. Not this time.

"Lenin?"

And so began nearly three hours with Berman, a decent Jew whose soul couldn't abide the sight of a crying child hanging onto her grandfather's pants. "I watched you with your girls," he said, "and I knew I could trust you." I ordered more tea. Berman, holding his piece of Lenin up to the light, offered expensive foreign cigarettes.

"Ah, the war, Simon Moskovich," he began, rolling up his sleeve and showing me his numbers and the scar along his cheek ("a Hasid's mark"). Then, sewing this, mending

that. The Kirov in Leningrad, where he was "a useful tailor," better than most. "I hid and made beautiful costumes. No one bothered me." And so on: our Alexandr Davidowich told me how he had made his way from one year to the next, from one stroke of luck to the other: a gentile seamstress who had once pitied his cadaverous shape and let him sew until his eyes stung ("She saved my life, Simon Moskovich, and so I'm here with you"); forty years of forgetting who he was because "to see the Hasid's head explode was enough Jewish history for me"; the moment when he agreed to take in a little extra work in a great museum; something about marzipan cookies, gnats, and a Kaddish for a babushka ("Did I have a choice about this? Would you have done differently? You're a good Jew, yes? She was so sick. Did I do wrong?"); and, for the last button on this incredible suit, so to say, something about a small scroll that popped out of a jacket, unwound itself, and revealed a fragment about a Jewish boy who got taken away by the czar. Then there was Lenin's suit, a vision in Red Square, and a "plan known only to Vladimir Ilyich."

"Lenin? A plan?"

"I slipped him a letter telling him about all of this."

"You did what?"

"A letter. I wrote it before we arrived at the mausoleum."

"How?"

"Fate presented an opportunity."

"How?"

"I sneezed. It was the perfect moment!"

"And?"

"I put it under his shirt. And then I told him to screw himself. The nose squeezing was an afterthought."

With that, I'm sorry to say, my hand began to shake and I dropped Lenin's nose into the dregs in my dirty glass. Berman, however, ignored this monumental loss.

"Look, Alexandr Davidowich," I asked, trying frantically to find a gram's worth of Ilyich's beak in a soggy mess of tea leaves. "What do you take me for? What is this plan?"

In all the long history of the Jews—those rotten trips through deserts, the Almighty showing up from time to time with another harsh request, insane goyim making massacres and burnings, ten million Shabbes evenings, my girls learning Hebrew songs in a Moscow synagogue—there must have been many such moments, when real trouble began, when, as they say, some Jew risked all, took a deep breath, and put his skinny soul on the supper table. For just as I was about to excuse myself—I was tired, enough was enough, already—Berman, his eyes dilated (a very bad sign!), grabbed my hand and said his plan required that he return to Pushkin, put on some old black coat inside of which he'd found his scroll, and go out looking for Jews who have more stories to tell "before there's no one left."

I must have choked, because Berman pounded my back and held his glass of cold tea in front of my mouth. "It will be a simple trade, Simon Moskovich—a story for a tailor's skills. Who could refuse such a proposal? And I swear that I won't ever lose another story. I want *them* to remember that we were here."

"Them?"

Berman pointed to the Russians crowded inside the lounge.

"Ahh. And then?"

The tailor rubbed shoulders with me like a black marketeer with some stolen vodka to sell. He smiled. With a single movement of his arm he pushed aside the glasses. "I visit a few places and do a little rearranging and some sewing. Do you have a car, Simon Moskovich? Would you be willing to assist a Jew in traveling from here to there?"

And so on and so forth.

God help me, I ordered another glass of bitter tea. A waitress who told us "we couldn't sit forever without spending a few more rubles," emptied poor Lenin's nose, adrift somewhere in a soup of tea leaves, into a pail of refuse.

"Fuck him," Berman laughed as he watched me stare into the woman's pail. "His story we already know too much about."

Some people are born with luck riding on their shoulders. The world may turn on its slippery heel and give them a kick from time to time—and here, my friends, I place myself—but they get up, curse, have a few drinks, smoke some cigarettes, find a lover, play a tune, kiss their children, and grow old with a few basic tricks still left to them. Their lives are blessed.

But then there are others, like this tailor Berman, whose lives are suddenly thrown off center by a dream or an undigested piece of boiled beef. This is a dangerous situation: having survived the worst the world can dish up, having finally inched their way into a safe place—a warm room at the Kirov, valued skills, a decent flat with a workable flush toilet, a garden, even a small pile of hard currency—they suddenly have crazy visions. "Help me," they cry. "Help a Jew!" In such strained circumstances, one must try to be hard. Still, despite the heartache that follows, this much I know: it's another Jew's duty, a mitzvah, to save such a fool from drowning (or so I once told Bodikian, who asked about Jews, listened to what I have just told you, and then, blowing a little puff of smoke from his eyes, told me I was "full of shit").

"You're an idiot, you know that!" I yelled at Berman. "You've no idea about anything."

Berman sank in his chair and spilled his tea. The drunks at the next table stopped belching and turned around. "Piss off out of here," one of them shouted. His mate flicked a cigarette butt at my feet. A baby began to shriek.

"All right," I said, pushing away from the mess and grabbing Berman's sleeve. "You come with me. Now it's my turn to talk."

At this point, Berman could have run away. How was he to know what I would do? But he didn't protest, not even a groan or a whimper's worth. As I've said, one must be hard—especially when one sees a Jew coming too close to the edge of nothing. "Outside. Now!"

Dragging behind, Berman followed me to my old Lada in the carpark. He stopped briefly to watch another group of nervous Jews shlep their cardboard suitcases and plastic sacks into the terminal. "Don't worry," I heard him say to a young mother holding a little boy, "I'll be here and do what I can for you." The fact that the woman grabbed her purse and looked at him as if he were a thief made no impression on him at all. I thought he was about to tell *her* about Lenin's damn nose!

"Now hear me out, Alexandr Davidowich," I said when the tailor was locked safely inside the Lada. "I haven't got all day."

Berman offered me a cigarette, which I accepted and he

lit. Then I opened up. I held nothing back. For the sake of posterity, what follows is a partial record as honest as any good lawyer's transcript.

"What year is it?"

"Ninety-one, I think," he said.

"Good. Now, do you want to see another?"

"I . . . "

"Well, friend, you won't. And here's why: you don't know the trouble you'll bring to yourself if you go through with this crazy idea. Forgive me, but what a load of shit you're handing me (Bodikian would have been proud). 'Dress up in an old coat,' you say. Wander around the countryside and 'gather a few stories.' Visit museums and 'rearrange.' What is this, some kind of show? Are you a fairy, or what? Do you imagine that once you're dressed up in your Jewish rags that you'll be a welcome sight to our Ivans and Mashas?"

Berman spread his hands in a gesture of helplessness. Smoke circled under his nose. I thought he waved to someone. "Why not, Simon Moskovich? I've got nothing to lose."

I should have pushed him out, or done my duty by advising a good clinic and a long bed rest in Pushkin. Maybe my debt would have been repaid if I'd offered him some money for a bottle of vodka. "What a nightmare you'll invent, you idiot. No one will care except the ones who want to break your Jewish face into pieces!"

Any normal man would have thrown a punch. But not Berman. No such luck. Instead, he leaned over the gearshift. "Psst, Simon Moskovich," he whispered. "Trust me, I'm an excellent tailor with a good eye, so what else do I need to worry about?"

"What else!" I shouted in Yiddish, pushing him away and reaching for my key. "What else? What kind of a schmuck are you? Look, Berman, mind the year we live in. Do you understand what's happening around us? Do you?"

The Lada swayed as I pounded my hands against the steering wheel and gave a brilliant summary of recent developments: the party spinning toward chaos; Gorbachev's so-called "perestroika" leading to nothing but trouble; Poland, Czechoslovakia, Romania; the wall across Berlin now little more than small pieces of colored rubble sold by Turkish merchants; decent food only a distant memory; marches in Moscow by fascist types screaming about kikes and holding up pictures of the last czar; angry Soviet colonels muttering about a coup, or worse; even a chorus of praises for Stalin; and the writing on my Tatyana's gravestone.

"Don't you read the papers, Berman?" I asked, knocking the cigarette from his mouth. "Don't you know anything? Do you have a tarp over your brain? Why do you think my children left?"

Meshuggener!

No, he had only seen a television once, he said. In 1967. "It was blurry, so what use was it?" How could he, a busy tailor swamped by work, keep up with politics? "I read a few books very slowly, never newspapers," he said. And then this: "Yelena Gailova did tell me about the minister with the white hair, the Georgian who worried about a new crop of little Stalins. But I was concentrating on a czarevich's vest and . . . "

"And nothing, Berman. You know nothing! No offense, friend, but you're beyond help. So from one old Jew to another, do me a favor: get on that damn plane and fly back to your Pushkin. Have a good sleep, a long rest, yes? Maybe even a weekend trip to Finland. Take a few of your dollars or marks and buy some powders for your head, bribe your way into a clinic. Or if that's too much, go back to your sewing machine and help the women keep their dresses in good shape. Forget about this insane business you've cooked up. Because if the comrades get one look at a costumed Yid like you, they'll eat you alive, and then I only hope you've got someone nearby who'll be able to recite a Kaddish for you."

Finished. Debt repaid! What more was there to say? My anger vanished. I took out my keys and started the motor. "Go," I said as I reached across for the door handle next to the tailor. "Please, go."

Alexandr Davidowich began to shake. His face turned as white as my hair. Given my state of mind, I was relieved when he finally opened the door, nodded, and took my hand. With one foot on the cement and the other still holding the Lada in place, he turned away and waved to another group of Jews assembling their luggage in front of the terminal. Then he stepped outside and pulled his dark hat over his forehead.

"Brothers and sisters!" he yelled. "I've got a story for you . . . "

Throwing his coat on the ground, Berman ran toward them as if he'd lost something. Although I was too far away to hear what he said, I could still see him holding his hands out, pointing at nothing.

Time and again I'll be asked why I didn't press down on the accelerator and leave, go home, buy a bottle of something, and think about my girls. To this I'll respond with a shrug. "I was never the smartest one," I'll say. "Besides, how could I stay away from a good performance?"

If I live to be as old as the patriarchs, I'll never forget what happened next. When I turned off the motor and left the Lada, I walked to where Berman, a suspect Moses in a dark hat too large for his head, stood among a group of Jews.

"He is about so high," I heard him say in a voice not quite his own, "and his father told me that he has long hair . . . like so . . . "

In the five minutes that Berman had with these Jews, he went over every detail he remembered about some boy who was taken away to serve in the czar's army. "His father spoke to me," he said. "It was all written down, I swear it. He wore crappy shoes, and he left without a proper coat because there wasn't enough time to prepare him." And that's not all: the tailor worked in the bump on the head Isaak's father had given himself, and the rabbi's wife, and a few odd bits about the other Jews who vanished along with the scroll. "I did what I could, but I lost all of them. Now I'm looking for them."

Without naming any one place, he described everything that might have been, and probably was: the look of the streets in front of Isaak's home, the location of the study house—"next to the small creek where the sunflowers grew every summer"—the muddy hillock where Isaak's father stood and watched his boy get sucked into the morning fog. "You must know this place, Simon Moskovich," Berman said, suddenly reaching for me. (How did he know I was nearby?) "Don't you remember how we celebrated weddings outside?"

What to make of this? There I was, center stage, as it were, on a filthy sidewalk covered by spittle, drawn into a supporting role I didn't want, listening to Berman imitate the groans and sighs of Jews I'd never known in a place I'd never been. Even in a world where two plus two end up as five, nothing could be madder. But the more Berman talked, the more I nodded at the mention of every name. "A beautiful place, our village," I added, "and even the peasants bought my mother's honey cake."

Honey cake!

And there was Berman, smacking his lips, his legs spread apart as if to anchor this fantasy to the shaky ground. Was it the honey cake I baked out of nothing? Or maybe my perfect pitch operating on another level? "Wasn't he a good boy, our Isaak?" he asked me. "Do you remember the day he flew a kite over the rabbi's house?" "Yes, yes," I agreed. "He was the pride of everyone."

As I watched Berman become someone else, I suddenly remembered how my old comrade Bodikian, soused on grain alcohol from a field surgeon's kit bag, his face as red as the clotted rags covering the soldiers' stumps, once recited Armenian poetry in the hospital tents. There, in that mess of pus and bandages gone sour from infection, no one could understand his language—but as he spoke, slowly pushing out each word in that stifling air, even the screamers, the young ones who would be dead by morning, stopped and listened. "Erevan, Erevan," he cried—this much I understood—and something in Russian about a harvest of grapes and a young girl's bridal night. Suddenly, I found myself translating Bodikian's strange poem into better Russian and not-so-good Ukrainian, and, after a few minutes, all of us in the tent were with him in a different place: warm, dry, and safe. "I learned that one from my father," he told me later before he collapsed, stinking drunk, by a latrine trench. "And he heard it from his uncle, who remembered it from his mother. Makes for a bit of peace in tough times, comrade bugler. Nothing more." Bodikian's smoke.

If it hadn't been for the sudden screech of the loudspeaker above our heads announcing some garbled messages about departing flights, I might have added a few lines from the Armenian's poem to Berman's show. But, having circled his invented lives like a balloonist hovering above the gaping mouths of stunned spectators, Berman was on his own, wringing his small hands in front of some strangers, reaching out for help.

How to describe what followed?

One of the Jews, a young man clutching a leather bag, pushed his way to the front of the group. "Bastard," he shrieked, grabbing the tailor by the arm. "We don't need this crap from you. Get the hell away from us!"

No juggler, Berman never had a chance to recover. Whatever he intended was lost when the Jew shoved him against a dustbin. Then the young man turned toward me and held his fist in front of my mouth. I froze.

"You want some of the same? Are you part of this game, shithead?"

"Leave him alone, Misha," an old woman in a frayed coat at the back of the group said. "No more!"

The commotion that followed—Berman gasping for air, I covering my face, our attacker's mother pulling him away before the militia noticed him, the other Jews scrambling to step aside from this final glimpse of Russian madness—ended with another screeching message from the loudspeaker. The angry man walked into the crowded terminal with his friends and family. Berman, fumbling for a hand-hold on the dustbin, was nearly run over by a baggage cart.

As I bent to pick up his coat, Berman got up by himself. His face was pale. His trousers were torn.

"Enough," I said, throwing his coat over his shoulders. "You see what happened. And they were Jews. Please, there's nothing more to do. No one needs these memories. Not even our own. Go home, Alexandr Davidowich!"

Berman listened, stunned. He shook his head. As he began to roll down his stained sleeves, the old woman who had saved both of us from a pop on the jaw burst through the terminal door.

"Hey, you," she shouted before her voice was drowned out by the loudspeaker. "I had a great-grandmother in Vitebsk who used to tell me about such a boy. I was only a little girl. I thought it was a fairy tale, but I remember . . . "

Berman staggered against a railing. I thought he was about to faint. As we were pushed to one side by a knot of loud soldiers and some Japanese businessmen, the woman retreated back inside, and Berman began to cry. "Help a Jew, bugler," he sobbed, taking my hand. "How could it hurt?"

"But what do you want from me? What can I do?" I asked, too close to him to back away. "What?"

He straightened his hat. Then he bent toward me.

"You drive me to Novgorod and a few other places. Think what I might have learned if I could have fixed that woman's torn coat. The whole story! Yes or no, bugler? Are you coming with me? I need someone to help me remember, and I'll even pay for your time in hard currency."

Forgive me, Papa, you know I never had much sense. Only God understands what kind of medicine you would have prescribed for this crazy tailor who said he reshaped Lenin's nose and now looked for a lost boy in the air because he wanted to put everything under glass. And what would you have said about me and my taste for nonexistent honey cake? But try to understand that my Ida, who was then somewhere over the warm water with her children—my grandchildren—would have expected no less from the tumult of my brain-become-balloon. After all, Papa, if an old man is shackled to reason, what happens to memory?

"Help a Jew, bugler. How could it hurt?"

"All right!" I shouted, taking out my keys. "Yes!"

And then, even before we returned to my Lada, I knew that I, your foolish son, would probably be the one to say a Kaddish for this Alexandr Davidowich Berman.

Whoosh!

3

One hour before sunrise and the reawakening of Pushkin village, the widow Yevgeniya Vasilevna, who had been generously feeding Alexandr Davidowich's cat gristle and boiled fish heads for several days, saw two men stumbling up the stone path not far from her front window.

"I thought they were drunk," she said later to the women who came to her for ointments and advice about their husbands. "Especially when I heard one of them tootlin' away on some sort of whistle." Never one to stifle a bit of gossip, Yevgeniya Vasilevna remembered every detail.

"When they got closer, our little tailor clapped his hands, while the other one—him I never saw before— played this squeaky whistle. 'We're home, Simon Moskovich,' Alexandr Davidowich said to the tootler. 'Take a good look.' Just before they reached the door, here comes the tailor's ugly cat, flying out of nowhere like a giant moth and landing right on top of the tootler's shoulders. He shrieks like a girl, drops his whistle as if the devil himself had popped into his sorry life, and reaches for the tail covering his face. 'Psst, my love,' Alexandr Davidowich says before he starts to laugh. 'This is the well-known musician and actor Simon Moskovich Zorin.' "

Thus began, in a manner of speaking, the great tour: two old men—Berman of Pushkin, fondling his lonely, one-eared cat, and Zorin, recently of Moscow and a sane existence, smelling as ripe as the barnyard from too much travel, cigarette smoke, and lack of bathing. "Psst, little one," Berman kept saying as he buried his unshaven face in the cat's purring throat. "I'm home!"

"I offered you some help and a ride," Simon Moskovich said, brushing the dead leaves from his trousers and groping around in the darkness for his bugle's mouthpiece, "not the end of my life."

A brief argument followed, along with some arm waving. ("I must have lost my mind to come with you," said Simon Moskovich. "I didn't hold a gun to your head, friend," answered the tailor.) It ended when Alexandr Davidowich finally promised "the best compote" he could make. Simon Moskovich asked for some hot water and a few hours of undisturbed sleep. "And keep that damn animal away from me," he said. "I have a weak heart."

Four hours later, a decent enough waiting period for Yevgeniya Vasilevna and the neglected women of Pushkin, Alexandr Davidowich's homecoming was known throughout the village. "The tailor is here," they heard, one from another. "He's come back to help us."

Naturally, Yevgeniya Vasilevna was the first to arrive with a torn housecoat. "It was a present from my cousin in Bulgaria. My late husband couldn't keep his hands off me when I wore it." Next, while Berman was in the midst of pinning together her badly frayed hem, two women appeared with poppy seed cakes and, held behind their backs, some cheap winter coats and blouses about to give up the material ghost. "We can't afford new ones, Alexandr Davidowich. What can you do for us?"

Wearing Berman's cloth robe and felt slippers, his skin

red as a shrimp's from a hot bath, Simon Moskovich watched the continuous procession of Pushkin women pass through Berman's rooms. By midmorning, the tailor's first day back was already marked by the arrival of cake after cake, some fresh dill and dried mushrooms wrapped in newspaper, a jar of thick sour cream and onions, and a small tin of herring. Berman accepted everything with a bow. Then, because he had a mouthful of pins, he lisped his instructions. "Thstand thstill" or "Who thold thiz thoo you?" or "Thstop cryin', Anasthasia, I can fith it, I thwear!"

"All of this for helping to mend some dresses?" Simon Moskovich asked when he saw the tailor put his fifth sticky cake on the table. "The Messiah himself couldn't expect more."

"There are advantathes in being able to thow things," Berman said as he attached a silver bobbin to the Singer. "If I helpth them, I altho helpth thoo."

"What?"

Berman spat out a few pins. "Off the couch, bugler, we're running out of time. If you're going to be of use on our trip, you need to learn how to sew. First I'll teach you about a good stitch, and then we'll get your Lada ready for our special business."

It was next revealed to Simon Moskovich how a skillful tailor works. Standing in front of each of his "customers," his work lamp pointed in the proper direction, his new "assistant" breathing close to the problem, Berman carefully measured what needed to be done. "Be thtill," he ordered, as he pinned each fold and anchored it into place. "This ith a very delicate operashun. I like to usth the baker's thtich." Working like a young apprentice anxious to earn a Hero of Labor medal, he threaded a long needle and repaired Anastasia Stefanova's coat, her cousin Svetlana's bolero jacket with the cheap satin trim, and Valentina Petrovna's two precious blouses from the DDR. Simon Moskovich was told to practice on a torn petticoat. "Her Sergei was a bit too rough last weekend," he was told by a laughing Yevgeniya Vasilevna, who stayed close by to spoon out dollops of sour cream on top of the herring and supply a running commentary on the prior life of each garment. "This Sergei is as useless as a bent fork."

"Shh," Berman said. "Shh."

All things considered, Simon Moskovich caught on to first principles without too much suffering or humiliation. Berman taught him the crossover stitch—"it hides any errors"—and how a tailor must learn to grasp a piece of material between his fingers and align his pins in a straight line. "In this kind of work, bugler, no one ever forgives a mistake."

But that night, his right hand stiff and bandaged from his first lessons with the needle and with Yevgeniya Vasilvena's fish concoction churning in his gut, the former bugler and glassblower, now a tailor's obedient assistant, awoke a dozen times, twice banged his knees on the worktable, and was bitten on the toes by Berman's nervous cat. Before he drifted into a heavy sleep on the lumpy couch, Simon Moskovich, like an explorer who has just set foot on a newly discovered island, took stock of the tailor's cluttered world.

On the wall behind him, a ten-year-old calendar announced an upcoming season for the Kirov Ballet. On the other walls, hanging from long nails, were thin strips of muslin, cotton, and dyed wool. The floor was covered with little piles of crumbs, a few stray cat turds that had rolled behind an ashtray, a well-sucked fish head, and snips of material from the day's work. Galoshes and a black hat crowned a simple pine bookcase—Simon Moskovich counted eleven books, each one showing its spine-bent age—supported on one side by a large wooden crate filled with Berman's collection of Melodia records. A black-and-white poster advertising a 1946 production of *Cinderella* covered the washroom door. And, tacked to a piece of black velvet above an old windup Victrola, was a faded studio photograph, dated 1903, of Berman's parents posing stiffly next to a stuffed dog wearing a clown hat. The sewing machine occupied center place on the thick worktable, along with the remains of two cakes, a record jacket, scattered needles and spools of thread, and, carefully folded inside a plastic bag, a blue-and-white tallith. No newspapers, no radio, no television. This is a man who knows nothing, Simon Moskovich thought as he considered the sum of Berman's pitiful estate. Then, aloud: "This is a man who needs my help."

"So write down your ideas, bugler," Berman shouted from the other room. "Don't leave anything out."

"What? Speak up."

"Ideas, thoughts, plans, put them down. Who knows what will be useful."

Moving one step closer to a lasting commitment because of a helpless meshuggener's request, Simon Moskovich found an old school tablet. "First things first," he mumbled so as not to forget where to begin. "If you deal from the heart with a stranger, you risk pissing away your life in someone else's pot."

In the coming days, other details followed.

*   *   *

Sitting on a broken wooden chair next to Berman's worktable, Simon Moskovich munched on raw sunflower seeds
and watched the tailor's hands working one needle after
another for the attentive women of Pushkin. Dresses, crino-
line slips, school smocks, and the trousers of numerous husbands became the objects of Berman's disciplined attention
from early morning until the arrival, sometime after midday, of one of Yevgeniya Vasilevna's greasy herring stews.
"Now, you," Berman would say, as he stood over the bugler
and dropped a piece of torn material into his lap. "Clear
away your bowl and try some stitching. Who knows when
you might have to take over."

If a good bugler sits close to a good tailor, he soon learns
how beguiling the art of the needle can be. In spite of the irritating droplets of oil that flew out from the old Singer and
covered Berman's forehead and spectacles with a shiny
film, Simon Moskovich was hypnotized by the steady
rhythms that brought cloth together with cloth to make
something out of nothing. And since this was a tailor who
could only do his best work while listening to music—
Mozart or Bach for blouses, shirts, and torn collars; Verdi
and Shostakovich for the big jobs, like Anatasia Federovna's
winter coat—everything he did was timed to the second, a
final stitch always achieved when twenty violinists drew
their horsehair bows over the last two notes.

There was something to be said for learning a new trade
with all of its complicated hand and eye movements. This
"slides into" that, Berman would tell him. Or such-and-
such material had to be cut "along the bias" with a small
pair of scissors. Cotton can do this to make a "good stretch"

above the breast; wool "must smell right before you begin sewing or it means bad luck" for the final product. It was no small feat to learn the correct way to hem a skirt, or to be able to tear apart a coat's panels and tighten its lining, or to tie off numerous threads better than a brain surgeon. Working without complaint, such accomplishments came easily to a bugler and former glassblower with steady hands and perfect pitch. "Ahah!" sighed Alexandr Davidowich every time Simon Moskovich finished a job. "Ahah!"

So passed those first days when, to be honest, Simon Moskovich thought mostly about his newfound skills, music, and filling his stomach. To soothe his daughters' fears, he wrote them how well he was and how, in time, he would join them. "I am on a holiday in Pushkin with an old friend. We listen to music and take long walks." He said nothing about politics. He drew a crude cartoon of himself strolling along Pushkin's streets, carrying his bugle case and some flowers. ("Papa at his ease," he wrote beneath his own likeness. "Weather is fine.") He never mentioned any-thing about Berman's "special business."

Somehow, in the midst of so much activity, not to men-tion the pleasure of companionship, education, and regular meals, Simon Moskovich almost forgot why he had come to Pushkin in the first place. Time just disappeared. Sewing was always done in the mornings—"apprentice lessons," Berman said—when Yevgeniya Vasilevna arrived early with yet another "friend" in dire need of the tailors' help. There were Melodia concerts while dresses were pinned against nervous hips, more food with tea, and cherry brandy toasts, until Berman, his back aching, announced that he was tired and ready for bed. "Chh, chh, chh," he called to the prowling cat. "No more for today."

But one afternoon when Berman was off on one of his pigeon-feeds on the palace grounds (or so he said), apprentice Moskovich sat in front of the sewing machine to try and master a steady rhythm on the treadle. The ancient machine had a life of its own, and no matter how many times he attempted the simplest job, he failed, either because his foot slipped or because he couldn't coordinate one movement with another. This time, however, he patiently threaded the bobbin, aligned his material in the proper position, and slowly pumped his right foot against the wrought-iron treadle. Three centimeters into his victory against the machine, an oil bullet shot out from some hidden gear into his nose. His index finger, "the guide that controls everything," Berman always warned him, slid beneath the Singer's plunging needle. Sharp as a dagger, the needle pierced his fingernail and connected Simon Moskovich to a portion of Ludmila Stefanova's fancy black skirt with the Gypsy trimming. The bugler's eyes filled with tears. He saw everything through a reddish haze. The pain that flashed from severed nerves to brain to open mouth came out as a loud wail that made Berman's cat race across the room and hide.

In one of the few lucid seconds that he had—even the Almighty allows an interval of understanding before the end—Simon Moskovich had enough strength left to work the machine's wheel up far enough to free his skewered finger, with thread still attached, from the needle. He shrieked all manner of blasphemies, most of which involved severe injury to Berman's body parts; and then, with his heart pounding, he raced to the WC, dropped to his knees, and immersed his throbbing finger in the toilet bowl. Beneath the surface of the water, his swollen finger was the size of a pink tadpole attached to a thin, black tail. "Son of bitch," he kept saying between beats of pain. "Son of a bitch."

In the midst of this humiliating moment, Simon Moskovich suddenly regained some common sense. Suffering mightily with his hand submerged in a toilet, one thing became clear: there would be no more bullshit, or he would be back in Moscow by the next day. No more sewing lessons, no more injuries, no more gossip from those old sows who pounded on the tailor's door, no more crazy scribbling in a child's tablet, no more waiting for the Angel of Death to issue reminders of his presence (the near loss of a finger he took as a warning) before the job was done. Without a break from one thought to the next, Simon Moskovich was ready to tell the tailor that the game was over. "Pack up that fucking machine and let's go before I decompose," he yelled, sending the frightened cat into a hissing rage. "Shit!"

It was in this pathetic state—his injured finger hurting too much to remove from the water, his heart pounding from the strain—that Simon Moskovich rehearsed his ultimatum and considered ways to rid the world of Berman's awful cat. Suddenly hot and nauseous, he tried to reach for a thermometer on top of the washbasin, only to drop it on the floor. Exhausted by one ridiculous failure after another, Simon Moskovich finally collapsed amid the tiny droplets of quicksilver. He considered crying. Instead, he kicked the door shut. Then he dozed.

At first, he thought he was dreaming when he heard Berman's muffled voice. "No, there's no charge, but what would you like me to do?" the tailor said. "How tall was he? His sleeves hung down where . . . ?" And then a response, several octaves lower than anything the tailor could muster in this world or the next. "Alexei never came back . . . Hindu Kush . . . late March . . . played his guitar for us. . . ." A woman's voice joined the conversation. "He'll help you, Oleshka. I swear it." Then Berman, "It was so? How so? Tell me."

It was the sobbing that brought Simon Moskovich back. That and the reek of cheap alcohol. Cradling his wounded hand, he opened the door and saw the fragments of his dream.

Berman sat on a low stool in front of a young Russian dressed in battered military fatigues, the kind of outfit soldiers wore to hide in hot, dusty places: dirty beige in color, loose trousers fitting over a pair of standard issue combat boots, red-striped undershirt beneath the jacket, soft-brimmed hat with a Red Star and a paratrooper's insignia in the middle. To the soldier's left, holding onto his long arm, stood Yevgeniya Vasilevna, bearer of salted herring, who couldn't stop crying or babbling instructions. The boy could hardly stand up.

"Tell him everything, Oleshka," she said. "Then you'll feel better."

When his mind cleared, when all memories of recent dreams passed away, Simon Moskovich saw an amazing sight: There was Berman, one hand inserting pins into the soldier's tunic, the other hand doing its own work independently of its mate and writing down everything the intoxicated boy said. Simon Moskovich now realized the soldier was only three, maybe four, steps past his peach-fuzz secondary school years. A boy who had seen terrible things.

"I know, I know," Berman kept mumbling as he reconstructed the tattered field uniform, with its singed service patches and black burn marks over the sleeves. "I was also frightened when I heard the mortars explode. Twice, I went deaf. My pants were always wet, believe me. Then I gave up on God. Was it the same for you? For Alexei?"

The boy—no, the man who had lost his boyhood but kept a boy's ability to cry, no shame in front of an old veteran like Berman—swooned as he went over the details of his loss. Ten days, he said, only ten days before his tour was up, he and his friend Alexei were on a minesweeping patrol in the Panjsher. Just nineteen, Alexei carried a letter of acceptance from the medical academy in Leningrad—"He knew every part of the body and was our unofficial medic, much better than those fuckers in the regimental hospital"—and had each remaining hour of his tour recorded in his diary. "Two hundred and fifty left, Oleshka," he'd tell me, "and after we have something to eat, a smoke, and a long piss, two hundred and forty nine."

Suddenly, at hour two hundred and thirty-six, Oleshka freed himself from Yevgeniya Vasilevna's grip and the tailor's pins. He cupped his hands over his ears and screamed. Flailing his arms at anyone thinking of stopping him, he stumbled into the corner and wedged himself between a bookcase and a small writing table. He lay flat on the floor. His aunt choked.

"Help him, Alexandr Davidowich," the old woman cried. "Do something!"

"No, let him be."

Berman backed away from the boy's aunt. He dropped his needle and thread. "Shh," he whispered, moving closer to the soldier, who was now somewhere else.

Notebook in hand, Berman carefully approached the

boy. Now both of them were in Afghanistan. Both were minesweepers in the Panjsher, hiding within a narrow corridor of sharp granite. Oleshka grabbed his friend's hand. There was no one else nearby to help them, no one to say, "Fuck this shit, let's get out of here," at least not until Oleshka and Alexei did what they were trained to do: feel the dirt until their bayonets touched something metallic, call out a warning to the others, and begin to draw a circle around the hated object. Berman gave the boy a pair of tailor's scissors.

Alexei, the future doctor soon to be back in Leningrad, only a meter in front of his best friend, began to probe around the perimeter of an antitransport mine, probably a TS-6.1, "the Italian." He called out the names of the squad members and told them he was defusing it. "I've got it by its prick!" he shouted. "Don't move forward." This was, he knew, warning enough to keep fifteen other soldiers in the rear, all doing their internationalist duty by eating dirt and smashing sand scorpions, from standing up. Oleshka drew back, turned his shoulders and waved to the men. "Stay put, we've got it!" he shouted. To Alexei he whispered, "Don't move!"

Berman froze and lay flat on the ground. He remembered. He heard a click.

It was Yevgeniya who first shrieked when the Italian exploded in Oleshka's memory, and he, like someone in the throes of an epileptic fit, threw himself against the bookcase-become-granite-wall. Several dishes of uneaten compote and Berman's beloved volumes—Gogol, Tolstoy, Chekhov, an entire set of Gorki—dropped over Oleshka's body, just as pieces of Alexei had once settled on his uniform, singeing his chest and arms in a rain of burning flesh, organ, bone. All happening during hour two hundred and thirty-six.

Simon Moskovich ran to help. He thought: Why in God's holy name do I get involved in such affairs? What's wrong with me? But with the boy's aunt collapsed in a chair, and the tailor kneeling, clutching Oleshka—"I know what it was like," he repeated as he stroked Oleshka's bruised head—who else but Simon Moskovich was capable of excavating Berman from beneath a pile of books, papers, and sticky compote?

Before Simon Moskovich reached the tailor, Berman looked at him and shook his head. "Get the notebook, please," he said. "Now!"

The bugler—he of the perfect pitch—suddenly knew what his job was, for he had just seen Alexandr Davidowich Berman, veteran of the Great Patriotic War and survivor of much worse, receive his first story as payment for repairing something. "He needs you," Yevgeniya had begged Berman when she'd brought her nephew to the tailor. "His head is about to burst. Do a little work on his uniform so he can have some peace."

"A job for a story," Berman had answered.

This was the day when a good tailor stole a nightmare and made it his own. And so Simon Moskovich forgot about his aching finger, his bitter ultimatum. Instead, he pulled away a volume of Chekhov, smeared with half a stewed prune, from beneath Berman's knee.

"Tell us everything," Berman said to Oleshka. "Leave nothing out."

Yevgeniya Vasilevna, an Old Believer with a pounding heart not long for this world, crossed herself when Oleshka, her only nephew, began to gather together what was left of his friend's body. "He moved," the boy whispered to Berman.

"I know, comrade. I know."

And that was that.

On the morning that Simon Moskovich's finger returned to its normal size, assistant curator Grigori Stefanovich received a cable from Vasilly Petrovich. It was, he knew, the news he'd been waiting for.

ARRANGEMENTS FINALLY SECURED FOR SPECIAL EXHIBITION. BRITISH ECSTATIC. FRENCH CERTAIN TO FOLLOW. ITALIANS STILL POSSIBLE. VICTORY IS OURS. HOME SOON.

Three hours later, a second cable—a postscript to the first glorious message—arrived.

INFORM OUR TAILOR. IF NECESSARY OFFER THE WORLD. IF THIS FAILS, BEG! CONTACT SOON AS POSSIBLE. ANSWER TO INSTITUTE SLAVONIC STUDIES, LONDON.

A third cable was sent because chief curator Vasilly Petrovich was beside himself with worry and too impatient to wait for an open phone line.

SUCCEED. THINK OF YOUR CHILDREN, GRISHA.

Whether it was wise or not, Grigori Stefanovich, sensing his own future riding alongside the curator's excellent fortune, reversed the assigned order of priorities. Why waste time when so much was at stake? Why even bother with silly offers of more useless rubles or, as seemed to work well in the past, a few months' worth of hot meals? In brief, why not strike before the flies gather?

The assistant curator brushed off his dark suit, and added a few important embellishments to his written instructions. He folded Vasilly Petrovich's first cable into a heavy envelope, practiced a brief speech, swallowed his pride, and, within thirty minutes, was sweating in front of the Jew. Well, actually, two Jews. Alexandr Davidowich was entertaining a friend.

"Esteemed colleague," the assistant curator began, carefully balancing himself on a shaky knee, "I have the pleasure of informing you that you have been selected to help prepare your work for viewing in the West. Vasilly Petrovich sends his regards from London, with this additional message."

Anxious to make an extraordinary impression, Grigori Stefanovich displayed the important cable and cleared his throat. To his left, the other old Jew chewed loudly on a heel of bread. "Our dear Sasha must know," he read as if the world turned on his words, "that he will be allowed to accompany us to England and. . . ."

The younger man stood face to face with the tailor. The one holding a tarnished bugle and a partially eaten piece of salted bread moved closer. Then came the biggest shock of all. Berman, wearing an old black coat smelling of mildew, put his finger over the assistant's mouth in the same way one might shush a noisy child. Next, he introduced his guest, "the great musician and craftsman, Simon Moskovich Zorin, who has recently become my apprentice."

Grigori Stefanovich never finished his invented message—never, in fact, got to the serious begging part ("I plead with you for the sake of our families, our future"), for

Berman immediately offered his hand to the assistant curator and pulled the poor soul to his feet.

Without stopping for a breath, and somehow swallowing the straight pins that adorned his mouth, Berman listed exactly what had to be provided for a skilled tailor called to service by what remained of the Soviet state.

"First, find a decent portable sewing machine made before 1937, one that I can carry without straining my back. I recommend that you call Moscow and place an order for a Singer Little Wonder with side bobbins, a rubber-backed treadle attachment, and a hard-shell carrying case. Next, so we can learn all there is to know about the old clothing, obtain a document that my apprentice and I can use to enter any major museum displaying royal garments. Finally, since we will need to travel, please find four decent tires for my apprentice's Lada, a new pair of windshield wipers, and a tape recorder to organize our thoughts as we work."

Grigori Stefanovich dutifully copied each request in his notebook. Minor needs—small sewing machine, a piece of official paper, tires, wipers, tape recorder. Everything could be arranged within two days, four if these Jews were picky about quality. But now it's coming, he thought. Now, they'll begin to haggle like peddlers.

"And?" he asked, his hand poised to note the exact amount of money, probably in hard currency. "How much, Alexandr Davidowich?"

Berman stood as rigid as one of his wire forms. His "apprentice" smiled.

"This may be difficult," Berman finally said, "and I hope I'm not asking for too much, but some things are necessary."

"Yes, anything within reason. You know I have Vasilly Petrovich's solemn word to move mountains for you."

"Five will do nicely."

Grigori Stefanovich gulped. His pen slipped against the notebook. Five hundred? Five thousand? Dollars? Marks? Not rubles? His chest began to collapse under the weight of so much responsibility. "Remember your family," he'd been warned. My God! Please, let it be rubles.

"How, dear comrade, shall this amount be paid?"

"In cartons, how else?"

In all his years of service for the sake of preserving Russian culture, during which time he had been forced to lick the behind of one fool bureaucrat after another, Grigori Stefanovich had never been in such dire circumstances. It all came down to this: agreeing to pay a bundle of notes wrapped in cartons to some Jew who knew how to sew. His mind raced: family, future, London!

"Fine, five . . . hundred did you say?"

Berman laughed as he picked up his cat. "Who could smoke that much, Grigori Stefanovich? No, no. Only five. If possible, find some Marlboros. The long filtered ones, yes? Is it too much?"

Grigori Stefanovich, his spirit soaring as high as a meteorological balloon, could not restrain himself any longer. The color returned to his cream-white face; air began to circulate in a normal manner through his lungs. He wrote down this final request.

"Done. But only five, you say? Why not six?"

Berman offered his hand. "Five, Grigori Stefanovich. Only five, though I could use a lighter or some wooden matches."

The assistant curator's fingers, the ones that still held the pen, shook when they reached the tailor. Berman leaned forward and sealed the bargain with a firm handshake.

It was this joining of clammy hands, ladies and gentlemen, that marked a singular and important moment in Russian history—for this was when Grigori Stefanovich, gold medal graduate in art history from Leningrad State University, descendant of a long line of anti-Semites, a believer in all the old, accepted verities (Red and White), learned that, despite what he had always believed, there were some Jews with absolutely no inherited ability to suck a blood ruble from a good Russian's purse!

Grigori Stefanovich was overcome by the exhilarating shock of his easy conquest—you think begging in front of an old Jew who holds the keys to the kingdom is easy?—and his head, heavy as pig iron, dropped into his hands.

"Trust us, friend," said the other Jew, offering the emotional assistant curator a full glass of the tailor's thick cherry brandy. "Provide for our needs and you won't believe what good work we are going to do for you."

4

Many years before the son of Sophie and David Aaronovich Berman decided to become memory's tailor, and long before Vladimir Ilyich took his first baby steps toward the spark of world revolution, the great Russian church historian Lev Krasny-Zlabatov, a true child of the Enlightenment, completed his life's work in a freezing basement flat in St. Petersburg. Educated in Berlin, Vienna, and Mainz at a time when his more literate countrymen considered serious scholarship the preserve of effete Frenchmen, or worse, Krasny-Zlabatov had already devoted fifty-three years to a study of the holy spirituality resident in blessed Novgorod, the mother of all Russian cities. "Who can resist the power of God and Lord Novgorod the Great?" Professor Krasny-Zlabatov asked anyone who cared to listen. "Who?"

With the blessing of His Imperial Majesty, Nicholas I, Czar of All the Russias, Lands Known and Unknown, Krasny-Zlabatov had received permission to catalog the treasures of the holy places in the ancient town—churches, monasteries, ecclesiastical libraries. "Our lifeblood courses through this place," Nicholas wrote to him in a parchment letter Krasny-Zlabatov kept locked away in a leather box as a testament to his ruler's faith, "as does the goodness of our Savior, from whom Our authority descends. Let nothing concerning Our Novgorod avoid your loyal gaze and scholar's pen."

Over the span of six thousand nights, well past the end of his youth, without a thought for wife or children or material comforts—he cared not for interruption in this world—Professor Krasny-Zlabatov toiled away, organizing history for the glory of his beloved czar and, he hoped, for the sake of the Holy Orthodox Church, whose devoted son he was. Nothing escaped his attention: not the intricate Byzantine mosaics that decorated the city's two hundred churches, the eleven thousand ikons, the lineage and teachings of the great monks and priests, the sarcophagi of the eminent metropolitans, or the three hundred and twelve statues of the saints. Starting with the remote past and working his way forward, he read every book, noted the contents of every document that passed from hand to holy hand, and personally authenticated the date of each timeworn fresco. And it was Krasny-Zlabatov, awed by the recent discoveries of French photographers and chemists, who was the first scholar to employ a Parisian photographer, a wandering drunk named Henri Paul Fouquet, to capture the faces of the living prelates and theologians. "Get close to the godly among us," he told the Frenchman, "and you'll make them live forever." Put to the test, Krasny-Zlabatov then astounded the photographer by naming each monk who had ever walked over the cobblestone walkways leading up to the Yuriev Monastery or the Cathedral of St. George.

As he entered his last boil-ridden years, however, having brought his monumental study within fifty years of his own birth, Krasny-Zlabatov made a fascinating discovery in a stack of letters hidden away by the monks of the Church of St. Simon. Beginning in 1703, when they were seized by a passion for "naming all of the Lord's enemies," the good monks had begun to document the presence of the "unre-deemed." Working in shifts so as to include a full account-ing of the various antichrists—Muslims, Turkmen, the odd Catholic merchant from Venice, Dutch Calvinists set loose within Holy Mother Russia by Czar Peter himself, and, of course, the devilish Jews—the monks scoured Novgorod from top to bottom in pursuit of their goal. No foreign name was lost, not one devil escaped their attention. Praise God, they never tired or gave up. They recorded their findings in Old Church Slavonic and always noted the exact location and manner of dress of any Muslim or Jew within the town's borders—"they who are," a certain monk named Cyril wrote, "our mortal foes must never be forgotten." Sometimes, an especially gifted monk would even make a small sketch of a Jew's head or "strange costume." And so on.

As he read through each such letter the monks had written—and, mind you, the collection spanned nearly one hundred and twenty years—Krasny-Zlabatov decided, in a fatal moment of inspired creativity, to include a selection of these missives in his enormous book. After all, the monks were very careful about details, and their observations on the town's populace would provide an interesting addition to his otherwise endless list of Orthodox holy objects and places. Elated by this scholarly decision, Krasny-Zlabatov titled his final chapter "The Strangers Among Us."

Perhaps it was his age, or maybe his failing eyesight or the burning pain of his lanced boils that made Krasny-Zlabatov so careless. Whatever it was, the devoted scholar eventually included one too many references to Jews in the final handwritten manuscript he submitted in three large bundles to the Office of the State Censor and Procurator of the Holy Synod. Carefully documenting the lives of an alien people who had lived in dank hovels within spitting distance of the town's Kremlin wall, or along narrow streets close to the River Volkhov, Krasny-Zlabatov wedged into his history the details of eighty-four Jews who, in one century or another, celebrated their bizarre holidays, baked matzos, stood on street corners selling feathers or salt (more precious than gold!), and, once each week, hid themselves from all earthly responsibilities and the monks' curious gaze. "I have done my best to describe all," Krasny-Zlabatov wrote in his last sentence. "May God and my czar be pleased."

His lifelong job finally completed just after the Orthodox Christmas—"My child goes forth into your hands," he told the procurator in St. Petersburg—Krasny-Zlabatov was so elated that he had his first drink in more than thirty years, ran out into the snow without a coat or hat, and, given the cold shock to his nervous system, was dead within the week. Given what happened shortly after his passing, poor Krasny-Zlabatov, who was buried with full ecclesiastical honors, one of his beloved Novgorod ikons resting atop his lifeless chest, was better off beneath the earth.

When Nicholas was first presented with the late Krasny-Zlabatov's monumental work, he was fully prepared to affix his royal signature, which would ensure publication and a pension for the scholar's widow. In fact, after the Procurator of the Holy Synod began reading those early chapters, the czar applauded and canceled important diplomatic conferences to listen to each beautifully written passage. For three days, as an audience of one, he was mesmerized by Krasny-Zlabatov's excellent narrative about the soul of Russian civilization. "Such patience and love he has given us," he said. "Such devotion!" He even ordered that a marble stone, sculpted in the shape of the Church of St. Sofia, be placed above this favorite scholar's grave. "Inscribe 'He Gave Words for the Love of Church and Czar' on the stone," he told the procurator, who passed on the royal command before he continued his reading. "The splendor of the Lord's Creation appeared in the frescoes painted on the walls of the Church of Sergei Radonezh," the Procurator read, "and these were dedicated to the munificence of the Holy Romanov Rulers." And so on, page after page, until, on day three of the reading of this great theological narrative, the disastrous moment struck the earth like a meteor.

"Read that again!" shouted Nicholas in his loudest martial voice. "What did you just say?"

The procurator began to shake. His face turned as scarlet as the several imperial medals against his broad chest. "This pierces my heart, sire," he said. "I had no idea."

"Read it again!"

And he did, repeating every last word composed by the dutiful monks of St. Simon in their quest after the strangers in their midst.

A certain Jew named Moses Schomberg, having been the first such Hebrew to appear next to the mighty Kremlin wall, in the otherwise peaceful year of 1494, was seen dressed in a black caftan and fur hat. Speaking an unintelligible tongue of dubious origin, said Jew held aloft three bunches of yellow feathers, which he offered the Believers for sale or barter. The Hebrew's five children sat by his feet and chanted mysterious words after their father, whose feathers, may it be known, interested none of the town's Godly subjects watching him from afar.

Poor Moses Schomberg, a hapless seller of yellow feathers from some exotic place, and the first of the eighty-four Jews to appear in Krasny-Zlabatov's final chapter, made His Imperial Majesty roar, then pounce. No fool when it came to the Yids and their pernicious influence in his empire—it was he, after all, who came up with the idea of conscripting Jewish boys, some as young as six or seven, into his armies for a term of thirty years—Nicholas snatched the manuscript from his terrified procurator. "He dares to include filth alongside purity!" he shouted as he riffled through each page, spotting one Yid name after another (the descendants of Moses Schomberg reappeared, among others of his faith, the feather-selling business having become more profitable and expansive by 1569).

The procurator, by now fallen to his knees in a fit of shame and remorse—he, after all, should have done his homework with Krasy-Zlabatov's manuscript!—was immediately stripped of his high rank and ordered to take up new duties as a minor court clerk in Vladivostok. And what was left of Krasny-Zlabatov, whose visible insult hovered beyond the pale of belief, was disinterred from a well-tended grave in his beloved Novgorod and, by direct order of Nicholas Himself, reburied in a nameless pauper's pit several kilometers from the eternal comfort of holy ground. Then Nicholas took the polluted manuscript and tore it into several sections until his hands grew weary of trying to disembowel such a thick pile of papers. What remained was only one thin section that, by God's grace, slid beneath an upturned corner of Chinese rug, where it rested for two months until the imperial parquet was waxed by a lowly serf who skated over the floor with soft rags attached to his feet. "Look, important papers," the serf said, fully expecting to be rewarded for his find. Without looking at his charge's discovery, a member of the household guard, fearing charges of gross neglect of duty, took the documents and deposited them in a leather box outside one of the imperial offices.

Things being what they were in those days of ten thousand inept bureaucrats, the last inflammatory words about Krasny-Zlabatov's eighty-four Novgorod Jews remained unseen for nearly seventy years in a damp basement storeroom of the Catherine Palace. Unlike the piles of valuable Romanov clothing, crated paintings, jewels, and goldplated dinnerware, the monks' reports about the various feather peddlers and other "strangers among us" never saw the light of day or felt the touch of another angry hand.

The Great Bolshevik Revolution, helped along in important ways by a number of persecuted Jews, finished off the last of the czars. And in one of life's incomprehensible dialectical ironies, all that remained at the bottom of the Romanov pot was eventually cherished by Soviet minions who lovingly rebuilt the czars' palaces, reset the nobility's jewels, applied new layers of gilt-edging to the plates, saw a future in displaying exquisite clothing, and, as Vladimir Ilyich himself once ordered, eventually got around to preserving and rebinding every last document from a thousand decadent years of imperial affliction—including a certain flyspecked sheaf of papers, once rescued from beneath a czar's rug, that ended up in a closed section of the Catherine Palace library. As for poor Krasny-Zlabatov, who gave life and soul for the sake of blessed Novgorod, the end beyond the end makes one shudder—for long past the day when his bones, and the splinters of his precious ikon, were relocated by an enraged czar, the paupers' graveyard in Novgorod was plowed under by the invading Wermacht armies of Field Marshal Von Paulus and turned into a series of sharp-toothed tank traps, a nightmare of reinforced concrete and steel.

In a driving rain that soaked through his shoes and fed his foul mood, Simon Moskovich packed the Lada's trunk with everything that was necessary: several cartons of cigarettes, the Singer Little Wonder, eleven bolts of cloth, the portable Victrola, several sealed containers of compote, two over-stuffed valises, a small plastic bag with goose feathers ("What in the hell is this for?" he asked), a few notebooks, and a small can of lubricating oil.

When he finished arranging everything for the twentieth time, he reattached his new windshield wipers, kicked the sides of each reasonably good tire, and only then felt secure enough to return to Berman's rooms. His money belt, filled with a variety of hard currencies, was strapped beneath his shirt. "Hurry up," he shouted to Berman, who was pacing back and forth.

The tailor waved. "Not now. Not today."

Then Simon Moskovich began to shake, less from the cold than from his frustrating memory of the previous weeks.

"Not now?" he asked the tailor. "We have everything we need and still no travel plan. When?"

Berman, as he'd done so often over those last weeks, would only say, "A bit more time . . . I'm almost finished." He shook his head and buried his face even deeper into some flyspecked sheaf of papers he'd borrowed from a closed section of the palace library. After he scribbled some notes, the tailor shut himself and his cat inside his bedroom.

Simon Moskovich kicked his wet shoes across the room. As many times as he had raged over the foolish delays, threatening to leave—"Listen to me or I'll walk out now! Well, certainly after it stops raining!"—the tailor's response was always the same. "Not today, wait a bit longer. . . ."

Simon Moskovich finally rose up in a fury. How many times had he already explained routes to Berman? This road to here? This place lets you get to that place? How many specific addresses had he gathered—museums, towns, apartment blocks in Leningrad and Moscow where he knew Jews still lived? ("They'll never stop talking," he said.) How many hours had he spent on his back beneath the filthy Lada, checking brakes, stopping oil leaks, sealing every last hole with putty? And for what? "'Wait a bit longer' isn't worth shit to me!" he complained in front of Yevgeniya Vasilevna. "I'm throwing the rest of it into the trunk."

Which he did, once again, swearing each time.

All madness followed this latest event, or so it seemed when Simon Moskovich, grunting his unhappiness in the face of Berman's unending pleas for more time, began to re- move books and other necessities from Berman's rooms.

"You'll never find your Jews in a book, Sasha. Now your apprentice is taking over," he told him, "and there's nothing to be done about it."

Whenever the tailor left for a long walk with Yevgeniya

Vasilevna's nephew, Oleshka, who had become devoted to him, or shut himself away with his damned book, Simon Moskovich stole a few more items from Berman's desk or the old trunk in which he stored the precious implements of his trade. First to go was the portable Victrola and some Melodia records, next the heavy volumes of old maps or histories—borrowed from the palace with the assistant curator's best wishes—the bolts of cloth, the wicker basket filled with needles and scissors and tailors' chalks, and, finally, the compact Little Wonder, all stacked neatly into the Lada's trunk or piled on its torn rear seat. Each day, something different was added. By week's end, Berman's world was stripped almost bare and the Lada's shock absorbers groaned under the weight of its cargo. Berman never said anything, nor did he complain when his voice echoed in the nearly empty room. But the one item that remained beyond the bugler's grasp was the book Berman took with him wherever he went. "A bit more time, that's all," Berman said as he tucked the volume under his armpit. "Be patient."

Finally, when there was little of value left to take, the Lada had just enough room for two old men. Simon Moskovich, running out of patience, slid into the mud beneath his automobile and took care of his mechanical business. "We leave for Leningrad in three days," he shouted when he saw Berman's feet shuffling past his head. "Absolutely! No more delays."

At the precise moment when the deadline was reached, on the first dry day in weeks, Alexandr Davidowich took his last early morning walk around the palace grounds. He wore his slippers so as not to disturb Simon Moskovich, who was still snoring, his forehead and hands stained brown from Pushkin mud and filthy oil. He opened Krasny-Zlabatov's manuscript to the proper page, the one with the sketch, and used a straight pin to attach a note, "You read this. I've gone to feed starving Soviet pigeons."

He took a plastic bag and quickly made his way through the gate, down the stone path and toward the palace park. The one-eared cat followed close behind. As always, he met Yevgeniya Vasilevna's nephew in the appointed place. They embraced, veteran to veteran, next to a wrought-iron bench outside the Jew's workroom. As always, Oleshka wore his paratrooper's tunic and striped undershirt.

"It's today, yes?" Oleshka asked. "Everything is ready?"

Berman nodded. He showed Oleshka what he had in the bag. "This is the best I can do."

Oleshka unfolded the material and held it up against the tailor. His finger got caught in one of the holes. "And the hat? You made the hat also?"

"Yes, of course. It's perfect."

"Everything fits?"

Berman smiled.

"And Simon Moskovich? He knows?"

"All things in time, Oleshka. Our friend is very nervous these days."

"When do you think they'll arrive?"

"Soon. The older visitors always come by nine."

"Then I'm ready, too," the minesweeper said. "I'll stay out of sight."

Alexandr Davidowich let himself into the basement entrance. He walked to the storeroom where he had found the Jew's black coat and the much-missed scrolls, and where, many years before anyone had ever heard of Berman, Krasny-Zlabatov's eighty-four Novgorod Jews had once lain forgotten, a toilet for roaches. He unpacked the plastic bag, took a deep breath, and smoked one long Marlboro after another.

Surely you understand that anticipation raises a flag that spreads itself only in the right sort of breeze—too much wind and the material can tear, too little and nothing can be seen. The brain says, do only so much; the heart, speaking for all that is crazy, blows and blows. It is a tailor's job never to do anything hastily. Alexandr Davidowich, who tried to calculate everything, creating his costume according to the sketches of Krasny-Zlabatov's observant monks, sought to act somewhere between extremes. This is what happened: he finished his smokes, then took from his large pocket a small makeup case he had kept from the Kirov—"Take this with you, Sasha," Baryshnikov told the tailor before his last performance in Leningrad, "because it smells like the stage." Finding just the right shade, he daubed a dark shadow under his eyes, a little red over his cheeks.

Next, he rested against the wall while he put on the trousers from another life. He slipped a poor man's blouse over his head, and beneath it tucked the tallith, inside the black linen coat with wide pockets that he'd fashioned. As for shoes, no change was necessary. He knew from studying the monks' sketches that even in the old days Russians had made anything out of leather look like shit, so his poor Soviet hardsoles, bearing the weight of much history, would do as nicely as eighteenth-century originals. Now that he knew he was ready, all he could do was wait for the right moment. After he put on the hat, he also remembered to thread a good quality needle and pin it inside his frayed lapel.

In the carpark by the Gatchina Gates, the first bus

arrived. "Don't rush off!" the tour guide shouted to the elderly Russians who had already begun to wander off in several directions. "We've got only two hours before we leave." Frustrated that her orders weren't being followed, the young Intourist guide poked her umbrella at one aged couple. "Please, just stay together." Then, to the driver who was searching through his satchel for his bottle, she said, "Take one more drink, Volodya, and this will be your last trip."

"Anything you say, Lydia Petrovna. Not a drop until after work!"

The guide, a tired young woman who saw her life wasting away on these endless, numbing tours for a salary that hardly paid for meals, gathered her charges together for the long walk to the palace. "They serve tea somewhere?" one of the pensioners asked. "Maybe a sandwich?" "I need some relief," another grumbled. "How long do I have to wait?"

The guide held her umbrella over her head. "This is the road over which Czarina Catherine herself once walked," she said, keeping one eye on the old man who seemed ready to urinate in a drainage ditch. "This was once a very special place, so please. . . ."

On the bus, Volodya took a long swig from his bottle and laughed. "Stupid bitch."

The wind grew stronger; dust blew everywhere; and Lydia's charges, carrying their bags and half-eaten bits of breakfast, wandered off by themselves. Despite her instructions, they had no interest whatsoever in staying together as a group. One old couple, who had only joined the excursion five minutes before the bus left Leningrad, clung to one another like lost children who didn't know the way home.

On this morning, by all accounts the four hundred and seventh time she had walked down Catherine's road toward the lovely palace, Lydia Petrovna would perform just like a trained monkey: giving out just enough memorized information to fill two hours, not a second longer; putting up with stupid questions; ordering fools not to smoke or touch anything once inside the royal bedchambers; blocking groping hands from stroking either her own buttocks or a precious piece of Romanov marble or silk; searching for some old fool who had gotten lost in the park. Then, her ankles swollen, there would be the long walk back to the bus, a forty-minute ride to Leningrad with that soused asshole Volodya, and, God forbid that anyone should be generous, no tips at journey's end. Always the same dead routine. "The park covers five hundred and ninety-two hectares," she began, after she crossed the Tower Bridge in a swirl of dust, "and. . . ."

Then she saw him. "Don't laugh at me," she would later tell ex-KGB Captain Viktor Semonovich Kostov, "there's nothing wrong with my eyes. He was dressed like someone from a Repin painting—a peasant, or a beggar who might have pulled one of those canal boats. You know Repin's *Along the Volga*? Just like that. But this one wore a slouch hat, with an old coat hanging below the knees. Oh, yes— there were feathers attached to the sides of his coat and some thin tassels sticking out from his waistcoat."

Alexandr Davidowich circled the group. He held a bunch of yellow and green feathers over his head.

"These I brought from Catalonia," he cried, swinging his wares from side to side as if to brush away an attack of summer gnats. "Have you ever seen anything so beautiful? Feathers, brothers and sisters? Maybe you want to touch one? Maybe you want to trade a story for something beautiful? Maybe you want me to mend your clothes?"

In his soft hat, good enough for fending off rain or even a few pebbles thrown by angry townsfolk at a stranger (Moses Schomberg was no fool when it came to protecting his head!), Berman twirled a few times in front of his customers. He reached into his torn pocket. A flock of pigeons settled by his feet while he broadcast breadcrumbs in a wide arc. One skinny bird, maybe drawn to a long-lost relative, settled on his hat and pecked at a bright feather.

The preliminaries finished, Berman held up a threaded needle. He sat down on a wooden bench and waited for a customer. "Feathers or repairs, brothers and sisters. Feathers or repairs."

"So I yelled at him," Lydia reported later. "It wasn't enough that I had to deal with thirty-eight old people and a drunk for a driver? This I needed, too? 'Leave us alone,' that's what I said. 'Go away!' "

Why waste time? You know how people treat a beggar or a Gypsy, yes? Feathers or no feathers, a thief knows no shame. "Go away!" a brave someone always cries. "Leave us alone." "Piss off out of here," another threatens, "or I'll call the militia." Sometimes people laugh.

But sometimes, when the stars are aligned just so, or the feathers are of good quality (what else would you expect from sunny Catalonia?), there might be one or two interested souls who will come a little closer and test the water. As you know, there are many pairs of torn trousers begging repair, in this world and the one to follow. Not to mention the lack of extraordinary and available feathers!

Lydia Petrovna was to tell the investigator, "He never

actually bothered us. I thought he was mad, and so I walked away."

Mikhail Denisovich, who had only longed to take a comforting piss, said, "You think I pay attention to half-wits when I have to worry about my bladder?"

And Volodya Sergeyevich, forgetting how his red cheeks had pressed against his bus windscreen from the aftershock of homemade vodka, mopped his sweating brown and insisted, "I was looking at a road map. No matter what she says, I never drink on the job!"

But one old man, supported by his wife in the glare of so much official bright light, told the determined Kostov, "My shirt needed mending. What's wrong with a little help?" Close to tears, his nervous wife could only add that she "always had a soft spot for feathers."

And so she walked along with her husband toward the curious old man who waved to her, pointed to his bench, and drew a needle from his lapel. "Alexandr Davidowich Berman, tailor," he said, spotting the tear in the man's shirt and beginning, even without permission, to work, before his new customers could escape. "No charge."

The old man blushed when he saw the tailor's tallith fringes touch the dirt path. He looked at his wife to be certain he wasn't dreaming. He bent over, pointed to the fringes, and, with some difficulty, put together his thoughts in a language he rarely used anymore.

"Those you shouldn't let touch the ground," he whispered in broken Yiddish. "My grandfather, rest his soul, always said they were like God's eyelashes."

"Tell me about him," the tailor asked, without looking up from his work. "Tell me what he wore."

"He looked like you," the old man murmured in the tailor's ear. "But he never stopped trembling in the face of things, even when he dressed in his best overcoat."

And so on and so forth, mouth to ear, a whispered story as payment for three large feathers and a sewn shirt that, this tailor promised, "would last forever."

Jobs do get finished. Feathers get carried away. A tailor offered his thanks aloud, first in Russian—for the sake of the old woman, a non-Jew—and, next, a quiet "zeit gezint" in Yiddish to her husband. Alexandr Davidowich bowed politely, and before he gathered his kit he left a few feathers and a bag of breadcrumbs for the children who might wander into the beautiful park.

Before Oleshka and Simon Moskovich reached him— Oleshka jumping out from behind a low hedge, crying, "It worked!"; Simon Moskovich doing a quickstep from the car park—Alexandr Davidowich took out his notebook and made a few scribbles so he would never forget about the grandfather who once told a little boy about protecting God's eyelashes. For what it's worth, he also wanted to remember how to improve the quality of fringes.

Breathless and flushed, holding Krasny-Zlabatov's manuscript over his head, the bugler yelled, "I've read it! So now we know where we're going? Is it finally settled?"

"To Novgorod," answered the crazy tailor. "Where else?"

Simon Moskovich stared at the tailor's strange clothing and shook his head. He grabbed the minesweeper's outstretched hand. He picked up a feather lying on the bench and shook his head. "Then tell him that we're fucked for sure, Oleshka," he said. "No doubt about it!"

*   *   *

For an excellent tailor and a retired glassblower to attempt to depart from the roles that society assigns them is to violate gravity.

Today, in the wash of other momentous world events that dwarf their strange enterprise, it can no longer be determined exactly when A. D. Berman and S. M. Zorin finished their initial preparations for their very serious fight to preserve memory. (Simon Moskovich thinks it happened after Oleshka the minesweeper left Berman's room with a replica of his late comrade's uniform; Berman has other ideas having to do with feathers and eyelashes.) Does it matter?

This much is safe to say: two elderly Jews, both good with their hands, worked soul to soul, argued and threw smoldering curses at one another (preserved on tape provided by the ever-grateful curator of the Catherine Palace Museum), and made plans according to ancient maps and one old manuscript. Berman kissed Yevgeniya Vasilevna, hugged Oleshka, and begged both of them to take good care of his cat and the few remaining sunflowers in his garden. "But what's the animal's name?" Oleshka asked. "Call him Doctor Alexei," said Berman. "He'll like that one."

In the end, however, on a foggy Tuesday afternoon, gravity was overcome—by a packed Lada equipped with four slightly used tires and, securely locked in a compact case, a 1935 Singer Little Wonder in near-perfect condition.

Please, consider the possibilities.

5

In Budapest, on a miserably cold day in 1956, KGB Captain Viktor Semyonovich Kostov, his stomach gurgling from lack of decent food, first thought about Greece. Seated next to his mentor, Yuri Vladimirovich Andropov, Kostov was supposed to be taking careful notes on the important interrogation. ("Watch his face and describe everything you see," Andropov had quietly ordered his favorite KGB aide, "and then rearrange it so this cowardly Hungarian prick looks guilty.") Suddenly, in the middle of poor Imre Nagy's failure to understand socialist reality and the presence of five Soviet armored divisions within his beloved city, Viktor Semyonovich had a startling vision that made his fountain pen slip in several places over the foolscap. "What sun," he wrote, "and such a warm, blue sea!"

Andropov, who noticed everything, poked his daydreaming captain and asked, "Have you been faithful to Comrade Nagy's words?" Viktor Semyonovich jerked his head away from the Aegean Sea and left tiny pools of black ink on the document. He returned to the job at hand, but not before he had written "Everything is better in Mykonos" three times at the bottom of the page and drawn a fairly good likeness of an overweight, beardless Zeus flinging a few thunderbolts from the heavens—a mistake he intended to rectify before the night was out. "Mykonos!"

Then, the vision fading in the room's stuffy air, Captain Viktor Semyonovich Kostov, the only KGB officer in Andropov's select group ever to read a book from cover to cover, looked at Nagy's sweating face and caught a whiff of the Hungarian's fear. "This asshole knows he'll be dead within the year," he wrote in Russian and Magyar. "He trembles like a good Jew on a holy day."

Captain Kostov was wrong: Imre Nagy lasted until 1958, refusing to the end to confess to imaginary "counter-revolutionary crimes." It was Andropov himself who tired of the charade and ordered the Hungarians to bring in the proper verdict. With the information included in Captain Kostov's painstaking documentation on the origins and consequences of the Hungarian revolt, Nagy and six of his closest associates were found guilty in a carefully staged trial, secretly dispatched before they could see their families, and buried in unmarked graves that even a dog wouldn't piss on. "I don't give a damn what Khrushchev thinks about our methods," Andropov told Kostov after he looked at the corpses' photographs. "I wanted this to be done properly. Forgive the pun, Viktor Semyonovich, but this was our last shot! Send your edited report to Moscow."

"As you wish, comrade," Kostov answered, gathering his papers together. "I'll take care of everything."

But Viktor Semyonovich, riding the crest of so much trust and affection for his competence as a superb investigator and linguist, overlooked a few details. In the last-minute rush to document Imre Nagy's outrageous crimes against the people, the foolscap sheets with the bored captain's doodling—all of that nonsense about Mykonos being a "better place," plus that small drawing of a clean-shaven Zeus—were somehow included in the folder Kostov submitted to the highest authorities on the Central Committee. "What is this crap?" Nikita Sergeyevich bellowed like a Ukrainian peasant. "Is this me?" he said, pointing at Kostov's drawing. "Who wrote this shit about Greece and some praying Yid?"

Let's just say that, following the First Secretary's comment, Viktor Semyonovich's career suddenly became as valuable as a clogged drainpipe. Orders were issued from KGB Chairman Shelepin's office. Andropov was immediately summoned to explain the secret and mysterious Greek code. And poor Viktor Semyonovich, once a rising star, who already enjoyed life in a large three-room, high-ceilinged flat close to the Kremlin on Marx and Engels Street, found himself in warmer water than any fisherman from sunny Mykonos. "You stupid son of a bitch!" Andropov shouted, as he waved the crucial sheet in front of Kostov's face. "Did you have to draw a cartoon of the First Secretary? Is this what I get for a father's love?"

"I'm fucked," Kostov told his wife after the interview. "I don't know what to do."

But Chairman Shelepin did. Only a few hours after Andropov washed his hands of the foolish captain, Viktor Semyonovich lost three ranks and several years' worth of pension. Relocated to a stinking communal flat on the other side of the Moskva River, he was reassigned to the netherworld of the Moscow City Militia—a humiliating demotion, beyond his understanding. "From now on you'll deal with traffic violations and drunks who leak all over themselves," Chairman Shelepin told him. "Any questions, Comrade Zeus?"

During the two-month descent into self-recrimination that followed his disgrace, Viktor Semyonovich—a double diploma holder in classical and modern languages from Moscow State University—drank as much as the old men whose vomit paved the rank holding cells he was forced to clean. He struck his wife whenever she looked at him. He refused to speak to his parents. He bathed only two or three times, and then only after he was reprimanded by the prostitutes whose phony names he entered in the precinct ledger. He never read anything. He even considered electrocuting himself by licking the wall socket in the WC.

But on the day that his long-suffering wife locked herself into a closet to escape yet another beating, Viktor Semyonovich punched the door and, finally, had the second great revelation of his life—a moment of truth born from memory and sore knuckles.

"It . . . wasn't . . . Zeus!" he yelled, pounding his fists against the door.

Now he knew. Dismissing his careless, bourgeois romanticism about a small Greek island, Viktor Semyonovich was certain that his plunge from favor after that fucking Hungarian mess resulted from his comparison of the late Imre Nagy to a praying Jew. "I should have written 'old Yid' instead of 'good Jew,' Natasha," he confessed to his wife through a crack in the closet door. "Then you deserved what you got," she sobbed, "but I never did."

Two days later, Viktor Semyonovich's wife walked out with her dishes and wardrobe. "You're a fool," she wrote him from her sister's home in Rostov. "Deal with it by yourself!"

Which he did, for over nine years. Working like one possessed by a demon, he swore off drink, rediscovered regular bathing, kept his uniform clean, and kissed the ass of every half-witted, illiterate militia officer he worked under.

Although he was assigned to the worst possible duties, he became the scourge of the drunk tanks in several of the worst precinct stations in Moscow. "You drink, you die!" he screamed at anyone who staggered in front of his desk. "Here, comrade, there's no middle ground."

Still, he earned respect and favors because he passed on to his superiors any bribes he received from fixing traffic offenses or for overlooking the activities of the wealthier pimps working the hard-currency tourist hotels. Year after year, his record was perfect, as pure as the Ural snow. And on every one of his former mentor's namedays, he sent at least one apologetic, pleading letter to Yuri Vladimirovich Andropov, who had, by 1967, risen to his rightful place as KGB chairman. "Dear Comrade Chairman," he wrote, "I, V. S. Kostov, am a new man, chastised by your wisdom and guidance. All I ask for is another chance to employ my skills in your service. I have, you see, become something of an expert on our homegrown Zionist conspiracies."

In each letter, Viktor Semyonovich detailed how, working long hours on his own time, he had mastered both Hebrew and Yiddish, studied the history and "religious practices" of the Jews, and otherwise turned himself into "a fount of information" on the illicit activities of secret Hebrew schools and the underground network of Jewish book peddlers with ties to the West—"I can," he wrote, "supply names and addresses of probable Zionist agents."

Keeping the original cause of his terrible demise in clear view, Viktor Semyonovich Kostov was a man who lived only to rectify a youthful indiscretion, the result of a flight of fancy nurtured by terrible Hungarian weather, bad food, and too many books. Beneath a framed photograph of the KGB chairman that he kept over his bed, Kostov pledged his undying devotion to the service. "I beg of you to let me help in any way I can," he told Yuri Vladimirovich. "My loyalty is absolute!"

No record exists of a direct reply from the chairman to the lowly Moscow militia lieutenant (junior grade) who spent his days wallowing among the city's vile scum, his evenings searching out Yid conspiracies. But shortly after a host of Moscow-supplied Arabs were humiliated in six days by the Israelis, and Jews throughout the Soviet Union danced in quiet celebration, Kostov's superior officer received a cryptic phone call from KGB headquarters in Dzerzhinsky Square. "Tell Comrade Kostov to keep his eyes open," the quiet voice ordered the nervous captain, "and urge him to send letters home to his old father on a regular basis."

"Don't fuck up," the captain told Viktor Semyonovich after he relayed the important message, "or you'll be cleaning up puke in some Vladivostok precinct!"

Kostov's eyes teared over. If he hadn't thought God was only a delusion held by stupid peasants, or a wandering air bubble on the brain of certain intellectuals, he would have fallen to his knees and kissed the hem of a priest's cassock.

"The postman," as Kostov was soon called, was a redeemed man. Reassigned to a better office, given the use of a ten-year-old Zhiguli sedan to help in preparing his "letters" and a phony document identifying him as a plumbing inspector from the municipal water authority, Viktor Semyonvich, who could now gain admittance to any flat or office, began his new life three days after his fortieth birthday. Dressed in a cheap Gum Department Store suit and hat, a well-worn prayer book under his arm, Kostov often wandered past the Great Synagogue along Arkhipov

Street on Jewish holidays, exchanging greetings in Yiddish with the old men, several of whom actually invited him home for a nice meal and a sabbath chat. "I come from Riga," he told them before offering a traditional Hebrew toast over a glass of sweet, syrupy wine. "My mother, God rest her soul, was a Jew." He even hissed at the Russian cretins sent by the Interior Ministry to throw snowballs or taunt the faithful who gathered outside the Central Synagogue. And on one memorable Jewish holiday, he hugged a little girl who, the remains of a mud ball dripping from her face, calmly looked at her assailants and said, "So long, comrades, it's been fine to know you."

Year after year, using his various contacts, he devoted himself to ferreting out minor examples of Zionist behavior among Moscow's many Jews: a shipment of Hebrew primers discovered in the suitcase of a Lithuanian Jew stopped for a traffic violation on Leninsky Prospekt, a scientist at the Petrochemical Institute who was noticed praying secretly in an institute closet, an actress from the Gogol Drama Theatre who received three letters from "a colleague" in Warsaw's Yiddish Theatre. "Irina Rosenkovskaya needs to be watched," he noted about the actress, "since her contacts are very suspicious." And while his letters about this and that went unanswered, and he was never rewarded with anything more than some relief from breathing noxious odors within the drunk tanks, Viktor Semyonovich knew that his messages—all of which he posted, not without a trace of irony, on the Jews' sabbath—were being read by the right people, maybe even *the* right person. "Have discovered a cache of Hebrew record albums (newly pressed) in the basement of the Mayakovsky Library; translations and names to follow."

Truth be told, hundreds of names always followed—such was the result of diligence, faith, and hard work. It was Kostov who suggested that more care—"use darker ink"—be taken in stamping internal passports with national designations. "Don't be fooled, comrades, identities must be established."

But as the "years of stagnation" passed, and loyal Viktor Semyonovich never received even the slightest response or encouragement, his bitterness grew and his interest waned. His Jewish suit became frayed and dotted with grease spots. He began to drink again. He often called in sick so he could recover from the previous night's retching. He kept some of the bribe money he had once turned over to others, and, despite frequent calls to the right offices, he was never offered a way out of that shithole communal flat he shared with two crazy old women and a retired oiler from the Baltic fishing fleet whose arthritic dog crapped in the front hall. The postman despaired and stopped sending letters.

It was in the above mood that Viktor Semyonovich, then the oldest junior lieutenant in the Moscow Militia, one too many dog turds sticking to his shoe as well as to his soul, once again contemplated suicide. He oiled his revolver, drank his way through a half-liter of vodka, turned up the radio's volume, and spent the morning of November 10, 1982—the twenty-sixth anniversary of his great Hungarian sin—wrapped in his dirty wool blanket in a blur of self-pity and sweat.

Then he heard it! "Comrades, we are overcome by grief when we tell you that our beloved First Secretary, Leonid Ilyich Brezhnev, whose guiding light illuminated the path of world internationalism and the struggle for Marxist-Leninism, has died."

Kostov threw off the soiled blanket and grabbed the radio. His throat constricted, his revolver fell to the floor. The announcer paused, lowered his voice after a few funereal bars of music, and suddenly delivered the message that gave Viktor Semyonovich Kostov a new foothold on the Soviet earth. Comrade Chairman of the KGB, Yuri Vladimirovich Andropov, a survivor among sharks these many years, had just been named First Secretary! That said, Viktor Semyonovich, wearing only his underpants, ran into the communal kitchen and kissed the old women. The oiler, a veteran sailor who didn't give a shit for such displays, turned his cheek and held onto his dog when Kostov came toward him with wet lips and blazing eyes. "Fuck Mykonos!" Kostov shouted over the radio's static and the dog's howling. "The postman is back in business!"

Three weeks later, a letter written on the finest heavy bond paper was delivered to Kostov's office by a messenger known to work for the highest authorities. The messenger walked through the crowded, rank-smelling precinct room. All conversation ceased when he dropped the missive on Viktor Semyonovich's desk, saluted the junior lieutenant, and left. His legs shaking, Viktor Semyonovich ripped open the envelope, waved aside the foul cigarette smoke that swirled around his head, and read the only order he would ever get, you might say, direct from the horse's mouth. "So?" the letter began. "Anything new for Papa?"

Viktor Semyonovich had, once again, a purpose. He did as he was asked: he found a reliable dry cleaner to refurbish his suit, he took better care of the Zhiguli, he gave up complaining about his flat, he studied confiscated Hebrew and Yiddish books. He hunted Jews. In letter after letter, he reported the results of his labors in clear prose. "The Zionists may be everywhere," he wrote, "but they are always easy to find."

As they were, indeed. In Moscow's many scientific institutes, permeating the structure of every branch of the civil service, at the MosFilm studios, even within the army itself. Buoyed by the faith he knew was placed in him by very important people, Viktor Semyonovich wore out several sets of tires in his work. He kept careful records ("A secret Hebrew class is being taught by a certain V. M. Bar-shavski, a biomathematician at. . . ."), wrote detailed notes, compiled translations of Israeli newspapers smuggled into the country by American Jews, and still found time to melt into the crowd of young Jews lining the quarter-mile length of Arkhipov Street to celebrate Simchat Torah, or to share a glass of nice honey wine with a fellow Jew too stupid to pick apart his phony Yiddish accent. Although he never received any direct instructions, he knew he had decades' worth of work ahead of him until, as he noted in one letter, "the Zionist stain is erased."

Thus fortified, his reputation grew whenever his hard work resulted in new arrests, trials, a few more Yids traveling first class to the wastes of Perm 31, or the howls of outrage that appeared in the international Zionist press. "I salute your fine efforts, Viktor Semyonovich," an aged militia colonel whispered to him at an official reception. "Tell me, comrade, have you ever been to Leningrad?" Viktor Semyonovich shook his head. "But as you know, comrade colonel, I would welcome any new assignment."

The next day, Kostov took delivery of a factory-fresh black Zhiguli with comfortable seats and a working heater.

Unfortunately, even the crappy replacement tires Kostov bought for his new Zhiguli lasted longer than Yuri Vladimirovich Andropov, whose amazing ascent to power was cut tragically short by a weak heart after only fifteen months. In the old days, such a momentous change would have frightened Viktor Semyonovich. But even when the party elevated that doddering old fart Chernenko to the mountaintop, our Viktor, now roaming Leningrad streets in a clean suit, close to the synagogue on Lermontovsky Prospekt, was too busy collecting names and possibilities to care. After all, who in his right mind could deny his value? The Central Committee might change like the leaves; the Jews lasted forever. But out of respect and fond memory, in his flat he draped Andropov's rosy-cheeked portrait in black bunting and always kept a few fresh flowers nearby.

Viktor Semyonovich celebrated his good fortune in Leningrad, and his sixtieth year of life, by attending, three times in one week, performances of *Swan Lake* and *Eugene Onegin* at the Kirov, where he admired the grace of Russian dancers and the beautiful costumes that shimmered like ice crystals dropping over the Neva River.

A policeman's life is like a well-made automobile that moves over smooth streets and, a moment later, gets stuck in an open hole with jagged edges and nails. One kilometer's worth of satisfaction is soon offset by three clicks of frustration, discomfort, and loss. And so it was for Viktor Semyonovich. In Peter's glorious city by the Neva, after many years of dedicated service, he was finally slowing down. Plagued with varicose veins and prostate problems that made pissing a nightmare, the only recently promoted militia captain rode through his days toward a pension, a medal (he hoped), and frequent visits to doctors. Even after Chernenko's death and his replacement by Mikhail Sergeyevich, Viktor Semyonovich was determined to do his duty until the end, albeit with no great interest or hope for much.

What else was there to do? Despite the terrible setbacks to Lenin's dream—disaster in Afghanistan, that faggot Gorbachev's lawyerly weakness, ingrate Polacks and Balts spitting in the face of Soviet generosity, and continuous disruptions within the KGB itself—Viktor Semyonovich would never again, he promised himself, give in to despair. He had accomplished much in Leningrad, where he had lived for several years as a part-time Latvian Jew with close ties to the frightened community of Yids—not to mention the expert advice he still gave to the local militia on the proper handling of drunks, prostitutes, and Zionist hooligans. "I'm like a computer, comrades," he wrote in a postscript to a recent letter naming names. "What could possibly replace my memory?"

Three months short of his sixty-fifth birthday, Viktor Semyonovich's prostate took a turn for the worse. He was admitted to a special militia clinic. "It feels like it's going to fall off," he complained, wincing with pain as he stood over the toilet holding his limp member. "It's like our current government, eh?" Specialists were consulted, the captain was anesthetized, and a biopsy performed. Viktor Semyonovich, still woozy from the drugs, was told he would have to wait until the next day for the results. "Then turn on the radio and let me sleep," he mumbled. "I feel like shit."

In his dream, which he would later recollect as the most

vivid he had ever had, he was drawn, naked, into the blue Aegean. Hour after hour, he swam alongside the fishermen's boats. "I'm from Latvia," he told the Greeks who offered him food and wine. "My mother was a Jew." Then, what must have been hours later, tired from his constant swimming, his belly filled with heavy black olives, he floated on his back toward the shore. "Go ahead, bite my ass," he shouted to the fish. "Mykonos is mine!"

No one was more surprised than Viktor Semyonovich when the fish spoke back, calling his name over and over as the warm water lapped over him. "Are you there? Can you hear me, Kostov?"

Boats floated past him. As if a plug had been pulled, the water began to drain away. Viktor Semyonovich felt his left side sinking. In a panic lest he disappear beneath the waves, he began to stroke against the current. Then a cool, soft hand rubbed his face. "Up, up, comrade, you have a visitor."

The light in the ward was blinding. Two men stared down at him: one told him there was no sign of cancer ("Only a small blockage, so you'll live forever, comrade!"); the other, more familiar in a militia uniform and a cap the size of a dinner plate, bent down and pinned a silver medal on Viktor Semyonovich's stiff hospital gown. "A well-deserved tribute," the colonel said. "Now, what do you think about this?"

"Comrade?"

Through the haze that was once Mykonos on a beautiful morning, Viktor Semyonovich managed to prop himself up against his pillow and regain some sense. The medal poked into his breast. When he turned to his left, he saw that the fish that had called him a few minutes before was only a thin folder with documents sticking out. For the first time in a very long career, our Viktor Semyonovich had the pleasure of hearing a high-ranking officer beg his assistance.

"Study these, please," the colonel said. "Then tell us if we should be worried. Things being what they are, we can't afford to take any chances."

"Sir?"

"Just read them and let me know."

His backside aching, Viktor Semyonovich offered a weak salute to the busy colonel. When he was finally alone in the room, he rang for some brandy and strong tea. Although it took every bit of his strength to reach the window, he did so and, in the sunset glow that turned his hospital gown as pink as Lenin's holy tomb, thanked his mother's God for a few more years. He even cried. Pain or no pain, he breathed deeply and took a long, satisfying piss in the sink.

It was there that he opened the folder filled with reports and odd bits of junk—lengths of thread, two needles, a cheap cassette, a filter from an American cigarette. Some of the sheets fell into the sink, others he saved; the cigarette butt disappeared down the drain. Even with his mind dimmed by drugs, brandy, and residual pain, Viktor Semyonovich, as only a good officer could, began to sort things out for those too stupid to understand what was happening in front of them.

He emptied the folder's contents onto his bed and read about a series of malicious acts of hooliganism in Novgorod that had baffled local militia officials. Beginning three weeks before Viktor Semyonovich first felt the hot premonition of his own end, the initial report included the testimony of state curator P. V. Chulenkin, "a longtime party member," who discovered the rearrangement of two exhibits in Novgorod's Kremlin Museum. Said exhibits displayed the priceless fourteenth-century clothing of several czarist boyars. Comrade Chulenkin reported that "the clothing was removed and replaced by ragged coats worn by the Hebrew traders who once lived by the city's old gate." Pinned to one of the Jews' coats was a note: "They lived here, too." No other tampering was discovered, although "a loose silver button was reattached to one boyar's vest, and two ruby chips were refastened" to their original mooring in the noble lord's fur cap. Folded neatly and set on the floor next to their former place of glory, "the exhibits were otherwise undamaged." The militia officer who took the report noted the discovery, however, of "several lengths of thread, two long needles, and a crushed feather." A thorough search of the museum's premises failed to turn up any additional physical evidence.

There was more: in four other state museums—the Archbishop's Palace, the magnificent Palace of the Facets, the Dukhov Monastery, and the Guard House on Zastavnia Street—responsible officials complained of similar incidents of tampering. In the Archbishop's Palace a porter discovered an old skullcap wedged into a display case; in the Palace of the Facets, a babushka cleaning the floors removed a flyspecked leaf containing a Hebrew prayer ("translation unavailable") that was tacked to a stucco wall; in the former Imperial Guard House, a vigilant Young Pioneer found a cassette recording dangling from a portrait of the First Secretary ("of an unnamed person speaking in a hushed voice about a secret Jewish ceremony"); and, in the Dukhov Monastery, a priest found a Jew's prayer shawl placed on a silver stand next to a holy ikon of St. George, along with an explanatory note: "Dear Good, Russian Fathers, this might have been worn by Moses Schomberg, late of this city, who once sold feathers not more than five meters from this very place. Some time ago."

Viktor Semyonovich read each report like a schoolboy doing his assigned homework. He studied the handwriting on the two notes and concluded they were written by the same person. He held the thread up to the light, pulled hard, and knew it was too good to have been made in the Soviet Union. He thought about the repairs to the boyars' clothing, stared at the amateurish photograph taken of the prayer shawl, and, specks or no specks, his Hebrew was good enough to allow him to read the Kaddish that some poor babushka had plucked from a palace wall. As for the skillfully decorated skullcap, Viktor Semyonovich, impostor Jew at many holy day services, could only conclude that this had been made by someone who wished God to smile upon his head. He listened to the tape recording and smiled. In a weak hand, he scribbled a note he would later recopy and send to the Novgorod Militia: "Some Jew wants a place in the sun. Who is Moses Schomberg (get name, address)? Be vigilant. Your hooligan knows how to sew."

All of this effort pushed Viktor Semyonovich to the ends of his strength. He had enough will left to dribble another pale rivulet into the sink. He took a gulp of brandy to ease the pain and collapsed into a chair. His head filled with ideas, and he dozed along the edge of sleep for several hours until the door was flung open. Opening his eyes, Viktor Semyonovich saw the colonel's shaken white face.

"It's worse than we thought," the colonel said. "They've gotten to Lenin!"

Viktor Semyonovich pulled his gown down so as to cover himself. He asked permission to remain seated. He ignored his physical infirmities and the call of certain fish, and listened with grave attention to this latest problem.

When everything was said—"a letter discovered inside Lenin's shirt . . . left by some bastard Yid . . . a trusted tailor . . . repairs"—the officer kicked over a nightstand. Captain Viktor Semyonovich Kostov, so close to the end of his career that he could almost taste the Greek olives and feel the warm water, laughed.

"This you find amusing, Kostov?" the colonel shouted, holding up a photocopy of the letter written over a blueprint of the great Bolshevik.

Viktor Semyonovich took the letter from the colonel's sweaty hand and read each of the Jewish names a certain tailor felt were so important. He urged the officer to maintain a professional calm and share a glass of brandy with him. "I will need to interrogate this fool academician, Pudenkin," he said. "Also, you must get for me a new suit, appropriate for a prosperous nobody. And it would not hurt, colonel, if you could provide me with a new Zhiguli sedan."

"You know what this is?"

Naturally, his years of ordeal had taught Viktor Semyonovich to choose his words carefully before speaking. "This," he said, without any fear of being misunderstood, "is what I have been waiting for my whole life."

6

Olga Mikhailovna's angina began to act up as soon as her older daughter told the news about the tailor who was fixing everything. Carrying two skirts and one of Dimitri's jackets, Raisa was frantic to find a place in the queue. "Hurry, Mamushka! He won't stay too long. Bring him your wedding dress."

This is when Olga Mikhailovna's pains started, like small forks twisting inside her chest. She sat down a few meters away from the closet where her dearest "memory," wrapped in a torn flour sack, was hidden away from prying eyes.

With only three pills left until her son-in-law Dimitri visited the pharmacist in Borki, Olga Mikhailovna had to decide how to deal with her heart: take one pill now before she unlocked the closet and looked inside, or save the whole lot—one to get out the door, two for the walk—until later. The Devil's arithmetic.

Olga waved her hand and stayed put. Carefully, she crossed her legs. She knew her limits and how to consider the consequences of any decision involving movement. From what she had already heard, *he* wasn't going anywhere, so why rush?

Dimitri stumbled in. "Tatyana Stefanova has given the Jew her cousin's dress," he said, his breath already reeking from vodka. "Trust me, with all the material involved for that one, this Jew will be here for at least two days! Besides, his Lada is screwed over."

So, again, she thought: one pill to get out the door? One for the walk? Keep the last one under her tongue while she cradled the package and remembered? Beg Dimitri to come with her and watch whatever happened? Maybe this tailor would cheat her? What if he asked for too much? Should she offer the amber necklace Fyodor had given her before the war? ("It's worth more than you think, sir," she would say. "You see how perfectly preserved the fly is? It came from Poland. What more could you want for someone special?") Maybe she should take a nap? Heat water for tea? Eat a small piece of day-old bread? Would her knees support her?

She closed her eyes and took small gulps of air after every pain, just like the doctor advised. Then, between jabs at her heart muscle, she rehearsed some words.

"Sir, my name is Olga Mikhailovna. I was born on this collective farm. I know everyone. How could I not? Everyone, you see, has eaten the bread I baked in the farm ovens. In better times, I made the crusty dark kind with honey, sometimes molasses; ryes, whites, rolls for weddings with drops of sugar, mint, or poppy seeds. During the war, those shit Germans took everything worth stealing, even my oven. Five days after my twins were born—only five days!—I dug a hole, lined it with tin, and mixed coarse wheat husks with sawdust. If the children choked on it—this happened, sir, in August of '43—I soaked the stuff in my own milk. Or I chewed it for them, with a little bit of apple or berry . . . whatever I found nearby in the orchards. You ask any of the older ones on the farm about Olga

Mikhailovna's war bread. I baked, they ate. Some of the children lived . . . people remember such things. As God is my witness!"

Olga Mikhailovna then saw herself holding out her package, which she would unwrap fold by fold to show him how important this was: Chinese lace, embroidered satin her mother bought in Odessa (at least two meters' worth!), brushed muslin lining, and some pressed lilacs. How could this Jew tailor, whose old car ran out of steam on the Borki road, refuse to charge her a fair price after he saw what she had?

However, if words meant little and he took one look at her wedding dress and began to bargain like a blackmarket street merchant, she would groan and offer fifty-three rubles from her purse. If this didn't satisfy, then she would part with the amber. Maybe she would mention her lost milk again? Or something about her wedding day? What else was there to give?

"Please, sir. Please!"

Suddenly alert, Olga Mikhailovna, People's Heroine during the Great Patriotic War (and rightly so) forgot about her heart pills, the need to ask Dimitri to help her walk, or the details of her beautiful wedding day and night. She got up and found her birch cane, the one Fyodor used during his last two years, God smile upon his soul, and the plastic bag with the English words on it. The closet key she removed from the chain around her neck, where it rested, as always, in the loose skin between two moles.

For luck, she kissed the key and crossed herself. She opened the closet door and pushed aside her old work aprons, raising a small cloud of flour dust, a baker's snow, that still clung to them and settled on the sack wrapped around her dress. Because the smell was still fresh, she stuck out her tongue and tasted honey and dill.

Then, in a moment of heaven-sent inspiration, Olga Mikhailovna pried open the chest on the top shelf and found the one item that any Yid would swoon over. "For this," she said as she stuffed the musty coat into her plastic bag, "I'll get whatever I want."

About this coat, and the contents of its pocket . . .

They say that one of Napoleon's misguided officers, some stupid fop of a marquis in charge of a decimated cavalry brigade of two hundred Lyonnais, got lost during the terrible retreat from Moscow during the early winter of 1812. Equipped with bad (but beautifully drawn) maps purchased in a Lyon antiquarian's shop and a compass he never understood—well, have some sympathy, the poor man had already lost three fingers for his little emperor— the marquis, half-blinded by pain, ordered his dragoons to ride north instead of due west after they left our beloved Moscow in flames. Toward "Pologne," he assumed; toward his garden, wife, and mistress.

But almost as soon as he passed through the outer suburbs, the marquis was plagued by constant, cowardly attacks on his men. If they stopped for a piss or a moment's rest for their horses, Don Cossacks sniped at their rear, killing animals and men. With the little sense that remained to him after forty-three of his men froze fast to their horses while crossing the Volga, the marquis followed a frenzied spider's-web route to safety: turning back, losing horses in snowdrifts, reversing his route eight or nine times depending upon the direction of musket balls, and eventually forgetting in which direction the sun, when it could be seen, actually set.

"He's fucking us real good," a young sergeant shouted, after which the marquis, finger stumps burning, mind raging, dropped his worthless piece-of-shit compass, rode next to the unfortunate sergeant and shot him through the eye. After that, no one (there were still one hundred and twenty-two men alive) complained about anything more for at least six hundred kilometers.

During the seven weeks it took the marquis to lose fifty-six more of his men to a small detachment of Volga Cossacks, the commander's face froze into a maniac's grin from which Satan himself would have fled. The marquis ranted at the slightest hint of insubordination; he had three frantic dragoons shot for insisting that, given their current position beneath the north star, France probably lay to their left. Each time one of his dragoons breathed his last, the marquis, in an ingenious stroke of military cunning, removed the dead man's trousers or coat. He ordered another survivor to wear it and never remove one article of clothing under penalty of death. "Even if you have to mess yourself," he grinned. "Even if your prick can't move under the weight." And this is why the sixty-six remaining dragoons, still riding in the wrong direction, shat themselves in the bloodstained coats of a hundred others and lost the ability to locate their privates. Setting an example for the men by attaching eleven swords from his own several uniforms, the marquis, who could hardly move for all the clothing he wore—"If those pigs think we're well fed," he told his adjutant, "no one will bother us"—looked, from a distance, like a huge summer squash atop an emaciated gelding. "We must kill the fat one," the Cossacks said whenever they planned a new skirmish, "but save him for last."

In this amazing journey toward oblivion, the marquis dispatched every Russian peasant he came across. He even executed some dogs by hanging them from the rafters of an Orthodox church in Krestoy. Good liberal that he was, he decapitated an old priest because the poor bastard offered the grinning Frenchmen a bowl of goat's milk, which the fool thought was poisoned. With sixty-six fat Lyonnais dragging behind him, the well-insulated marquis, now riding due north on a mound of his own crap, covered a thousand kilometers in the wrong direction, knowing that any day he would hear Polish spoken and, God willing, find someone to run a hot bath for his battered and filthy body.

One bright morning in late December, having accomplished the impossible, the overburdened dragoons finally reached the limits of chance at the banks of an enormous frozen lake as blue as a precious moonstone. Since the marquis had long ago lost track of time and geography, he was certain that Poland was within sight. "*Ici est Pologne, mes amis,*" he called out to his exhausted dragoons. "*Pologne!*"

Dismounting with difficulty, the fat-seeming Marquis packed his nose with the last of his expensive Parisian snuff, sneezed loudly, and caught a whiff of sweet smoke wafting above a dozen poor huts—miracle of miracles, what smelled like baked pastry. After months of consuming horseflesh, boiled leather, and perhaps a few choice bits of recently deceased dragoon, the aroma of bread and sugar was more powerful than a whore's perfume. And this is when the marquis knew that, finally, without any doubt, he had reached safety, and the comfort of hot water.

Tears formed in the marquis's eyes. He tried to remember a few words of Polish. When the rich smell became even stronger, he began to drool in anticipation of an excellent meal. He also thought about soft, white linen, and the possibility of a woman's thighs. As he approached the largest hut, he shed one coat after another until he was as naked as a newborn. Not more than ten meters behind him, several of his dragoons, following their commander's lead, did the same.

"Take whatever you need!" the marquis shouted as he waded through the snow toward the smoke and the cake. "Trust me, these Polish animals love us more than life!"

Two steps away from the hut's door, the foul-smelling marquis, wearing only the tattered remnant of his plumed campaign hat and carrying just one tarnished saber for protection, fell across the threshold. "Good morning, me need a fat pig," he said, in the only Polish words he knew. "Fat pig."

Two weeks later, as he awaited his own execution tied to an apple tree in front of a snow-covered hillock, the marquis would remember two images. The first being the two weeping willows in the garden of his lovely beige chateau in Lyon; the second, no less powerful because it was so recent, the screams of the eleven frightened Jews who scurried away from his nakedness in that hovel that was supposed to be in Poland.

As you've already guessed, the marquis, a fool to the end, had never left the borders of Holy Mother Russia. The Poland of his long-deferred dreams was far to the west; what lay in front of him was a poor Russian shtetl, thirty kilometers southeast of Novgorod, where on that particular night some peasant Jews were about to celebrate the Hanukkah feast with candles, potatoes fried in oil, and freshly baked poppy seed rolls formed into the exact shape of the marquis's ridiculous hat. "Russia, Excellency!" one of the Jews shouted. "This is our Russia."

In an explosion of curses brought on by madness and disappointment, the marquis slashed at the Jews, killing several closest to him. Although he chased the women into the snow for his dragoons to deal with as they saw fit, the old men and their sons he saved for himself.

Trapped in a land conceived in hell, the marquis forced the Jews to remove the corpses of their brothers and then to boil some water for a bath. Next, still smiling as he babbled, over and over, his Polish sentence about pigs, and the Jews begged for mercy, he made them take off their clothes and face the wall while he took his time washing away months of encrusted dirt. In his flowery and not untalented hand, he drew a little sketch, and wrote a precise description in his leatherbound journal, of the cowering, naked Jews.

The execution of the frightened Jews as spies, which the marquis recorded in his journal as a necessary "military measure" to safeguard his surviving men, has long been forgotten. What has been remembered, however—what lingered far beyond a marquis's dementia brought on by months of snow and lost borders—were the black coats and fancy hats he took from four of the Jews who most closely approximated the size of his own thin body.

Newly clad in the Jews' holiday coats, to which he attached his several sabers and pistols, even the marquis couldn't postpone the terrible fate which awaited him in the following days. After stuffing his saddlebags with still-warm rolls and silver candlesticks, his smile washed clean by tallow soap, he finally located the direction of the dying sun and rode west with his dragoons, only to be surrounded and captured five days later by some very angry Cossacks.

Although when they shot this mad French dog who kept mumbling in Polish he was slightly thinner than they expected, the Cossack officer left the Frenchman's body tied to a broken wagon, not only as the deserved result of his crimes against the Russian people, but also because he took away from the Cossack the pleasure of killing his Jews. Before he rode off with his new French sabers and silver candlesticks, the Cossack ordered the serf who had watched the whole business to "leave this scum where he is for two days."

Order issued, the officer then cut off the marquis's ring finger for a souvenir, polished the silver candlesticks with oil, and set off to find the rest of the doomed Lyonnais.

Yuri Ivanovich Stepov, the serf who had the bad luck to witness such horrible scenes—he was only sharpening a scythe when the Cossacks arrived with the grinning prisoner trussed up like a squealing sow—never did learn the true nature of the marquis's crimes. After all, what was Yuri Ivanovich in the scheme of things other than some miserable piece of property with a game leg and ten hectares of black soil to manage for an absentee nobleman? Still, an order was an order. So he waited for two days and forbade any of his eight children to poke the marquis, whose frozen body he covered with hay and sticks to show signs of disrespect. He then built a fire of birch logs, let it burn constantly to thaw the icy ground, and hacked away at the earth until the frozen marquis's hole was prepared.

At such times, Yuri Ivanovich, who was no less than the great-great-great-grandfather of our Olga Mikhailovna —she, the future heroine-baker of a much later war—

had to think about his own needs. This is why, just before he dropped the marquis into the earth, he peeled away the thick tangle of black coats from the body until he reached the only one that wasn't too soiled or mangled by rifle balls and powder burns. Having removed this quality, prize coat, Yuri Ivanovich mumbled a few Christian words over the corpse, covered it with dirt and charcoal, and had his five sons push a large boulder over the mound. "Even this one deserves a resting place," he told them as he fondled his new coat and the contents of its pocket. "Leave the rock where it is or I'll beat you until you scream."

Three days later, before he could even enjoy some warmth from a dead Jew's best coat, Yuri Ivanovich's weak heart gave up the spirit during the second hour of a howling blizzard. His grieving widow locked the coat in a small trunk, which she hid in the rafters, because she was too sad to pass it on to one of her sons. This is where the coat remained, unnoticed and unworn, through the lives and deaths of four generations of Yuri Ivanovich's many worthy descendants and a host of unlucky czars.

It was Olga Mikhailovna's own mother who rescued the old trunk, oiled the wood, and gave it to Olga Mikhailovna before her joyous wedding to her beloved and handsome Fyodor Nikolayivich. After the Nazi fascists left in 1944, having offered their farewell by shooting a dozen old men and boys in the collective's flowering apple orchard, Olga Mikhailovna, her breasts depleted of milk and warmth, hid her lovely wedding dress beneath her great-great-great-grandfather's prize coat, because, as everyone knows, the past must be treated with due respect. Failing that, Olga Mikhailovna, baker of sawdust bread for paper-thin children, knew that the fancy coat (and the sheet of paper she found inside its single pocket) could always be traded someday or sold for something better.

Rumor has it the Americans have developed high-powered spy satellites that, from thousands of kilometers above earth in God's space, can determine a dog's sex or the license plate numbers on a military vehicle. If this is so—and who in his right mind would deny the Americans such feats of technological genius?—then it's possible to imagine such an instrument, swinging in orbit somewhere over blessed Novgorod, snapping, just by chance, a crisp black-and-white photograph of two old men (could the Americans tell they were Jews?) standing beside a smoking 1973-production-year Lada with a broken oil gasket and a bent tailpipe. One of the men is about to kick the car's side.

This much you already suspect: Berman and Simon Moskovich, recent rearrangers of state and church property, were lost in a minor sort of way. Seeking the road west from Novgorod to Luga—"There's a museum I want to visit," Berman said, "but I promise not to touch anything this time"—Simon Moskovich became disoriented when a cloud of black diesel smoke exploded from the exhaust pipe of a Bulgarian truck and obscured his failing vision at a crucial roundabout.

Unable to see well, the bugler mistakenly drove south toward Borki on a rural road designed in hell or Moscow. This was the terrible road that made the oil gasket give up the ghost. Worse, in a series of potholes no one ever gave a shit about fixing, the Lada's tail pipe was twisted into a piece of macaroni very close to the exact spot where, many years before, the marquis had his last, sweet vision of French willows.

"Have a rest," Berman told an exasperated Simon Moskovich, whose toe ached from the energetic kick he'd administered to the Lada. "Stay with the car. I know what to do."

Daylight was hanging by a thread, so to say, when Alexandr Davidowich left Simon Moskovich and his damaged toe to seek help. Carrying the Singer Little Wonder and some extra material, he crossed through an apple orchard, waved at a large woman changing a tractor tire, and offered to barter his services with anyone on the collective farm who knew something about metal and oil.

"It won't even cost you a kopek," the tailor said, pointing to his sewing machine. "I can fix anything made out of cloth." As a demonstration of his seriousness and good faith, Alexandr Davidowich showed the woman a color photograph of one of the Czarina Elizabeth's court gowns. "You should have seen this before I mended it," he said, putting it into her soiled hands. "It was a mess!"

Whether for good or ill, our Russians are a hospitable people. As long as they don't have to deal with Gypsies or Germans, they'll give a glass of kvass to the thirsty, a chunk of bread to a hungry beggar, a linen dressing to the wounded. Then, having pleased the Savior, they turn away. But to someone who says "I can fix anything made out of cloth" . . . well, let's just say that their world opens up, because who among them doesn't own a torn dress or a suit that might, in the hands of a skilled tailor, once again turn into something useful. Or beautiful. Or both.

"Alexandr Davidowich Berman, from Leningrad," he said. "I once made costumes at the Kirov. Can you help me?"

The news that a Jewish tailor from Leningrad had arrived—"You should see this picture he has," the woman yelled—moved around the communal outbuildings on the First of May Collective faster than a telegraph message through copper wire. "Lydia, Natasha, Liudmila," she cried. "Come quickly, there's a tailor here who doesn't want money."

In all the excitement, Alexandr Davidowich, now an honored guest despite his suspect surname, momentarily forgot to remind his hosts about the poor bugler's swollen toe and his crippled Lada.

Inside a tractor shed illuminated by a hissing kerosene lamp, Berman hunched over his amazing portable Singer. In what must stand as a new all-Soviet record, the tailor required only two hours to finish mending seven dresses and three jackets for the patient dayshift women of the First of May Collective farm.

"I'll help everyone," he said. "Put on what needs to be fixed."

And so they did. Wooden chairs were arranged in a semicircle around the tailor, who made his machine hum. He shared a package of cigarettes with the men, and, when it was offered, accepted a bowl of cold cucumber soup and thick bread. Between mouthfuls of soup and bread, he pinned hems and attached small buttons to blouses. He transformed a father's trousers into something his thinner son could wear to a dance. He reattached a sleeve to a suit-coat, and removed another for a man recently deprived of his right arm. Twice, he heard someone clap. He never asked for money. He just sewed, ate more soup, and swatted at the moths flying into the bright lantern's sun.

Ladies and gentlemen, when the long-neglected Simon

Moskovich came limping up the collective's main path, a barking dog yipping at his heels, Berman suddenly felt all the shame that was due. Even though his own legs ached from sitting on a large boulder, he ran to assist in any way he could.

"This is my apprentice, friends. A talented tailor. He is the one who needs your help!"

If one tailor can slow down the world, two can make it stop. Such a fuss!

One of the men brought out a canvas chair and a bottle of pepper vodka. Someone else offered a stool. Before the apprentice could form the first words of a violent curse for being deserted in the dark on some godforsaken road, Simon Moskovich's foot was undressed by two women and placed, as gently as a baby, into a pail of warm water.

Although he was grateful for a bit of relief and a soothing drink, the bugler made Berman bend down so he could hear one more request: "Go screw yourself, Sasha," he whispered in Yiddish. "And when you're finished enjoying yourself, beg one of the comrades to fix that piece of crap I left on the road."

Irina Valentina, who was not more than a week away from giving birth, approached the second Jew. She held a tiny baptismal gown. "Please, sir, could you mend this?" she asked.

His toe throbbing along with his anger, Simon Moskovich—master of three basic stitches and the rudiments of simple repairs—pointed to a chair. "Sit, sit," he said as he unfolded the torn gown. Then he smiled and asked Berman for a length of thread and a "good, sharp needle for the little mother."

Work, you see, is a balm.

Thirty stitches and five carefully mended tucks later, when all that could be done was done, Simon Moskovich's Lada was finally towed behind a tractor into the courtyard. Advice was offered about leaking oil and twisted tailpipes; tools appeared. Dimitri, a tractor mechanic in a newly repaired, double-breasted jacket, slid beneath the Lada's undercarriage with a flashlight. In the shadow of such competence—his own as well as the grateful mechanic's—Simon Moskovich's toe stopped aching, although anger still buzzed somewhere inside his head when he looked at Berman.

"Mamushka!"

You would think the arrival of an old woman, even one as well known to everyone as Olga Mikhailovna, would hardly cause a ripple of attention. But when Olga Mikhailovna slowly walked into the crescent of light surrounding Berman and his tired apprentice, all talk stopped.

There was a soft moan when Olga Mikhailovna, who had somehow managed to squeeze her large body into a much narrower dress, approached the two Jews. Dimitri the mechanic, viewing everything upside down beneath the Lada, bumped his forehead when he tried to get a better view of the linen and silk that whisked past him.

"Mamushka!"

No, not this night. Here, as any fool could see, was a bride. A lovely bride. Long, white hair braided into a bun. Flowers, too: jasmine, a few yellow roses, some violets from the box garden outside her window, even the smell of mint, which she chewed to cover her breath. This was something to see.

Still and all, poor Olga Mikhailovna, her heart racing because she was so nervous, holding onto an old coat and the assorted flowers, had to swallow her last pink pill when two seams, stretched to their limits across her waist and alongside her ample hips, ripped apart.

Olga Mikhailovna's face turned as white as the jasmine. This was a tailor's emergency!

Under the circumstances, no formal introductions were necessary.

Everything that Berman did that night—fixing the ordinary as well as the extraordinary—was done without complaint or question. Although his back ached from so much concentration, and his eyes occasionally went out of focus, he measured and cut the way careful tailors do when a seam requires a new life. "Take hold while I sew by hand," he told his apprentice, who hobbled over and stood next to him. "More light . . . more light."

From one side of the courtyard to the other, the collective's workers gathered to watch the Jew alter the old woman's special dress to fit her new requirements. "His name was Fyodor Nikolayivich," she told her tailor, "and I used to bake bread. . . ."

"Shush, Mamushka," Dimitri said when he pulled himself from beneath the Lada. "Shush."

This is how things ended: Olga Mikhailovna went inside a neighbor's house and removed her fine dress. Then Berman went to work, because for some women everything should be done: realigning layers of material, a new white button, a few extra inches let out along the bustline, a careful ironing of ancient creases and unnecessary folds from top to bottom.

After one hour, Olga Mikhailovna was finally able to show off her flowing Odessa wedding dress. "Mamushka!

Look at you," her daughter cried. As promised, no rubles jumped from one pocket to another, and the old girl didn't even have to part with the amber necklace that displayed a small ant's golden tomb.

And this is how it would have ended, toward dawn, if Olga Mikhailovna—all mint, jasmine, and a waterfall of silk—had simply taken what was hers, thanked the Jew, and walked home to sleep with her memory.

No, let's be true to events. You take, you give something in return—just as Olga Mikhailovna did when she turned to Alexandr Davidowich and gave him the musty coat and one loose page from the marquis's long-forgotten campaign journal.

"My mother told me it once belonged to one of your kind," she said about the coat. "All I know is that it kept someone warm. There's also a small cap inside the pocket. The paper means nothing to me."

No longer feeling her age (or the dangerous lack of tiny pink pills), Olga Mikhailovna left Berman in the shed before he changed his mind and recalculated the value of his expert work.

The next day, Berman and his apprentice were given a basket of sausage, a container of fresh kvass, a bowl of sour cream with cucumbers, and some apple jam. After a few tries and a lot of smoke, Dimitri fiddled with this and that bolt and finally succeeded in giving Simon Moskovich's Lada the spark it needed.

Simon Moskovich would surely have driven away earlier than he did, but he had to wait until Berman scoured the collective farm to find a schoolgirl who, the year before, had won a third form gold medal in French.

"Tell me what this means," he said as he gave her the soiled page from Olga Mikhailovna. "Is it an old recipe for stew or bread?"

The girl did what she could to decipher the intricate script. Although she missed a few verbs, and she had no idea what "five cowering sons of Moses" meant, the gold medal winner did an admirable job of translating the two paragraphs that the marquis, sitting in his dirty bathwater, had composed about the naked and shivering Jews who stood in front of him, their best coats piled at their feet, while he washed the Russian shit off his sore backside.

" 'This was in December after we left cursed Moscow,' " the girl read, turning the page over to finish all that was left before the sentences, lost to water stains, gave out. " 'This hovel also stinks of the Jews' candles and burnt sugar.' "

Berman smiled and, for her trouble, gave the girl a silver button he said would bring good luck. "It comes from Leningrad."

"There is a small sketch and one more line," the girl said. "Should I translate?"

Berman nodded. A picture? He had never looked on the back of the sheet.

She proudly counted aloud in French. " 'Ils sont ici,' " she read. " 'Cinq Juifs.' "

"What?"

" 'They are here five Jews.' "

Much later, long after the tailors left, the little girl who had won both a medal and a silver button told her sister she had no idea why the old man who fixed Olga Mikhailovna's wedding dress for the price of an old rag suddenly counted to five and then started mumbling in a strange language that sounded "like German."

And as for the little cap he put on after the counting was finished—well, all she could say was that it was strange for a Russian man to wear something on his head that was so much smaller than a Frenchman's beret.

"Don't be so stupid, Tamara," her sister laughed. "That tailor was no Russian."

7

To those of you who were lucky enough to witness the recent dismantling of the empire built by numerous revolutionary cockroaches—in Poland, Czechoslovakia, Romania, East Germany, even in great Russia herself—we say: how astounding! Can you believe how the world has spun around? It was like a World Cup match, yes? Boom! A good kick to freedom's goal in Warsaw, and Walesa, the Polish electrician from Gdansk, wins the match. Whoosh! The Czechs let Havel loose—a fantastic kicker of words, no less!—and beautiful Prague is awash in the old flags and a pink tank. The poor Romanians bleed over the pitch until Ceausescu, that bastard who built palaces and made orphans, is put against a wall on Christmas morning along with his guilty wife. Point! The Germans, working like a well-oiled Mercedes sedan, finally decide the party is bad for business, and then even they break through the Wall to ignite fireworks over the goal itself.

And, in the Soviet Union, where Mikhail Sergeyevich lets in a bit of fresh air before it's too late, the players gasp for even more as they walk past Lenin's granite warehouse (our Mother Russia's pathetic goal) on the last May Day. They take a good look at the assembled leaders and party hacks wearing red carnations. They point their fingers.

They laugh, and, after seventy years, some of them even shout: Fuck you!

But when all of the champagne is drunk and retched over the remains of the cockroaches, and the people begin to dream about denim jeans, decent flats, and honest newspapers, questions must be asked: Who was responsible? Who let *Them* in the door in the first place? Who gave the party's gravediggers uninterrupted employment in a thousand unknown places? Who let *Them* try to kill God and His Only Son with numerous Five Year Plans? The score must be settled, friends. This is 1991: Now you tell us, who gave the comrades the idea for all of this shit?

Leave it to some Russians (it was their bad seed, don't forget) to work their deluded historical imaginations into a frenzy, and say: Are you blind? Insane? Look around, brothers and sisters. Stand with us under the Romanov double eagles and proclaim the truth. The door is open, the record is clear. Check the names. Can't you see how the germ spread from place to place? Lenin, with those Oriental eyes of his: a Jew on his mother's side; Trotsky (remember this swine, who used to be called Bronstein, Lev Davidowich?), a 100 percent Jew; the early killers in the CHEKA or the NKVD, Stalin's lapdogs—all Yids; Litvinov, Molotov (a Jewish wife, so the toady was a 50 percent Jew—by choice), Kamenev, Bukharin, the whole lot: from 15 percent to full-blooded. Stalin knew about all of this because he started his young life in the Holy Church before he went bad, stinking like milk left in the sun. We always knew. Please, don't be fooled by sob stories and exaggerated claims about Yid losses during the war. The Hitlerites may have been pigs and looters—God knows how we suffered under them, how our mothers cried—but, after all, *We* know something about the ZhidyYidkikeHebZionistMarxists who built up this bed of filth. From the Baltic to Odessa, we shout: God save our late, Jew-murdered czar: to his last breath the "little father," Nicholas II, understood where the vermin lay!

Match point.

Not too far from Dulovka, on a road only slightly better than the one that recently brought Simon Moskovich's old Lada to its rubber knees, Berman the tailor, overtired from his late work, took a long nap in the back seat. "I need some rest," he told the bugler. "So forgive me if I don't talk for a few hours. You drive, I'll snooze."

After Berman promised to keep quiet, his eyes were soon shut. Although Berman began snoring, a bit of drool sliding down his unshaven cheek onto a bolt of dark cloth, Simon Moskovich could clearly see the tailor's wrinkled lids fluttering, like someone conjuring up plans for a few more episodes of historical sabotage.

No spring lamb himself after his bout of drinking to cure a painful toe, Simon Moskovich parked the car under a tree to give the tailor a smooth sail into sleep. God only knew what Berman, with his fancy black hat covering his mouth and nose, was dreaming about between snorts and gurgles.

Simon Moskovich drew out his notebook and decided to take stock. How could it hurt? Better someone should know what was what. Yes?

Yes.

"My Dear Arkasha," he wrote at the top of the page, "your father-in-law sends to you his love and regards. You will please forgive me for not writing sooner, but I have been on holiday. In the countryside. Who needs Moscow during the summer? To all of the children and my daughters, my hugs and a whistle. True, a hug and a whistle . . . mention this to Ida, she will understand what I mean. I think of you day and night under the sun with your Hebrew verbs, or in shul, or walking past some golden dome (remember the photos of Jerusalem that you showed me? I do, for sure), or taking afternoon strolls past Arabs tending stalls in the market. I see all of this, and more. An old man's constant thoughts about his family give comfort. Always!"

Simon Moskovich added a few more light bromides about "the humid weather" and the "high price of petrol." Knowing how much Ginzburg hated the party—"They're a bunch of parasitic slugs," he once told Simon Moskovich— he cagily invented a few code words that any censor would pass over because they made no sense. "They say the duck in Gorki Park we used to wonder about won't be able to fly much longer because he's losing his tail feathers." So much for Mikhail Sergeyevich.

As you know, Simon Moskovich was a sentimental man. This is why he suddenly stopped writing and placed a photograph of his daughters and grandchildren on the dashboard, balancing it next to a slowly cooking cucumber salad. He considered inventing a few ingenious lies to ease his son-in-law's mind—"I received a special bonus from the factory . . . a long rest in the north, at a spa with mineral waters as good as the Czechs have in Marienbad. I sleep ten, twelve hours a day and eat like a stag!"—but thought better of this ploy, because Ginzburg the physicist would know curative waters were nowhere to be found anywhere north of the Black Sea. Even in Israel, where he and the others

215

were making a better life (Simon Moskovich had to believe this), the bugler knew his fantasies would be recognized as concrete boats, sinking within seconds. Given a half-minute's pause after finishing such rubbish, Ida would be shrieking her father's name and asking to come home.

So, given the limits of his vocabulary and recollection, Simon Moskovich told the truth, mostly. Maybe Ginzburg, a very good scientist with a mystical bent of mind, a secret Cabalist who could dream about fiery chariots and still know everything about cosmology and the beginnings of the universe—he, of all people, would understand what was happening to Simon Moskovich. And why.

There was much to report: the airport departure—"Do you recall the old Jew who danced with the girls?" A piece of Vladimir Ilyich's waxen nose lost in the tea dregs. Berman with his camp numbers, his mumbling about a Polish Hasid's broken head, his gnats, his incredible tailoring skills, his plan to provide the Romanovs with some Jewish company inside a few exhibition cases. All the rest, including a taste of imaginary honey cake and a near clomp on the nose by an angry Jew. The more he wrote about Alexandr Davidowich, the more he realized how insane this would appear, even to someone like blessed Ginzburg, who understood freaks of nature and other dangerous earthly phenomena.

In the midst of connecting one thought to another, Simon Moskovich closed his eyes. He would later deny he ever fell asleep, because what he saw was in full color and included smells and a cold, tingling sensation along his leg.

This is what overtook his several senses: He was standing, bootless, rank from nervous sweat (this is what he smelled) in the dirty snow on Moscow's Arkhipova Street, within sight of the old synagogue. Ida, a little girl again, about the age she was when she liked to twirl tallith fringes and sing, was standing on the synagogue steps. But this time, his feet stuck in place, Simon Moskovich couldn't reach his daughter. Someone threw a mudball with shards of embedded stone at her, then another. "Fuck off!" the bugler shouted as he tried to free himself from the snow. A voice yelled back: "Go home, big nose! Who gives a shit about a kike!" More mudballs followed, and two reached their target.

Simon Moskovich jumped in his seat. He probably shouted Ida's name. The cucumber concoction, now a ripe brew from being in the full sun, spilled over the photograph, then onto his lap. But his letter to Ginzburg, which escaped a dousing of dill and cream, survived.

Holding up the notebook so he could finish his letter, Simon Moskovich ignored the goo soaking into his trousers. Soon, he had completely covered two pages with everything that had happened and might happen. Everything. He crossed out any reference to Berman being a "meshuggener," substituting "visionary." "I am," he wrote, "helping Berman to remember."

Demons come and go as they please, even in Ladas parked in the humid heat. Who knows what such heat will do to an old man? It's certainly possible that the brilliant idea that flashed into his head, so recently overcome by several colors and pungent smells, came from nothing more than a thread of First of May Collective vodka still coursing through his bloodstream. It may have been a slight touch of food poisoning, or a bruised toe's final shriek inside the brain. Are first causes so important?

"You see, Arkasha," he wrote after he had fully

described his precise and frightening dream, "what we are doing comes to this: If the Almighty could make an orchid for you out of nothing but gas and other stuff (the technical terms are foreign to me), then He can also allow his servant, Simon Moskovich Zorin, master glassblower and bugler, to make a sign. Please don't worry, good friend, I'm no fool."

Anyone blessed with perfect pitch knows that once a clear and piercing note is formed in the brain, nothing can interfere. So, too, with Simon Moskovich's intention to do what he was about to do.

Sliding across the mess of cucumber and cream, he left the car and opened the Lada's trunk. Strong beyond his years—this was, you see, for little Ida's sake—he pried a meter square top from a wooden carton filled with extra material and a few of Berman's special feathers. Placing the wooden top on the ground, he considered where the words should fit. This was very important, so he paced back and forth, stepped aside to get a decent sense of perspective, and put thumb to thumb together in a director's frame that would have made Eisenstein himself proud.

"Ahah!"

Although he wished he had more than one color of ink, the lettering itself was easy enough to accomplish once the feather's quill was sharpened (he remembered doing this as a boy, when new pencils were as rare as oranges). As Berman might have said, You make with what you have. Blue is good, he thought. Blue is what I have. Blue will catch their attention. Blue is a Jew's color.

"Ahah!"

Preparations made, Simon Moskovich got down on his knees to make some extraordinary words, born of a mud-ball and his daughter's frightened face.

"Oo-oo-oo," came a groan from above him. "Oo-oo-oo!"

Any child knows that Russian letters are beautiful. With their swirls and little tails, swooping lines and sharp peaks (these, the splendid gifts of an inspired Greek saint who wanted to give Christ's Gospel to the wild, pagan Slavs), our script is a work of art, especially when it emerges from the tip of a goose quill dipped in blue ink, each letter joined to the next. Just like ballet dancers on a stage. Fantastic.

So thought Alexandr Davidowich Berman. Slightly woozy from his nap, he stood above the bugler and watched the words appear. It was he, as you might have guessed, who thought about dancers and moaned "oo-oo-oo"—most certainly because Simon Moskovich, who had once turned molten glass into tiny animals, knew how to make a handsome curve. But also because—and this is very important—Alexandr Davidowich was now looking at the first such tailor's sign to appear in all of Russia since the Bolshevik Revolution proclaimed personal advertising a filthy capitalist crime or maybe a Jewish trick.

A.D. BERMAN & FRIEND,

Tailors & Costumers

No Charge for Work Done

Ida Says:

"They Make the Old Like New"

Just then Simon Moskovich finished. Ignoring the tailor's appreciative groans, he wedged the sign into the space between the license plate and the Lada's trunk.

Simon Moskovich moved back a few paces to check his work.

Berman, cleaning his teeth on a bent embroidery needle, said, "Now we're really in business."

"But we do nothing stupid," Simon Moskovich told Berman. "Everything gets old—automobiles, sewing machines, your eyesight, my patience. Remember, please, this old Jew wants to see his grandchildren someday."

Berman promised: Nothing stupid.

Then, smelling the sour odor that wafted toward him from Simon Moskovich's messy clothes, he suggested his apprentice wear the slightly used black coat that Olga Mikhailovna, bride of brides, had saved from Gehenna.

"Sasha!"

"And if we're lucky, I can fix up a very nice hat with a brushed fur trim. Your Ida would love it."

"Sasha!"

"It's just for business," Berman replied. "Nothing more."

Shortly before posting his letter to Ginzburg, and while Berman adjusted the coat Olga Mikhailovna had given him so that it fit him like a glove, Simon Moskovich reread what he had written. For the third time in a day, he made a few changes. "Meshuggener" replaced "visionary" in several spots because, as the Talmud instructs, a Jew's last will and testament should always follow a straight path.

8

In a little-known publication that miraculously escaped the censor's axe during the worst years of the Georgian executioner, a certain Veronika Rusknanskaya, at thirty-eight years of age only a few months short of her last Easter, confided an important memory to a young Moscow journalist. The lucky writer—his name was erased sometime after 1934—had somehow discovered that the prematurely aged woman was the last person in this world ever to speak to the great Tolstoy. An accident of history, surely. But it happened.

Veronika Rusknanskaya, who was only fifteen at the time of her encounter with greatness, and who shuffled through life with one leg shorter than the other, scrubbed floors and emptied spittoons in a provincial railroad station in Astapovo, Ryazan Province. Already pregnant, the illiterate char had a hard go of it whenever she bent to empty a bucket of dark water or reached above her head to polish the glass-encased photograph of the bemedalled Czar Nicholas II, her "little father." Despite her discomfort, she worked with care and attention, as her sort did during those distant years. She loved her czar and thanked the saints who made him and who gave her the continuing strength to earn a few rubles. "A clean spittoon and floor," she told the journalist, "meant good health for his passengers." As simple as that.

When Leo Nikolayevich fled Yasnaya Polyana and his grasping family to make his peace with God, he took ill with a high fever on the train. Stopping at Astapovo, a nothing town, the beloved writer's doctor begged the stationmaster to provide a clean bed for his patient. Naturally, the man was honored by such a request, and he promptly ordered Veronika Rusknanskaya to change the linen in his spare room, arrange a bed table for the aged count's few belongings, and empty his bedpan whenever necessary. "This is a famous and holy man," he told the girl. "So give him whatever he needs."

To bring this sad story to its point, Veronika, as always, did as she was told. She spread the stationmaster's best sheets over an iron cot, found a chipped bedpan, ironed some towels, and then, after the noble person was established in his room, waited for further orders outside the door. Shortly before the little station was swarming with journalists who had caught wind of a great story, Leo Nikolayevich's lungs, struggling for air, began to deflate.

In those final moments, while his bereft wife, Sonya, waited for a last audience with her husband (which was never granted), the old writer begged for a glass of water from the dimly seen peasant girl who wiped his forehead. So careful was she—so tender was her touch—that Leo Nikolayevich, now very close to his God's throne yet still capable of stringing a good sentence together, opened his eyes and took the girl's hand. "Remember, child," he said, "real genius strikes at the heart with a cool cloth and a simple message."

Whatever else was said was soon forgotten in the rush

of weeping family and curious witnesses—including a famous painter—who surrounded the great man's bed.

Many years later, Veronika Rusknanskaya, widowed and very ill herself, mentioned the "cool cloth" to a journalist who wanted to reconstruct the writer's last hours. After careful questioning, the old woman clasped her hands together. Her eyes brightened as she took a tea cloth from the table to demonstrate for the journalist exactly how she had wiped Leo Nikolayevich's brow and lips. "Spit and I'll give you a wipe, just like I did for him," she said, pressing the damp cloth over the journalist's face. "Go on, spit."

The unsigned article was written and published in an obscure Moscow literary journal, a torn copy of which fell into Alexandr Davidowich's hands in early 1952. As you know, the tailor cherished anything by the old count, especially those sections in which the master lovingly described what his characters wore. During that brief period of retired sanity in his Pushkin garden, he reread his favorite passages—the last few chapters of *Anna Karenina*, the early parts of *My Childhood*, and the article about Veronika Rusknanskaya's sweet memory—to the late Yelena Gailova of blessed memory. "Truth is as truth does," Yelena said after Berman finished. Then she repeated one of Father Grigori's favorite aphorisms. "The Lord's heart is always simple."

Long after this, as he stood next to Simon Moskovich's brilliant sign advertising his skills, Berman naturally thought its peculiar genius—its "simple message"—was similar to the comfort afforded by a "cool cloth." This is when he cooed like a young lover and said, "Now we're really in business."

In a poor country now overburdened with sellers of anything that could be eaten, worn, rebuilt, or rubbed into a sore, we're certain that a good tailor was worth more than a thousand dazed economists. A tailor offering his valuable skills for nothing at all was a prince among the helpless. From Novgorod (there was some backtracking) south to Valdaskaya by way of Staraya Rusa, and then northeast to Luga and other places, Alexandr Davidowich and his apprentice covered more ground than a Panzer division. They blew two tires and lost both windshield wipers (thieves were everywhere) and several bolts of material that were stolen when, suffering from the runs, Berman and Zorin had to make an emergency stop and stupidly left the Lada unlocked for fifteen or twenty minutes. Berman's back gave out in Volot and had to be massaged by his tired driver, and, once—this was in Valdaskaya—the overworked Singer Little Wonder spurted some oil from a stripped pinwheel into the tailor's left eye, momentarily blinding him. In Dno, two drunk army conscripts, their heads already shaved to look like green peaches, staggered up to the tailor and his apprentice and called them "Yid bloodsuckers." Berman, looking up at the two boys, told them that their pants were too short and needed fixing; he also offered a feather, showed them his camp numbers and said that "God would be ashamed of them for insulting a veteran of the Great Patriotic War." Add to this ledger of troubles Simon Moskovich's sour temper, which lasted for nearly a hundred kilometers after he swerved to avoid squashing a dog in Simsk, and thereby drove into a road marker.

And so on.

But if such minor mishaps about pulled muscles, stinging eyes, cruel name-calling, and broken headlights are overlooked, you might notice the increasing load of minor treasures—dishes, old clothing, a chipped ram's horn, eleven hats, a few siddurim with broken spines, and a large oil painting, framed in carved oak, of a certain Aron Abramovich, 1847–1901 ("Smolensk Merchant of the First Guild")—that weighted down the Lada's rear seat and gave Alexandr Davidowich Berman reasonable satisfaction.

Frankly, why deceive you with fairy tales? Even if Simon Moskovich's original sign was inspired by a colorful thought about young Ida Simonovna, its open invitation created a strange capitalist revolution and a lot of fixed garments: all sizes, no charge for work done, silk is no problem, broken or jammed zippers liberated "one, two, three."

"A hem for a story, a dress for an epic, a lining for an old book," Berman would cry after Simon Moskovich found a suitable spot to park the Lada. "No charge." If a truckdriver in Ludza wanted his leather jacket mended, or the Lada's blue sign attracted the attention of a suspicious militia sergeant with tight pants in Palkino, Berman obliged. He did the necessary repair work beneath any available shelter, only demanding in return some simple information. If there was a spot in a market or a tram stop where Russian women stood in a pathetic line offering their old dresses or their husbands' slightly used underwear for a few dozen rubles, Berman, cradling the Little Wonder, said, "If I fix what you're holding, friend, you'll get a better price."

Poof! What an idea. The women flocked to Berman, got their sad stuff made presentable, even had a little work done on their own sleeves or ragged skirts. Then, this: "Are there any Jews left in this place?" the tailor would always ask. "Maybe a synagogue or a community hall? Do you know where I could find a twisted Jewish bread?"

"At 15 Karpovksy," someone would say. "A basement flat."

"Try the street behind the station. The Jews always go there on Fridays."

"The clerk at the telegraph office has a strange name, try him."

"Rosen the pediatrician knows everyone."

Or on one of those occasional moments when the earth began to shake beneath the tailor's feet: "How should I know? Maybe you need to look in the cemetery by the petrochemical works. Just follow your nose, brother."

"Karpovksy 15," Berman would tell Simon Moscovich after they finished their work. "In the basement."

Let's not be too hard on the scores of suspicious Jews who didn't answer their doors when Berman came calling with his apprentice, or told him to leave them be. And it doesn't do any good to wish ill upon the others who listened to his plea yet never invited Alexandr Davidowich in for a glass of tea, or at least a chance to sit down and rest on a soft chair. Be patient with them; they had their reasons for hiding.

For every nervous pediatrician, accountant, clerk, or elderly babushka who slammed a door because "nothing is done for nothing" and "what if this Jew with a sewing machine is really someone else?", there were two or three (this was in Porchov) who trusted the old man's eyes or noticed a touch of fringe hanging below his odd black coat. A few, thank the Highest, were willing to exchange a hem for a good story and a small helping of boiled chicken with kasha, maybe even a serving of fresh compote and the offer of a sofa to sleep on. But always: "Please, you won't stay too long . . . the neighbors, you see, are gossips and we try to avoid them. Now, what was it you wanted to know?"

Much to Simon Moskovich's annoyance—"Stop putting

your life on a plate in front of the world," he told the tailor—Berman always explained everything: about the lost scrolls and the sad stories within; the need to make a few adjustments for memory's sake; a great exhibition that, with luck, might cause many people to shiver and remember; and the wisdom of relying upon a good tailor "with connections in the right places."

"Let's not lose anything more," he added after one Jew or another handed over a photograph or even an oil painting that was gathering dust. "I promise a war against forgetting."

Then Simon Moskovich would stop chewing his chicken or boiled potato, look at Berman, and whisper, " 'War'? Did you have to say 'war'?"

"Psst, is this tailor on leave from the Kirov?" several Jews asked.

"No, just from his senses," Simon Moskovich said, while he grumpily measured a waist or used a tailor's chalk to mark a few lines. "But his heart is solid and he dreams about people like us."

One decent but slightly senile soul in Porchov, a former watchmaker, happily "willed" Alexandr Davidowich some old prayer books he had hidden for nearly thirty-five years, and a wrinkled, water-stained photograph of a rabbi holding a small bird. The old man pointed to the photograph and said, "He visited here in 1932 and performed some magic tricks for the children."

Alexandr Davidowich took out his tape recorder. "Speak up, friend, what was his name? What sort of tricks did he perform?"

The old Jew stared at the floor. He swatted at nonexistent mosquitos. "Good ones."

"What sort of tricks?" Berman asked again. "This is very important."

"He found a white bird in Isidore Kalmonovich's cap. He said, 'This one comes from God's breath.' "

Berman wrote: "Small bird. 1932? God's breath. Some rabbi!"

That same lucky day, Berman was given a chipped shofar from a retired civil engineer who, when his wife was searching for an old coat in the adjoining room, quietly claimed a Polish Jewish grandmother he had never known. "Put this in a museum," he told Berman, handing him the ram's horn. "I think it came from Kiev. My wife wants to toss it."

To make him feel a little better, the tailor did an excellent job of relining winter coats for the engineer's Ukrainian wife and her daughter. As soon as she went into the kitchen to model her new coat for the neighbors, the engineer proposed a strange toast in two parts: "Your health," he said loudly enough to please his wife, followed by a softer, "My name used to be Horowitz, but you know how it is. . . ."

Berman knew how it was. He gladly accepted whatever was given, even if it was little more than a name, a useless ram's horn, or a photograph of some ancestor who couldn't be identified. Simon Moskovich smiled, and, for the umpteenth time, repacked the Lada, but not before he reminded Alexandr Davidowich that their travel time was attached to a "short leash."

To this very day the bugler can still recall how, the next morning, Alexandr Davidowich insisted upon looking at each piece he had collected. Even though the sky threatened rain, he stood outside the Lada like a pawnshop operator checking his meager stock. While Simon Moskovich entered each item into the notebook, the tailor raised the shofar to his mouth and blew. Nothing emerged but air, dust, and a flatulent rumble. He tried again. Nothing. Two more attempts resulted in failure. Finally, he began wheezing and had to rest against the car.

"Amateur!" Simon Moskovich laughed. "Too much smoking, comrade."

So it was left to Simon Moskovich, a bugler with some experience in producing interesting sounds (and a nervous Russian Jew who also couldn't imagine explaining to the local militia that Alexandr Davidowich Berman, as red-faced as a Moscow circus clown, nearly expired after trying to blow through a dead animal's horn!) to grab the shofar, expertly cover the offending hole, and, after three tries, finally blow a long note that sounded like a diesel lorry's squealing brakes.

In the distance, a few frightened dogs barked. The engineer who used to be Horowitz (when, he never said) ran outside. The poor man was pale and sweaty when he reached the Jews. Given the circumstances, he could have shouted all manner of choice oaths, cursing the tailor who made dogs bark and suspicious neighbors pay attention. He could have said, "I took you in, fed you, gave you something, and now this!" Surely, someone would be told to "go to hell."

Simon Moskovich apologized without waiting to hear what was coming. "I was helping him," he said, pointing to the weakened tailor. Berman was still trying to catch his breath when the former Horowitz asked if he could have a brief "lesson on the horn."

"I drink a little in the mornings," he confessed, "so if my wife sees me she'll only think I got a little pissed for old times' sake with a couple of Yids."

Just as he had learned in Moscow many years before, Simon Moskovich explained how to make a decent sound. "Purse your lips like a baby over her mother's tit," the bugler instructed. "Bring the air from your chest, not your cheeks. Blow steady."

Berman, having recovered, lit a cigarette. He, too, added a kopek's worth of advice: "Have a little faith."

With a shuddering sigh, the engineer emptied his lungs into the horn for the first and last time, creating from this superhuman effort a decent sound—Simon Moskovich recognized a painful B flat—that would have been acceptable in any shul on Yom Kippur.

This time, only one dog barked.

Before the engineer left, he freshened his breath with a sip of vodka. "It's still yours," he told Berman, who was worried about having to return his only shofar. Although the engineer would have liked to try his luck one more time, his wife began shouting his name. Berman turned and saw a large, angry woman approaching.

"Take this address," the engineer said, quickly shoving a slip of paper into Berman's pocket. "Ask for Sasha Yurivich. If he's still alive, tell him that Ilya from the old days sends a hug. If he's gone, maybe blow the horn for him."

Berman looked at the note with a Pskov address. Pravdy Street. "What does he have to offer?" he asked. "Hurry, tell me."

"He lives next to someone who came back from the

dead and sleeps next to the evidence," answered the frazzled engineer over the sound of his wife's yelling.

Simon Moskovich, with his lips still wet from the ram's horn, moaned, "Oy vey."

In the seventy kilometers between a former Horowitz's Yom Kippur bleat and the ancient town of Pskov, Simon Moskovich made the tailor promise seven times, positively, without doubt and no monkey business, before they caused a real pogrom, that Pskov was the last stop before they returned to Pushkin. Finis.

Once again, Berman gave his solemn word. In fact, he swore each promise with one hand over his heart, the other covering the Little Wonder's hard-shell case. To keep Simon Moskovich from mentioning his grandchildren again, Berman complimented the bugler on his driving and—how could it hurt?—for his skill in blowing the ram's horn.

"Better than a symphony."

The Lada lurched onto the main road in a cloud of dust. Simon Moskovich managed a slight bow as he shifted into third gear. "Perfect pitch, comrade tailor. Perfect pitch."

9

Klozman had died, and there were seven left who could still chew and argue about nothing; but, for the sake of official records, eight total if Masha Viktorovna chose to be overly generous and include Elias Jacobovich, who was beyond help and only a few more days away from his own long rest.

"Go ahead, count again," begged Sasha Yurivich. "I see eight."

Masha Viktorovna sighed and walked into the dimly lit hallway. Sasha Yurivich, always a puppy dog, followed her. After minding these old Jews for six years, she could identify each one's labored snoring without even looking at them. Smells, too; she knew their damp, musty odors.

"One, two, three, four, five, six, and yourself makes seven."

"And Elias?"

Masha pretended to listen by cupping a hand over her ear.

"Seven and a half."

"Eight, Masha," Sasha Yurivich corrected. "Shame on you, how can you make Elias a half-person?"

"Well, go and look at him. You think you'll find a person there?"

"Shush, he might hear you."

"Hear me? He can't even see me. You know that."

"Who needs sight? Please, one more time and then we'll play cards."

"One, two, three, four, five, six, seven, and Elias Jacobovich is possibly eight if he could do his business in the chamber pot to save me trouble every four hours. There, satisfied? Eight, more or less. Done."

"You count like a real genius. You admit to eight, yes?"

"Eight," sighed Masha. "But I know where you're leading me. I tell you I'm not going to beg anything from that Gypsy thief you saw outside. Did you see his hat with the feather?"

The Jew lied about the hat. "Yes, I saw. A hat's a hat."

"Romanian or Moldavian scum who mate with their mothers . . . the old, experienced kind that can lift a purse before you finish a sneeze. With things like they are, those two must have come sneaking here from across the border. My sister told me there are secret crossing points that even the KGB can't find."

"Mashenka, what Gypsy? Go take another look. He's a Jew, one of us. I'm sure of it."

"And what about the other one who sits in the car, waiting like a vulture? He's probably the one who holds the knife or maybe a gun to your throat. These mafia types always work in pairs."

Sasha Yurivich walked over to the dirty window. He breathed a bit of vapor over the dirty glass and used his torn sleeve to wipe it clean. It was raining, and a yellow fog began to settle over the street, making positive identification difficult.

"Mashenka, look, I'm reading what's on that sign. Even with these shitty glasses, I can see the words. That's a Jew's name. 'A.D. Berman.' What kind of a Gypsy name is that, eh?"

"And what else do you read?" she said, moving next to the old glazier who would never let anything be. "Read the rest."

" 'Tailor' and . . . something. 'No charge for work.' Also a Jewish girl's name. Maybe she does the actual sewing? A seamstress, right?"

Masha Viktorovna, close to winning this one, puffed on a loose cigarette. She stood next to the Jew and cleaned off her own place on the window. The one streetlight on Pravdy flickered on and off. Still, she knew what she knew.

"That's how they'll trap me, Sasha. I get all excited by a sign that offers free tailoring, I walk close, and, pop, I've been had. Another decent Russian loses the few things she's got. Then they drive off with my stuff, which they sell by the railway station, or take back to some caravan for one of their own to use."

Sasha Yurivich stared out the window. Even in the bad light he could see the Lada was piled high with junk. Stolen? The Jew with the feather was smoking; the other one, sitting in the front seat, seemed to be speaking into his hands. He couldn't see the girl who must do the sewing. Maybe Masha was right about them. Everyone charges something.

"What if I come with you when you ask him?" he said, enlarging his grimy porthole with his better sleeve.

"No."

"Do I have to beg? Klozman is dead. We're short two for the minyan. You know what this means to all of us."

Masha Viktorovna began to eat a sour apple. She spat

out the seeds and told the Jew to hush. No deals today. "Let's play cards, Sasha. You promised."

Sasha took off his wristwatch, the one his nephew in Odessa had sent before he left for Austria.

"Here, take it," he said as he offered the thin timepiece with the black leather band to the caretaker. "This must be worth two hundred, at least. It glows in the dark and has a calendar. Please."

Masha inspected the watch, returned to the window for another look, and then faced the pestering Jew.

"But you'll come with me?"

"Only one step behind you."

"And this watch is mine, with no whining about getting it back?"

"When Sasha Yurivich gives, it's forever."

"So what do I ask him, Sasha? What if he doesn't speak good Russian like me?"

"He'll understand. Just tell him that inside No. 16, on the top floor, there are seven . . . no, eight Jews who have some clothes for him. Tell him that we need to dress decently if Elias Jacobovich dies and we have to do a burial. Tell him we need to be proper about this, then . . ."

"What? There's more?"

" . . . tell him that if it wouldn't be too much, we could raise a small sum to pay the two of them to stay with us. So we could have enough for a minyan for Elias. Do you understand?"

"The watch is mine?"

"Yes."

"Then you stay close to me, Sasha. You take a stick with you . . . and if that Gypsy thief raises even a finger toward me, you hit him before the one with the knife gets out of the car."

Masha Viktorovna put on her jacket and tied a babushka over her head. She gave Sasha the long, hooked pole she used to lock the high window in the kitchen.

"You smack him good with this, do you hear. No funny stuff. And if he is one of yours, none of that Jewtalk in Yiddish. I want to hear everything that goes on."

Before she could put the new watch in her pocket, Sasha was already in the hallway, waiting next to the lift that might, if God was smiling, be working.

"What's that?" he said when Masha met him.

The caretaker frowned and sniffed at the fetid air.

"Yevgeny Lazarovich. Too many fried onions for supper."

Because Elias Jacobovich's late father was an expert in assuring the sanitary conveyance of the people's waste from one place to another, without a single recorded accident, he was, by order of Stalin himself, declared a Hero of Labor in 1947. Absolutely loyal to the party and to the Soviet dream, engineer Jacob Edvardivich Ravitz cannot be said ever to have made a willful mistake in his official duties as chief engineer of the Moscow city sewers. He knew the strengths and limitations of pipes and valves; he also knew that the revolution couldn't proceed towards its inevitable victory if shit, which always followed the path of least resistance, began to flow in the wrong direction.

A Jew in name only, engineer Ravitz always said that God had even less value than a five-meter length of poorly designed sewer pipe. In his early days of militant enthusiasm, after the trials of the murderous traitors Bukharin,

Kamenev, and Zinoviev, when he would have gladly offered up his life for the party, he openly denounced his father's religion as a cancerous wart and a medieval curse. "I hate my name," he often told his Russian wife. "But they won't let me change it. It sticks to me like concrete." And what is more important, he convinced his only child, Elias, that the only rewards in this life came from Stalin—"who has made this world for you"—unceasing labor for the people, hatred for those who betrayed the party, and service to the Soviet Union. "Nothing else matters," he repeated. Then, his paternal duties finished, engineer Ravitz left his wife and son, often for weeks at a time, and disappeared beneath the streets of Moscow and into the intricate network of catacombs he loved and understood so well.

All of this, of course, brought rewards to Elias Jacobovich. As the son of a party member who worshipped Stalin, the boy was sent to the best schools, with other children of the elite, where he distinguished himself in every subject, especially languages, drawing, and zoology. He wrote poetry praising the wisdom of Comrade Stalin as the "Great Mountain Eagle in our sight/who gives his life for children's rights." Like Lenin's martyred brother, whose sepia-colored photograph he pinned to his bedroom wall, Elias Jacobovich spent his summers at the family's dacha outside Moscow making precise drawings of the flatworms and ticks he observed through an excellent Swiss microscope. In all that could be judged, Elias Jacobovich Ravitz was marked for glorious things: university, party membership, the best life.

At the outbreak of the Great Patriotic War, Elias Jacobovich, then sixteen and too young to serve, fled the capital with his mother for a safe haven east of the Urals.

Unlike the Mountain Eagle, whose nerves and stomach were as thin as watery gruel, engineer Ravitz stayed in Moscow to watch over his beloved sewers. Covered in thick muck, he devoted himself to his duties, even to the point of planning a great underground explosion should the fascist bastards enter Moscow. "They'll be wallowing in backed-up excrement for years," he wrote to his wife. "Just let them try to flush a commode anywhere in Moscow!"

But it never happened, did it. Repeating Napoleon's fatal mistakes, the Germans lost it all—a million men and enough steel to rebuild ten Leningrads—in the mud and deep snow. The Mountain Eagle, now our generalissimo, shoved them into hell. Engineer Ravitz, his skin permanently discolored from lack of sunlight and constant contact with unmentionable stuff, his legs afflicted with a form of gout that comes from so much bone-turning dampness, emerged from his sewers in 1945 and immediately took to his bed for three weeks. When he finally awoke, still dazed, he didn't recognize his adult son or fully understand when he was told that his wife had died the previous year from a severe vitamin deficiency in Sverdlovsk.

Thinking he was in the middle of some sewer crisis, he shouted, "Check the main pipe beneath Leningradsky. Hurry, comrade, we're running out of time . . . "

In the several years it took engineer Ravitz to reclaim partial use of his legs, Elias Jacobovich, son of a crippled hero who couldn't tolerate bright light, completed his studies at Moscow State University. Praised by his professors as a poet with "exceptional talent, in several areas," he earned three gold medals and an invitation to pursue his academic work at the Gorky Institute and, honor of honors, to apply for provisional membership in the Communist Party. His father was ecstatic. "All my life," Jacob Edvardivich cried, the better part of his body trembling, "I have looked forward to this moment."

In the midst of this celebration, engineer Ravitz announced his willingness to return to his sacred duties. His superiors realized that no one would ever bring such pinpoint accuracy to diagnosing the complicated business of sewage control management, so he was wheeled underground in a special chair built just for him. With his several medals affixed to his engineer's smock, wearing tinted bottle-thick spectacles, Jacob Edvardivich rolled through the mighty Moscow sewer system, shining a strong flashlight on anything which displeased him.

The day that the light finally turned on him—when, as you know, the Mountain Eagle sent his minions after a new batch of Yid doctors and engineers—Jacob Edvardivich was being helped out of a shit-smeared apron. "Get out of that fucking wheelchair," the KGB major ordered. "But I am absolutely loyal," engineer Ravitz said. "I tried six times to change my name!"

They took the engineer to the Lubyanka Prison, where, as best we know, he vanished for his crimes against the people—after a thirty-minute trial in which he confessed through swollen lips that, yes, he was part of a conspiracy to flood the Kremlin with noxious, deathly substances. "And you had a plan you personally worked on during the war, correct?" The engineer, his legs swollen, nodded. "To blow up our entire system?" Yes. "To poison members of the Central Committee and their families?" Yes. "Spell your last name, slowly."

And that was that.

The willing son of a traitor, Elias Jacobovich Ravitz got

ten years for failing to report his criminal father and, after a KGB guard kicked him in the back while calling him a kike cocksucker, a damaged kidney that made pissing a bloody nightmare for the rest of his life.

Ten years and thirty minutes to the day after engineer Ravitz made his last plea to his executioners, his son was released from a camp two hundred kilometers southwest of Novosibirsk. Although he was only thirty-three, he looked like an old man. He limped from a broken foot that had never healed properly, he had only three teeth left, his face was pockmarked with frostbite scars from the endless Siberian winters, and his damaged kidney chewed at his side like a hungry wolf. If the world he hadn't seen in a decade required quick movement from place to place, Elias Jacobovich was doomed as a straggler.

"You can't return to Moscow," the camp commandant told him. "This is forbidden under the criminal code. You're now a Siberian citizen, comrade . . . here to help us build socialism in the East."

Elias Jacobovich was given the ill-fitting clothes he was wearing when he was first arrested, and twenty-five rubles. He was astounded to find in an inside pocket the expensive fountain pen his father had given him after his graduation from university. As a final word of advice, the commandant warned him to keep his Jew beak out of trouble. "Stalin may be gone, comrade, but the memory lingers on in your face and name. Welcome home!"

In the old days of the czars—decades before the battered days of Elias Jacobovich—released and hungry exiles often settled in small Siberian villages to live out their last days. Decembrists, anarchists, members of the intelligentsia who had written a displeasing tract or poem, liberal aristocrats and God-crazed peasants all planted their gardens in a hundred nameless villages. They played chess, wrote long letters, were even happy. Elias Jacobovich, reduced to eating soft food and praying for the health of his remaining teeth, did the same. He accepted a job teaching Russian and biology in a small village school close to the Ob River and wished for nothing more than to be left alone to read the few books he had collected, drink, keep a tidy garden, and fish for carp from the river bank. As the months passed, he even tried his hand at a few poems and pencil sketches of the river and woods, all of which he immediately burned for fear of being caught with seditious material. Aside from his students, he spoke to no one. In his need for security, he kept his "Jew beak" pointed away from the wind. He sought to render his existence wholly useless, and therefore safe.

The years passed.

The turn in Elias Jacobovich's story—the part that eventually brought our tailor close to him—came on a morning during a terrible storm that forced the river Ob to flood the low areas. Because he lived on a bluff above the river, Elias Jacobovich saw the steadily rising waters wash over the banks. The spring wind was as strong as he had felt in twenty years. It ripped shingles from the roof of his cottage; a stray dog, howling for its life, scratched at his door until, out of pity for another exile, Elias Jacobovich let it come in and sit next to the wood stove. "You like oatmeal?" he asked the mangy, shivering creature. "Bread soaked in milk?"

Maybe it was foolish to do what he did for a dog—God knows, Elias Jacobovich should have lived only for himself—but when there was a break in the storm, he knew he had a brief period of grace in which to gather more fire-wood from the pile. Five split pieces will do it, he thought. Five good pieces and we'll make it through the night.

The rain and hail, however, began to pour down again. Elias Jacobovich took his walking stick and crossed the limb-strewn area in front of his cottage. He moved as care-fully you might expect: eyes on the ground for hidden dan-gers, he prodded the mud for slippery spots or holes, and counted the paces to his covered woodpile at the edge of the bluff.

What Elias Jacobovich saw when he reached his pre-cious fuel made him scream even louder than the wind. He clamped down on his jaw so hard that he cracked two of his remaining three teeth. He covered his face, counted to ten, and hoped against all that was holy in this world that what he had seen was an illusion, a trick of nature.

Three bodies, entangled in driftwood and branches, their hands tied behind their backs with thin wire, bobbed against the riverbank. The Ob's strong currents washed over the mummified corpses. Several pairs of what used to be legs were chained together and weighted down with rocks. Elias Jacobovich fell to his knees. For the first time in his life, he mentioned God's name and cursed his own. Then, because this is what he had to do, he limped back to his cottage for a strong length of rope. Returning to the em-bankment, he tied one end around his waist, the other to a birch tree. Nearly blinded by the driving rain and ice, he carefully lowered himself toward the horror.

Over the next two days, during the worst storm anyone living close to the mighty Ob ever remembered, Elias Ja-cobovich pulled seven corpses from the river. He tore his clothing, cut his leg on a sharp branch, broke a finger on a stone, and was twice sucked into the current with one of the corpses. He stayed where he was, minding the dead and those that might yet arrive.

Elias Jacobovich, a decent man for all of his earlier false illusions, dragged each corpse to a high spot above the river. During his ten years behind the wire, he had heard thousands of shots; now, after another ten during which his mind had slipped from numbness to a frozen state beneath absolute zero, the ground was spitting up what it couldn't hold any longer. "We did fifteen last night," he had once heard a drunken guard tell his sergeant in 1954, "and it took nine hours to dig a fucking pit."

Because the shits who caused this to happen thought no one would ever find their victims in a Siberian wasteland, they couldn't have cared less what the Mountain Eagle's enemies carried to the grave. But Elias Jacobovich saw. Placing each body next to the other, the engineer's son studied the evidence before he began to dig holes and weep: three of the corpses' Polish army uniforms were still recognizable—these poor bastards had escaped Katyn only to end up here—as were the ranks on their torn epaulets. Two captains and a major. The remaining four, all civilians, wore the clothing they had on when they were arrested.

God forgive Elias Jacobovich for what he did next to disturb dead. Before he buried them, he inspected their shrunken faces—each body had, in approved style of the NKVD's executioners, one, sometimes two, bullet holes in the base of the skull. He removed their clothing and searched through their pockets, collecting a small pile of documents. On the Polish officers, he discovered material miraculously preserved in lined leather pouches: photographs of wives, fathers, children; several crucifixes;

ration cards and stained maps; a small volume of poetry; a cigarette lighter—"To Dr. Piotr Krajewski, on the occasion of his graduation. Krakow, 1937"—a pair of wire-rimmed spectacles. On three of the others, there was nothing but their clothing and a small, rusted penknife. On the last corpse, the thinnest and smallest of the lot, he found a small Hebrew prayerbook printed in Pskov and, locked in a gnarled hand the engineer's son had to pry apart with a stick, two small black boxes tied to some broken leather straps.

"You should always wash the dead," a tubercular Pentecostal had once told Elias Jacobovich in the camp. "We need to meet the Lord cleansed of filth. Even the Jews believe this. If I let you eat my soup, will you promise to wash my body?" Elias Jacobovich ate the soup, but the Pentecostal was taken away before he could keep his end of the bargain.

As gently as any priest or rabbi, Elias Jacobovich washed each corpse—head, trunk, legs—and then snipped the wires that bound their arms behind their backs. He tore linen sheets from his bed, the curtains from his windows, and covered each man. Making do with nine fingers, he dug seven deep graves until his hands bled from open sores. The dog, a bit stronger from the mush he'd eaten, and enjoying the man's silly game, sniffed each body before he jumped into the fresh graves to scratch at the ground alongside Elias Jacobovich.

After the graves were covered with dirt and a layer of rocks so that no one would ever find them, Elias Jacobovich drew several pencil sketches of what he had seen: the corpses entangled in driftwood and chains, the dog helping to dig a grave, the piles of artifacts he had found. Then he held a solitary service. It began quietly enough for the officers and the Russians with a verse in Polish from Piotr Krajewski's book (maybe something about trees or the afternoon light) and continued, slightly louder, with a half-remembered prayer he had once heard the Pentecostal mutter in his sleep ("God the Holy, in Christ's bosom reclines . . . "). But the little Jew, buried alongside the others, had his rest disturbed by an awful wail that sent the dog running howling toward the river. "I don't know what to say for you, no one ever taught me!" Elias Jacobovich screamed, over and over, until something in his throat tore apart and he spat blood into his filthy hands.

If the former poet and student of flatworms hadn't made so much noise and rolled on the ground, the grateful dog, hiding behind a fallen tree, might have returned and stayed with him until the end of his time.

That Elias Jacobovich, his voice now reduced to an inaudible rasp, left the secret graves is well known. That he dragged what was left of himself in front of the local authorities and resigned from his teaching post due to his peculiar malady is understood. That within two months this rehabilitated, formerly "Socially Harmful Element" was finally given official permission to seek medical treatment elsewhere in the socialist paradise is also noted.

But that he had gathered at least one item from each of the corpses—some clothing, spectacles, Polish verses, the Jew's prayer book and strange boxes—tied them into a tight bundle, which he always kept within reach, and was able to walk, silently, from the tundra to the west, has never been discussed. Given the distance and the hardship for a man with a bad leg and an aching throat, it's just too hard to believe in such a miracle, so few ever did.

Yet it happened. Just as it happened a few years later to that crazy young German who, evading our great Soviet defense system, landed his tiny airplane in the middle of Red Square, Elias Jacobovich became a flea that fell unharmed through a thousand checkpoints and traps. One year later, having been taken by anyone who saw him as a benign, wandering idiot who could only communicate with hand signals and illegibly scrawled notes, Elias Jacobovich arrived, smelling like death, in the old city of Pskov.

Fortunately, Elias Jacobovich came to rest on a broken bench by the railway station on a festive May Day, his unsightly appearance and terrible odor an insult to several good comrades recently arrived to celebrate this glorious holiday with speeches and proclamations. Not wishing to cause an embarrassing scene in front of some visiting Cuban guests, the militia gently removed Elias Jacobovich to the local city hospital to be bathed and disinfected before he was taken to a holding cell for the city's alcoholics and wife beaters. Frantically writing one verse after another from Pushkin and Mayakovsky, the old Jew convinced several doctors that he was not crazy. "Then what do you want?" one doctor asked. Elias Jacobovich opened his bundle and showed the doctors the prayer book and the small boxes. "To return these," came the scrawled response. "I am an honest Jew."

One thing is clear—Elias Jacobovich was a lucky man. Because the psychiatric wards and drunk tanks were overflowing with blind fools who drank cologne or lighter fluid, the overworked physician who examined the Jew made a few phone calls. "I've got a wandering mystic of yours in ward eight," he told a prominent member of the dwindling Jewish community. "Come and get this toothless old man before I change my mind and keep him here forever."

So be it. Elias Jacobovich, disinfected and shorn of his hair, was given a bed in a communal flat for elderly and infirm Jews on Pravdy Street. Along with ten other aging Jews too old to be cared for by their families, or left behind by sons and daughters who finally received permission to leave for Israel or New York, Elias Jacobovich was given a clean bed. Holding onto his bundle as if it were some sort of passport or official document, he curled into a fetal position. Except for the squeaks he made when he was hungry or needed a chamber pot from the Russian woman employed to care for him and the others, he was silent and caused absolutely no trouble for anyone.

True, Alexandr Davidowich was a bit worried when the old Jew who looked like an African warrior approached him carrying a long stick. You wouldn't feel the same in a strange place?

Also true, the tailor had to explain this mishegass in front of a Russian woman who kept staring at Simon Moskovich and speaking to him in baby-Russian ("Gypsy, yes? Romania? Moldavia? No funny business, understand?").

Meanwhile, Sasha Yurivich read the sign, three times. Then he dropped the stick. Crazy or not, he had his two Jews. And if Elias Jacobovich was still number eight, now there were enough men for a last minyan. "Klozman died over Pesach, may he rest in peace," he said when the tailor asked. "But maybe you got some time to sew for the rest of us? You know a few prayers?"

Sasha Yurivich explained all that was necessary for Berman to hear. Berman, in turn, asked about the one who "came back from the dead," the one he had come so far to meet. "Did I hear right?"

"Listen, this cost me a good watch," Sasha said after Masha Viktorovna left. "Please, stay and help."

"The one I heard about," Berman repeated. "He's here?"

"He's here and he's not here. Come, you'll see for yourself."

It wasn't easy on his spirit for Simon Moskovich to follow Berman upstairs. The smells of advanced age, which became stronger after each labored step—unwashed underwear, old medicine, greasy dishes stacked on tables, disinfectant, sour milk—made him see his own end waiting around the corner. But he had Berman's sworn promise, so he held his breath and did what he could.

Masha Viktorovna grudgingly brought out seven suits from the closet and threw them on a cluttered table. "No charge, right?" she asked.

The four Jews who still walked under their own power gathered around Berman, while two in wheelchairs were helped by Sasha Yurivich.

"You can fix this?" one of the men asked. "It cost me two months' wages. I am Dobrakind, Josef Isidoravich."

"He can do anything!" Sasha Yurivich said, shouting to make himself heard. "You think I didn't get references? He has a sign!"

Introductions were made, with added commentary whispered into Berman's ear by Sasha Yurivich. "This one used to work in leather . . . two sons in Haifa send him money that never arrives. Right, Yaakov?"

A blank stare from Yaakov, a few handshakes from Dobrakind the butcher ("He could take apart a cow in thirty minutes!"), Feldman the clerk ("Good handwriting"), and Volovsky the botanist ("He still knows his chess moves . . . a real brain"). From Meyer and Goldenburg, polite bows ("Meyer, the schmuck, once tried to get into the party, and Goldenburg, an agronomist who knows Talmud, won't ever let him forget it").

"And the one I came to see?" asked Berman.

"Sleeping, dreaming . . . who knows."

Experienced apprentice Moskovich measured waists, pulled at excess material around crotches, used the tailor's chalk to mark under armpits, and put a new cassette into the portable tape recorder. Berman cleaned his glasses and then set up the Little Wonder on the table. Soon, his mouth was filled with pins.

Berman slid Goldenburg's old suit under the needle and began to work. The agronomist wheeled toward him and whispered that what he was doing was a "mitzvah," but that he should be careful around Meyer "because he's still too stupid to understand anything about Stalin, his name should rot in every book."

Berman quickly conceded that Goldenburg was right, but, as all dues would eventually be paid in the next life, there was no need for such talk at the present.

And this was how the work proceeded: one suit after another went under the needle, each one needing to be taken in, frayed bits cut away, new cuffs fashioned, some kerosene applied to wash away old stains and grease marks.

"Tell me about what you remember," Berman would ask as Simon Moskovich held the tape recorder's small microphone close to his customers. "I get paid with words, so talk."

He also got paid with several photographs, a torn page from a volume of Talmud ("Listen, tailor, take this and put it under glass. Trust me, it's permitted"), and a tiny blue vest that Feldman found in the rubble of an old Jewish quarter in Lublin ("I was a tank driver in '44. I think you maybe can fix this and do something nice with it. I, personally, can't look at it any longer").

"Ahh!"

If truth were put to the wheel, and you asked Simon Moskovich why Berman disappeared for the rest of the night after he finished his work, he would say: "Look, he had to see number eight. So I agreed to play a few tunes for the boys. Don't ask, Berman's business was private."

Hours went by. Simon got out his bugle; good tunes were played. Filthy jokes were shared. Simon Moskovich even performed, several times because there were countless versions, his magnificent fifteen-minute interpretation of *War and Peace*, complete with sound effects and the appearance of the entire Russian army. "Not bad for an old man," Masha Viktorovna laughed when Simon Moskovich, putting on her babushka and raising his voice, became the beautiful Natasha Rostova. "For this I'll make some tea for the Gypsy."

While Simon Moskovich as Napoleon was retreating from Moscow toward Smolensk (*"Ah, quelle terrible chose la guerre!"*) and Pierre mourned the loss of his great friend Prince Andrei, Alexandr Davidowich, cupping his ear close to Elias Jacobovich's lips, praying that the microphone was good enough to pick up the scratchy whispering, recorded a very sad story. It may be that the tailor even had to get in bed with him so that the engineer's son could hear *his* story about the Polish Hasid and everything that came before."My father was a locksmith, and my mother taught me how to sew. . . ."

But sometime between the glittering moment when veteran actor Simon Moskovich re-created old Moscow before the horror and the final sweet embrace between Pierre Bezuhov and his beloved Natasha, Elias Jacobovich slowly, painfully uncurled his bony fingers. He released his soiled bundle into the Jewish tailor's care and, with the greatest effort, whispered, "Return this for me."

Thirty minutes later, his head resting on the pillow next to Elias Jacobovich, Berman stopped biting his tongue.

Enough.

10

Simon Moscovich had been back in Moscow a week when Berman's thin letters began arriving. "I take no apologies!" the bugler yelled before he stuffed them, unread, into his pocket. "Not even a word of goodbye . . . not a murmur of thanks for my trouble. Feh!"

Ladies and gentlemen, a few points need to be made. Simon Moskovich Zorin was very upset. And who would blame him? Who? Two months of his life thrown away for the sake of a debt to a crazy Jew, right? His Lada beaten into a sputtering wreck by so much traveling, not to mention the dent left along its trunk when he removed the tailor's sign (which he, after all, devised after a wakeful dream). The effort expended on a series of crappy roads, the heartache that came from being in Pskov with old Jews a fingernail's length away from their end, the nervousness his letter must have caused his son-in-law. Plus everything else he had endured to help the tailor: sore fingers, an aching spine from so much driving, a hole in his heart for his children, lost windscreen wipers, and the humiliating moment when, with ashes in his mouth, he had to explain to the old men in Pskov why Berman had stolen Elias Ja-cobovich's precious bundle of rags and vanished only three days before the poor bastard passed on. "He collects old material," was all he could shamefully admit to a room now, after Elias Jacobovich's passing, two Jews short of a proper minyan. "He meant no harm."

"Bullshit," Masha Viktorovna said. "Stealing from a dying man makes him worse than a Gypsy."

Sasha Yurivich, dressed in the suit Berman had fixed and pressed, his face colorless and drawn, the victim of a terrible hoax he could never forget, was even more direct. "The tailor didn't act like a mensch. He should live with that for the rest of his days!" Feldman and Goldenburg, their refurbished suits a bit too loose for their skinny frames, agreed. Then they accused Simon Moskovich of complicity in the terrible crime; Volovsky the botanist argued that "nature's laws are always kinder than the human heart." And Simon Moskovich, who had never wanted to be in Pskov in the first place, was forced to bribe a doctor to keep Elias Jacobovich in the morgue one more day so that a proper service could be arranged.

"I'm searching for two Jews to say some prayers," he told the doctor. "Some things are difficult to manage."

"Some things," answered the physician, "cost three hundred rubles."

Thus, of the ten Jews who eventually accompanied Elias Jacobovich to his grave, eight managed to say a Kaddish; one, Simon Moskovich, had to endure harsh stares and several insults; and the last two, a hospital intern just arrived from Moscow and a middle-aged furrier who claimed a Jewish mother but no other attachment to the faith, were hired at the last minute by Simon Moskovich for another one hundred rubles.

"Now, you leave us," Sasha Yurivich told the tailor's

apprentice after the brief service, when Simon Moskovich offered his hand and a kind word. "Never mind, never mind, there's nothing left to say."

Masha Viktorovna, who accompanied her charges to the cemetery for an extra week's pay, spat at Simon Moskovich's feet. "There, now take that back to your tailor!"

Just before he drove away in the direction of Moscow, Simon Moskovich removed and stomped on the sign, grinding his shoe over the letters. Without considering the consequences of his anger, he threw away the junk left by the tailor: an oil painting, some scraps of material, and two boxes of rubbish he didn't bother to look at.

"You prick!" he shouted as he ripped the sign apart. "Look what you've done to my beautiful Lada!"

During the long, exhausting drive to Moscow, Simon Moskovich, suddenly freed from all obligations and debt, wept in frustration. Then, like someone who has just taken a good purgative, he vowed never to believe anyone who didn't have a blood tie to his own person. And if I do, he thought, let my sagging balls fall off and roll into the Moskva River.

Once, long before Alexandr Davidowich Berman was even an irritating speck on the bugler's consciousness, and two years prior to his Tatyana's death, Simon Moskovich had finally saved enough money to buy a black-and-white television set. The result of three months of stinking overtime work at the bulb factory, the Polish set was given a place of honor in the Zorin household, next to a collection of tiny glass zoo animals he had personally created for his three daughters. "It's magic," the girls agreed when they tuned in their first program. "We're never going to give this up."

But they did, quickly tiring of the long, boring programs extolling the virtues of steel production in Sverdlovsk, concerts featuring a hundred overweight "Soviet Heroes of Labor" from Minsk singing praises to the leadership, or the endless coverage given to party hacks crooning loyalty to Soviet greatness and the various Five Year Plans for wheat or barley harvests.

However, if the fruits of labor are only enjoyed by those who sweat, as Vladimir Ilyich himself always said, then Simon Moskovich fully intended to suck every ounce of juice from his prize. Raising the television's volume to a decibel level only slightly less than that of a whining jet engine, he watched everything he could.

"It's like a drug for you," Tatyana complained. "What will happen to your mind?"

Simon Moskovich made sure the girls were in their room, then he answered. "I want to see for myself how these shits lie themselves blue in the face. I'm collecting their bird droppings for my grave."

And such images, too. Year after year, one flickering picture after another proclaimed the inviolability of the internationalist Soviet state. He listened to the liars defend the invasion of Hungary in 1956, watched the bright vapor from socialist hydrogen bombs exploding in test sites somewhere in the East ("Bastards!"), and was driven to a frenzy of anger when he first heard about Soviet tanks pounding their way into Prague in 1968 to prevent "Zionist manipulations."

Simon Moskovich, who often drank too much while he was watching, was transfixed by the monumental crap dished out by the party stalwarts. But no matter how much he complained or yelled his feelings into the noise—"You asshole, Suslov, your mother weaned you on sour milk and blood" or "That droopy-lidded assortment of criminals that calls itself a Central Committee should kiss my ass!"—he, like so many others, was certain that the mountainous pile of dung created by the party would never, ever topple in his lifetime or during those of his amazing children. "It's not worth having your heart pop," little Ida said, worried when her father's face turned scarlet after watching Brezhnev address the Supreme Soviet. "But they lie, sweetness," he moaned. "They lie and there's nothing to be done about it!"

Ida, then in secondary school, wiped her father's chin. "And his grammar is awful, Papa," she said as she pointed to the television screen. "Really awful."

"Bravo, sweetness! Bravo."

But if the lifespan of the Soviet state can be compared to the days of the week—Lenin's Bolsheviks winning out in 1917 on a Sunday, Stalin's terror and filthy muck by Tuesday, the Nazi invasion and the Great Patriotic War on Wednesday, Khrushchev followed by Bushy Eyebrows himself Friday morning until midnight, Andropov and stupid Chernenko holding on for a few dawn hours on a Saturday—then Simon Moskovich, angry and tired as he was, had returned to Moscow (after wasting two minutes past midnight, Saturday, with Berman!) to witness Mikhail Sergeyevich Gorbachev's Sunday morning. Full circle, so to say. Can you believe it?

Simon Moskovich believed it, and this is why he trusted to luck and purchased every newspaper he could find. He rode the Metro from one end of Moscow to the other in search of fresh news. "What's happening, friend?" he asked at any open newspaper kiosk. "Is it over? What's the truth?"

"Some are full of shit, some lick the truth," he was told by the vendors. "Read for yourself."

Which he did, collecting enough newspapers and journals to insulate a windy flat during winter. Over the next few weeks, during the great unraveling of the Soviet Union, Simon Moskovich took one hot bath after another. He balanced a bottle on the tub's edge and moved the television set into the doorway. Soaking himself to the texture of a sun-dried plum, he drank, watched, and read everything: *Pravda*'s mindless defense of the party, neo-fascist tripe in *Nash Sovremnik*, attacks on the Communists and support for Yeltsin in *Ogonyok*, poems written in memory of that swine Stalin in some military monthly, and—this is when he gagged on a heel of bread—a warning in some nationalist rag about the imminent threats to the Motherland posed by the "Jew-vermin despoiling our nation." "Our home is already burning to the ground," *Sovetskaya Rossiya* proclaimed on the front page. "What has become of us, brothers?"

"You're fucked, that's what," a jubilant Simon Moskovich, onetime Hero of Labor, yelled from the privacy of his bathtub. "It's all over."

Most Jews will take a drink only on a holiday (there are many), to mark a birth (there are never enough) or, God forbid, to ease the pain following a death. Whatever the cause that brings a full bottle to the table, they avoid acting like peasants at a wedding and keep their brains working, their eyes open. This is a known fact, correct?

But when a world revolution is exploding in front of them—when seventy-some years of lies and losses begin to disintegrate like cobwebs in a sunny corner—who would blame a good Jew (there are many) for adopting a few bottles of vodka as his best friends?

Alone in his flat, surrounded by a growing pile of newspapers and stale bread, his antique Polish television sending a sickly, pale glow over his face, Simon Moskovich Zorin used his weeks to toast the end of Lenin's paradise. "Stick it up your ass," he shouted at the fools on *Vremya*'s evening news broadcasts, "you've had your day!" Each time he heard Yeltsin's name mentioned, he played his bugle and didn't give a damn how many times his neighbors beat against his walls or pounded on his door. "Celebrate, celebrate," he mumbled before opening another bottle. "L'Chayim, Boris Nikolaiyevich."

"Shut the fuck up, we're sleeping!" his most disturbed neighbor shouted.

"Go to hell, Ivan Petrovich," answered the bugler, pounding on the floor with his wet feet. "This is no time to sleep."

Although it took nearly ten hours to place a telephone call to Israel, Simon Moskovich was too excited to care if it was monitored. "Ida, Ida," he shouted over the loud whine and static during the one minute he had before the call was cut off. "The ones with bad grammar are dropping off the television screen, just like dead flies!"

"All of them, Papa?" she asked, knowing immediately what he meant.

"Every last one, sweetness."

"Are you well, Papa? Will you come to us soon?"

Simon Moskovich began to cry. He lost precious seconds trying to regain his voice and part of a sentence.

"Some of them are talking about bringing back a new czar, I've read this and . . . ."

The line began to click and buzz. Someone with no interest in Simon Moskovich and his sort laughed.

" . . . so your mama n . . . needs me here," he stammered, pulling the receiver away from his good ear. "How c . . . can I leave her t . . . to the mud-throwers?"

"Papa? Papa?"

"Ida. . . ."

In the midst of this bittersweet celebration, Simon Moskovich, alone of all his neighbors, began to receive letters and postcards inside his rusty mailbox. Deposited in batches of two, sometimes three, and never enclosed inside the same size envelopes, the letters and cards were addressed to "Simon Moskovich Zorin, Bugler & Tailor's Apprentice," and bore a simple name on the reverse side: "A.D. Berman."

Day after day, regular deliveries: some glued together on the outside edges with cellotape, some stained with tea rings or cigarette ash. For whatever reason, A.D. Berman was quite a writer. Maybe he was in trouble? Maybe he had a new plan? Maybe, as Simon Moskovich justly felt, the tailor should just fall over himself and be done with it. "Screw you, Sasha!" he shouted as he stuffed them into his pocket. "Deserter! Thief!"

How to describe Simon Moskovich during these important weeks while he kept his joyful death watch? He didn't shave. His stomach burned. His eyes were always bloodshot from reading or crouching too near the television screen, but he was careful to eat between drinks so that his senses wouldn't be too dulled. He steamed in his bathtub, carefully balancing newspapers on the dry spots of his knees. He took long walks to clear his head and to buy more newspapers. He tried, always without luck, to place another call to his daughters. Just in case something happened, he slept beneath an old blanket in his chair by the television. And because he wanted to remember what a fool he had been in many places, all of Berman's crumpled letters—at last count, perhaps twenty—bulged unread in his large pockets like uneaten rolls.

What more could he do?

Who knows why Simon Moskovich risked missing the final croak from the Soviet throat by leaving his flat to visit the synagogue? Perhaps to breathe some fresh air on the long walk to Arkhipova Street? To see who among the older Jews was frightened by recent events? ("Is it true what they say about the czars?" he might have asked. "Is the community in any danger from the fascists?") To bury himself beneath a prayer shawl? To ask, in a very quiet voice because one never knew who was listening, whether there was some prayer a not-so-good Jew could offer to thank the Highest for mercifully putting an end to the party? To remember his wife, of blessed memory?

Or, finally, to read Berman's letters?

"You prick," he said, as he fished out a crumpled post-card with only one sentence and a small patch of cellotape that held a thin strand of brown thread. "You. . . ."

"Dearest First-Class Apprentice," the tailor wrote on the opposite side of a faded color picture of V. I. Lenin arriving at the Finland Station. "Work continues between the living and the dead, so I beg forgiveness and send a thread from our late friend's mended suit."

Simon Moskovivch folded the card and put it back into his crowded pocket. It was, he knew, the only kind of apology he would ever receive.

The morning service had already begun when Simon Moskovich took a seat at the rear of the nearly empty sanctuary. A few dozen eyes watched him as he covered his head with the tallith. "It's Simon Moskovich," someone whispered. "His children used to come here in the old days." Several Jews, who hadn't seen him in several months, nodded; he waved and then rubbed the beard that was clearly visible on his face. At the end of his row, a well-dressed elderly man, who seemed to sit tentatively, as if his backside were hurting him, watched our bugler through half-lidded eyes, then looked away.

Even in a synagogue that had long been used to sheltering strange characters—the devout, as well as KGB informers checking up on dissident Jews, moochers waiting to prey upon foreign visitors, the occasional gonif or two, and the frightened ones who were afraid to pray too loudly—Simon Moskovich was immediately noticeable. He bowed his head—or so it appeared—at odd moments, inclining far more than was necessary; he stood when he should have remained seated; he mumbled when he should have kept silent; he kept raising slips of paper toward the dim light to help himself read. For the rabbi who droned on but fixed a cautious eye on the last row of seats and the old men who kept moving toward the ark—he, Simon Moskovich, was lost in wild, holy thoughts. "Our Simon Moskovich has become a true believer," said one elderly Jew when he saw the bugler's thick growth of snow-white beard bordered by a tallith. "And look how he concentrates—are those the morning prayers?" "We should let him be," someone answered. "That's his business."

You can imagine the nervousness that followed Simon Moskovich's constant shifting from side to side, especially when the bugler seemed to choke on something and sputter what sounded like a profanity. Then there was a loud groan and a crumpling of paper. Then some laughter. This was too much to bear.

"Shussh, you," the old beadle called from the sanctuary doorway. "Stop that noise!"

"Ayy!" Simon Moskovich said, waving his hand toward heaven's light.

"Have some respect for others."

"Ayy!"

You must understand Simon Moskovich's confusion and concern. Holding some of Berman's letters on his lap, dropping others into a pile at his feet, getting lost between pages because the busy tailor never dated his writing or completed all of his sentences—"and then when I danced, she began to. . . ."

"So what did she do?" he cried. "Berman!"

"Quiet."

"Yes, yes," he said, finally aware of the disturbance he was causing. "I'm sorry."

"This is a sanctified place, Simon Moskovich Zorin," answered the beadle, a Jew who had seen far too much in a long lifetime. "One more outburst and you will have to leave."

"Yes," Simon Moskovich said as he picked up the letters and hid them under his tallith. "Yes."

Several Jews who watched Simon Moskovich at that moment said, "He just got a bit carried away with his prayers." But if you had been next to him, brushing his quaking shoulders with your own, hearing his legs moving up and down, and, worse, noticing how he made a tent of the large tallith so that he could hide from the other Jews, then you would have known that he was, as we say, playing on another field, where there was no beginning and no end. "To my best apprentice," each hastily written letter began. "I have found myself moving beyond our plan in. . . ."

After a twenty-minute period of peace and ritual order, when the rabbi returned to his singsong work serving the Master of the Universe, and the other Jews avoided staring at the bugler's foolish movements, Simon Moskovich jumped in his seat, swallowed some air, and made such a commotion that the rabbi dropped his heavy siddur. Three elderly Jews, far too old to tolerate such goings-on, pounded on their wooden seats when Simon Moskovich threw some papers into the air and began to point to un-seen places on an imaginary map.

"Simon Moskovich Zorin!" the rabbi said. "Out!"

Through split, puffy lips—the result of too many hot soakings in his numerous baths—the bugler began to hoot like a common drunk.

"Out!" repeated the rabbi. "Now!"

"Yidn, take heart!" the madman shouted in Russian and Yiddish until his voice echoed in the sanctuary with all the force of a well-blown ram's horn. "The tailor Alexandr Davidowich Berman is dancing in his black coat for all of us . . . and he's doing it everywhere!"

Upstairs, along the edge of the balcony in the women's section, the rabbi's sister nearly fainted, and her sister-in-law, equally short of breath and teetering from side to side in her tight shoes, covered her face in shame.

Following quietly behind Simon Moskovich after he walked outside, the well-dressed older Jew, wearing the suit of a prosperous nobody, spoke to him as if he'd known the bugler for many years. "It's a mitzvah to forgive an old friend, isn't it?" he said, as he moved toward a new Zhiguli sedan. "So I wish you well, Simon Moskovich. *Zeit gezint.*"

What a night the bugler had after frightening eighteen Jews (sixteen men, two women) with his crazy noise and carrying on. Given his recent past—all of that drinking and cursing at a Polish television set, all of the near-drowning in a bathtub while the party hacks were two steps away from a long-awaited retirement, the outburst of joy in shul—you would think that he was dangling at the end of a frayed rope. Not so! Simon Moskovich had work to do: points to plot—towns, rivers, mountains—and notes to set down before he forgot, or decided he was dreaming. And all of this effort required strict attention, a good map, and no television. Vodka was another question.

Like those ancient scribes who must have labored without rest as they transcribed the rabbis' stories before they disappeared, Simon Moskovich tried to piece together the journey of Alexandr Davidowich. He flattened out each crumpled, undated letter. He tore an oversized map from one of his daughter's geography books, unfolded it along the floor, and stuck pins wherever Berman walked, sometimes danced, or, close to the Winter Palace, broke three fingers on a horse's tangled reins.

The pins, which soon took the shape of a skinny centipede, gave some idea as to the tailor's whereabouts. But how Alexandr Davidowich managed his movements from one spot to another was enough of a mystery to make Simon Moskovich shudder. "Did you fly?" he called out each time he inserted another pin. "Did you find some Aeroflot pilot with a suit that needed a fancier lapel? Was there a ride on the back of a truck? Did you catch the wind? By train? How?"

If the postmarks on the envelopes were to be believed—if Simon Moskovich's pins penetrated the correct spots on the colorful map—here was an old Jew who defied all natural laws that rule travel in our huge country. Shlepping a large rucksack filled with his Singer Little Wonder and a portable Victrola with a few scratched records, Berman apparently moved in all directions: north, then east for a brief visit to the spot where, as he noted, "the coat given me by Olga Mikhailovna was born," a southerly turn "through six or seven villages" toward the Byelorussian border into Vitebsk ("Do you know the name of the painter who once lived here?"), an enormous swing east to Smolensk, a jump to Kiev, a southeasterly trip toward Tula and several places "close to Moscow," and, according to the last letter Simon Moskovich received, stops in what was now St. Petersburg (street names were provided) and Berman's own restful Pushkin.

Simon Moskovich was nonplussed when he realized that, while Berman might have posted his letters from these various places, he might not have done his "work" there. The only clear details he provided came with a name, sometimes two, of the Jews he had met or, what was even more frustrating for the bugler, a vague reference to a river ("I ate by a very clean, glassy body of water") or a building (" . . . there was still some Yiddish lettering beneath the chipped stucco on the restaurant").

While you were safe at home, watching your children or enjoying some coffee (if such luxuries were available at your spot on the earth), our tailor, as best Simon Moskovich could understand from a reading of Berman's fragmentary sentences, was searching, God help him, for a chance to discover where the lost Isaak (among a number of others) might have come to rest.

"On a hot, dry day," he wrote from somewhere close to Vitebsk, "I met a Jewish woman—Anya Meyerova, maybe not so clear in her head."

"You want to see where a painter lived, the one who was born here and later went to Paris or some such place?" she asks after I mend her housecoat. "Of course," I say, "take me." She does. "Nothing left, tailor," she says when we go to the old section, "nothing left." To the synagogue next; "nothing left but a workers' club, go inside," she says. Then I read on the wall: "Education is the Path to Communism." Place after place: "nothing left," like a broken record. Anya Meyerova is lost. She says, "No children here, tailor." I answer, "A boy named Isaak might have passed by here" and then, because my sack is so heavy, I show her what he might have looked like by drawing a little sketch. "Taken by the Czar Nicholas, God forsake him for what he did to us," I say. She laughs, says, "Come with me, I have a picture inside an old book. Come." But Anya is confused. She shows me a picture of her dancing with her grandson, died in '56 from the pox. She cries. "I can fix other things, too," I say. So we dance to the Victrola . . . in a garden, my apprentice. I wear a feather; she holds two flowers. Then I think about the painter—do you know his name?—he would have enjoyed this. Nothing dies, apprentice. Here I have found. . . ."

"Found?" Simon Moskovich cried as if the tailor were still sitting beside him in the Lada. "Found what?" Like all of Berman's brief notes, this one was unfinished, a suit without buttons!

"Who invented my fate?" Simon Moskovich said. Then he began to drink. He followed the amazing pins.

In those unnamed villages (seven holes in Ida's map) leading toward or away from the Byelorussian border ("When did you arrive, Sasha? Tell me!"), Berman's great change began. Accepting his chosen lot, he became more than the teller of the story—he became part of the story itself. "Enough of mending," the tailor wrote in one letter. "Time to say what I know . . ."

. . . to Malka Abramova, and also to her cousin who walked with me by the river. I put on the scribe's black coat, Simon Moskovich, fixed to fit me now. And I say: "Isaak had bad shoes when they took him away from the village where the rebbezim kissed a goy. Close your eyes, friends, imagine what it must have been like." "Some story," the girl says. "But my grandfather—who wore a black hat—brought home a Polish singer from Krakow. Think of it: a Jewish girl with thin legs and rouge over her cheeks who could sing Hebrew songs. The Germans caught her and threw her into the pit beyond the wood. See, there it is, by the new cesspool that has a sign next to it. 'For the People's Health.' " The girl grabs my sleeve. "Can you make a dress like hers?" she asks. I say, "I can make anything." So much for deserting tailoring!

Two days passed. She has her dress. Now she wants to learn to sing in Hebrew. Where is my bugler when I need him, eh? A stone presses on my heart, Simon Moskovich, but I sing for her.

You should see my new sign.

Thus it continued for Alexandr Davidowich as he made his way from place to place: in the villages where he found only a few Jews and flies, he sewed and told a few stories. "Wore the scribe's coat," he wrote, "because it only seems right." And always he asked about Isaak. If there was someone who was old enough to remember Stalin's plague, he brought out the tattered prayerbook and the phylacteries that Elias Jacobovich, a peaceful rest unto him, had carried with him for so many years. "I asked if anyone recognized such a book . . . they said nothing. So I did it by myself. K for EJ and LJ. People were silent."

The code he began to use—"K for EJ and LJ"—was as mysterious to Simon Moskovich's understanding as the means of transport Berman used on his journey. The message appeared at the end of every letter. "By myself, in the rain, K for EJ and LJ."

There must have been a strong wind behind Alexandr Davidowich, pushing him this way and that until he reached Smolensk. Here, he stopped—an aching back? a turned ankle? a powerful sun affecting his brain?—and fell into a "dark hole." His handwriting became difficult to follow: the letters were smudged, the script was almost as illegible as a nervous schoolchild's. "Unwrapped his bundle at the edge of Katyn forest," he scrawled in a letter of only two paragraphs.

Walked carefully until I found where the Poles were taken. EJ told me about this. "Do this for Piotr Krajewski and two others," he asked. "Of course," I answered. Now I'm here. What kind of place could this have been for them? EJ had whispered before he fell asleep, "The Poles I found must have been here and watched what happened. Why were they spared? Did they see the bullets, hear everything?" Unwrapped bundle: put a small cross and tiny knife close to a fir tree. I remembered Polish word for God, and repeated: *Bog, Bog, Bog.*

You do for Jews; you do for Poles. K for EJ and LJ. Polish man came up to me, very old. "You know what happened here?" he asked in good Russian. "I know, I know." "What?" he says. I say, "Thirty thousand Polish officers murdered by Soviets." "Then why," he asks, "would a Russian Jew bother?" I say, "A *human being* bothered." I tell him about EJ who found what he found. A very dark hole, Simon Moskovich. I will leave here forever.

Simon Moskovich dropped the letter. A graveyard's thin pine needle fell out of the envelope. "Katyn," he yelled. "He went to Katyn!"

His face flushed by too much strong drink, Simon Moskovich remembered the stories he had heard from the old Jews in Pskov, and finally understood the code that drove Alexandr Davidowich through the huge open graveyard he had been moving across. "Kaddish for Elias Jacobovich and the little Jew," he said as he ran his hand over Ida's map, pushing the pins even deeper into the paper. "Ah, Sasha!"

And there were the other pins, too: in Kiev, where, from an open tram window, Berman heard a Yiddish song about Jewish boys taken away by the czar and marched southeast, toward Tula, "so I ran out and made a tape recording; many autos honked at us." Then, following a song's directions, to the "city museum" in Tula, where, despite his promise to leave things be, the tailor somehow found the time to "deposit" another memory inside an empty display case. "I found a synagogue and told the Jews inside to visit the museum. 'There is an exhibit you should see,' I told them. 'Go now before it vanishes.' I said, 'This I did for little Isaak.' " In his battle to preserve logic, as well as to keep the room from swaying beneath his shaky feet, Simon Moskovich covered his eyes. He tried to imagine the end of this episode. "Fool!" the Jews must have yelled. "Get out of here!"

When he was sure that the ground was stable, he finished the letter. At this stage, why rule out any possibilities?

"Three came, old friend. I stood with them. They read the small card, carefully printed (you would be proud!) that I placed on top of the jacket. 'For Isaak who is no longer with us and who passed through this place. Taken from his loving parents in the terrible reign of Nicholas I. This is true. Please, remember him.' " It was then that one of Tula's Jews—as old as Berman? another meshuggener who hadn't enough trouble in his life? a woman who understood?—grabbed the tailor. "For some moments," the Jew said, "we need to dance." And they did, arms swaying, maybe linked by handkerchief or a colorful scarf, in a nearly empty museum smelling of dust and old floor wax. Berman wrote a final sentence: "You see, bugler, it works!"

As it did, friends. As it did. For this was the same letter that made Simon Moskovich jump up in the synagogue. "Berman!"

But some omissions he couldn't forgive. Never. In the

letters that made their way from "places close to Moscow," Berman only wrote: "More events for the Jews. I am well. Stitching my way backwards!" In the two letters sent from Leningrad, eight scrawled sentences total: on one, "Borrowed a horse and cart (not too expensive) and made a display by the Winter Palace. 'Give a poor Jew a living,' I shouted. Three broken fingers—wrapped up and healing nicely." On the last one, a letter that made Simon Moskovich groan in frustration, only this: "Packed our items, with instructions for the British, into the curator's crates bound for London. Several of my coats (hidden beneath Menshikov's robe), a rebbetzim's dress (tucked inside Peter's green broadcloth Preobrazhensky uniform), some tapes, feathers, and hats (inside Catherine's coronation gown), a memory for Elias Jacobovich's little Jew. And something for my parents (left sleeve of Grand Duke Alexis's boyar outfit). I am well. So is my cat."

A sudden rush of wind through Simon Moskovich's window scattered the tailor's letters onto the floor. A distant rumbling shook his dishes and the empty vodka bottles. Simon Moskovich kept one foot on the map, the other on the last few notes he had received. The floor began to vibrate so much that a full bottle of vodka crashed onto the floor, its contents soaking into the cheap paper and Berman's various letters. There were several loud thumps against his door, followed by a muffled cry.

Simon Moskovich got on his knees to save what he could. He peeled the wet map from the floor and made an even greater mess, as everything west of Moscow fell apart in his hands. As he reached for the letters, he slipped and hit his knee against the table, bringing down several framed photographs of his family and three tiny glass animals.

The banging at his door continued. "Screw off!" he screamed after he cut himself on the shards. "Go away, I'm busy!"

"God damn you, Simon Moskovich!" his neighbor Martov shouted as he kicked the door one last time. "There are tanks on Kalinin . . . hurry!"

"What?"

"Tanks! Soldiers!"

And this was when a slightly drunk Simon Moskovich, a tiny unicorn's glass tail piercing his right palm along with two of Berman's pins, decided to join the revolution. Naturally, he took along his bugle and, for luck, a vodka-soaked photograph of his three daughters.

Whoosh.

II

The long line of mourners lowered their heads and whispered. In the distance, a church bell tolled.

Nadezdha Yefimova clutched my wrist, careful to avoid touching the dirty bandage wrapped around my infected palm. "Go ahead, play something," she said. "What better time is there than this?"

"I can't," I answered, "my fingers are too sore, and. . . ."

"Try, Simon Moskovich. People expect a little music. Something quiet and sad."

Next to us, in the small space we had to ourselves, seven or eight students formed a circle around me. Several others, seeing what was happening, joined their friends. A young girl clutching a white, blue, and red flag, the old Russian tricolor, kicked an empty champagne crate toward me. "Don't push the old man," she said. "He's the bugler who played for Yeltsin."

Nadezdha Yefimova gave me a sip of cold tea from her thermos and a lemon lozenge for my throat. "Rest a minute," she said, pointing to the crate. "Drink slowly and catch your breath. The tea and lemon will help."

"Quiet down," someone ahead of us called out. "The patriarch has his hands up."

Then, people moved closer together and kept their peace.

"Shh," my student protectors told the others when I began to play. "Shh."

Sometimes, history rains on our heads like a summer storm in the countryside. More often than not, we Jews find some shelter and wait until the worst passes—why get doused and risk a bad cold? Why put yourself in lightning's way? But this time, I was one old Jew who didn't care; this time, at the ass-end of the great Bolshevik fuckup, Russian Jews who had toyed with disaster during these past three days in August were either too drunk or too happy to worry about the consequences. "We've won!" people cried. "We've won!"

Believe me, friends, I'm no hero. My stomach is still shaking from the sound of tanks and armored personnel carriers, and I admit to you that I dribbled a little bit in my trousers as soon as I saw the soldiers, weapons pointed toward us, sitting atop their vehicles. "They're armed," I told Martov, whose face was as white as snow. "This is no joke." "Then blow that fucking bugle of yours!" he shouted, as he disappeared without me into the crowd racing down the Arbat toward the Parliament building. "Maybe the noise will scare them back to their barracks!"

"Go home, Simka," I heard my father telling me. "There's no chance!" Sorry, Papa, you know me.

I blew a long, loud C. Enough to scare the devil himself; worse, more than enough to make me, Simon Moskovich, the unlikely leader of a group of ten aging Muscovites (maybe they, too, had wet trousers!) with no plan in mind. "To the White House!" I shouted, not quite believing what had just flown from my throat. "Boris Nikolaiyevich needs us."

One thing was clear—I had no idea what would happen. When we crossed Smolenskoye, our small group became part of a large crowd that surged past a battalion of young soldiers. Some veterans from the Afghan war, dressed in their old tunics, told us from behind an overturned kiosk to cover our faces with wet handkerchiefs as soon as we smelled any gas. "Piss on them if you can't bring up any spit," said one veteran, certain of what would happen. "Don't screw with our old comrades!" another shouted. "They have their orders." "But they're our sons," people cried in response. "Not today," he answered as he tied a dirty scarf around his mouth. "Now they belong to the other side."

We moved slowly toward the troops. My chest began to hurt. I thought I was going to vomit when I saw the tanks, the machine guns, the Soviet flag. Then: "Hey, grandfather," one of the soldiers who stepped down from a metal ladder on the tank yelled to me. "Do you know any John Lennon?"

"Who?"

"John Lennon, come on."

"You can maybe hum a little bit for me?"

Thank the Highest for my perfect pitch and good ear. It was a nice tune. The soldier, a year or two younger than my Ida, a recent schoolboy in a tanker's tight leather cap, sang a little bit in English, enough for me to follow along and pick out the simple melody. "What's the song?" I asked him when he came next to me. "Imagine," he said, quickly translating into Russian. Someone gave the singer a plum and some apples, others told him to go home; a little babushka, gaining a foothold on the tank's tread, offered him a boiled egg and some dill. "Imagine!"

An officer yelled something at his men. The people next to me chanted, "Rossiya, Rossiya!" and "Shame! Shame!"

"We'll be safe now?" I asked the soldier. "You have orders about us?"

Out of his officer's sight, the young tanker stroked my tarnished bugle while a group of women surrounded the tank. "Soviet soldiers, we are your mothers," they shouted. The smell of burning gasoline wafted toward us. "Go, grandpa," the boy said as he wiped his eyes. "Remember the song."

My knees began to buckle and I dropped my bugle. On my knees, I felt the cement cracking as the tank lurched backward a few meters, then swerved to the side as its turret began to revolve. The soldiers closest to the tank scrambled behind its huge steel treads and cocked their weapons. The terrible grinding sound of the machine's engine drowned out the yelling around me. Exhaust smoke covered those of us too frightened to move. A moment away from being turned into nothing, I really soaked my pants and socks.

"Give me your hand," a woman said as she bent toward me and grabbed my arm. "We need to move away from here. Hurry!"

From behind the tank, a second woman, her face blackened by soot, took my other arm and lifted me up. Without their help, you would have known nothing about this or everything that followed. It began to rain.

"Run!" the first woman yelled, pushing me toward a passage between two of the tanks. "I won't let you fall."

Trust me, even an old man whose rubber knees are stinging is capable of moving like the wind. Arm in arm with my saviors—I had neither the courage nor the strength to look at their faces—I half stumbled, half ran toward the barricades at the end of Kalinin Prospekt. Although I was too nervous to look behind me, I heard some shots and screaming, then more distant shouts of "Shame, shame!"

"Hurry, friends," the people behind the hastily built barricades said when we reached the overturned trucks and kiosks. "This is where you need to be."

"Rossiya! Rossiya!" my women cried after they hoisted me over a bathtub placed at the top of the barricade. "Rossiya!"

Thank the Highest for women who help a bugler, carry him to safety, stay by his side and ignore the bad smell of his soiled clothing. "You're no sensation here," said the one who first picked me up by the tank and helped me to run. "You'll dry off soon, but you need to show me that bad hand of yours."

Nadezdha Yefimova, a pediatrician from one of the central hospitals, knew how to make a good bandage. She poured a little alcohol over my smarting palm and told me to look away while she tightened the dressing. "Here, take hold of your horn," she said. "Who knows when you may need it again." Above us, like a swarm of red ants finding the honey, thousands of people swarmed around the Parliament building, some carrying more junk to strengthen the barricades—blocks of stone, tree trunks, wire fencing—others huddled in groups and chanting slogans or singing. There were flags everywhere.

"We're screwed for sure," a man next to me cried as he considered asking my doctor for a swig from her bottle of grain alcohol. He beat his chest. "Who has something to drink?"

"Shush, you," Nadezdha said. "Stay sober or else!"

"What's happening?" I asked my beautiful doctor. "Is he right?"

"He's drunk," she said, helping me to recline against an overturned telephone box. Then, before I closed my eyes: "We've always been screwed—so what does it matter now?"

"Fuck Vladimir Ilyich!" a man carrying a crudely stitched Romanov flag and a small portrait of the last czar—his name should be blotted out in every book—yelled beside me. "Rossiya!"

"Rossiya, forever," answered the doctor.

"Ah, Papa, can you believe this?" I mumbled. "Vey iz mir."

I will remember those three days in front of the Parliament building as long as I live. But I won't lie to you: with each rumor that passed among the thousands of us who stayed in the cold rain, sharing food and drink and fear, hundreds of Muscovites left us, and one of them who stayed, your bugler, wasn't beyond considering an escape, because what good is an old glassblower when it comes to facing down tanks or commandos with blackened faces! And who could blame me? Every few minutes some new and ominous story passed from mouth to mouth like fire: Yeltsin was about to surrender; no, never, would our president give up his post?; Yeltsin had suffered a heart attack; a specially trained group of commandos, something called "Alpha Group," was only hours away from lobbing gas canisters into our midst ("Get your faces covered," we were ordered a dozen times by some of the Afghan war veterans. "Can't you smell the gas?"); the coup's plotters had already set up detention camps for us in the East; the KGB was enlarging its concrete cells in the Lubyanka ("Those bastards have our number," a woman told Nadezhda Yefimova. "Believe me, about them I know. Look around you, they're already here. Waiting!"). And, three times, this: "They say Stalin isn't really dead."

And yet, there were also the radio messages we received via small transistors that brought support from Rutskoi, our Afghan war pilot, and Khasbulatov: "Keep calm. Don't move from your place, but don't jump on the tanks if they break through the barricades. Practice civil disobedience, but do not, we repeat, do not injure yourselves or others. We are with you, brothers and sisters. Always."

On that first night, as I stood close to my good doctor, my hand still burning, I fell asleep for a few minutes to the humming sound of a hundred Russians, most of them young university students, singing some of Vysotsky's great ballads around a sputtering fire in a refuse bin. "We may be in hell," they sang, "but we stay together and embrace." Others chanted Yeltsin's name. Not too far from the singers, a group of women lettered banners with blue paint. "We will not move," one read; another, "Russian Soldiers Do Not Harm Their People." I awoke with a dry mouth only to hear one of the banner painters crying. "They've crushed three of us with armored cars on the Garden Ring Road!" she shouted above the din. "All dead!" Another rumor told us to prepare for an assault by helicopter, while a young woman ran from barricade to barricade shouting about infiltrators with small explosive devices. "Hold tight," our radio messages kept telling us. "Have faith. Trust us, you can sleep peacefully." Easy for them; not so easy for me. And worse, God knows, for anyone who stood in the way of a tank.

Before dawn—Tuesday? Wednesday?—my lack of sleep finally supplied dizzying, incredible visions to my brain. Pressed against one of the barricades alongside the loyal Nadezhda Yefimova—"You think I could leave someone who looks like my father?" she kept asking me—I thought I saw my old mate and fellow performer, Bodikian. Looking the same as he did when we were in the Ukraine in 1944, the juggler stood just above us, atop an upturned bathtub, his tunic unbuttoned down to his waist. He balanced himself on the huge basin's claw feet like some sort of African trained monkey, doing fantastic tricks for the crowd. Floating. His brilliantined black hair reflected the streetlights in every tight curl. He held an umbrella and a cigar. He spotted me and laughed.

"Hey, Simon Moskovich, you good-for-nothing Yid," he called out. "You look like shit. Worse than shit."

"Bodikian, Bodikian!" I yelled (or so I thought). "Get off that damn bathtub."

"Fuck you, Simka, I'm doin' my job for the boys here . . . same as always. And you?"

"Come down here!"

"Never."

The juggler swallowed a howitzer's worth of smoke from his black cigar. His cheeks filled up. I watched him squirm until his eyes, smouldering like spent shell casings, began to roll and give off smoke. The old trick.

"Hey, Simka," he shouted once the smoke cleared, "you just goin' to sit there in your soggy pants like a frightened rabbi? How 'bout some jokes, or maybe a few tunes for the ex-comrades here? Come on."

I felt a body moving closer, a head resting on my shoulder. Bodikian, feet as sticky as an insect's, was now standing, shoes together, on one of the tub's claws. He looked like a hood ornament on a Zil limo. I thought he was going to fly away. Just as he began to slip, he pointed toward an armored personnel carrier with a drenched Soviet flag hanging limply from a radio antenna. "Sons of bitches!" he screamed at the soldiers. "Your time's over!"

"Bodikian, you fool. Enough . . . ."

"Eh?"

"I said to stop."

"Then play something, rabbi."

"Fuck you!"

The juggler belched some smoke and laughed. "No, Simka. It's time to fuck *them*! Play."

And so I did—for the wounded boys in the hospital tent who couldn't see Bodikian's incredible tricks, certainly for my parents who clapped for me in our old Moscow flat ("Not bad, Simka," my father said), always for my girls who waved from the Jewish desert and said I should be careful ("Wear a hat, Papa!"), and now for Nadezdha Yefimova and her many friends, for the juggler himself, dead since 1956. ("My father spoke of you often," the postcard from Erevan sent by his only daughter read. "He would say, 'That Simka was one decent Jew who could carry a melody!' ")

Bodikian shouted, "It's time to fuck *them*, rabbi. Play!"

Dazed, I awoke and looked up to where the Armenian had stood in my dream. I wanted a wave, or maybe a kiss blown my way. But there was no juggler, just a limp,

bobbing barrage balloon, a green turd-shaped piece of rubber, sent aloft by the Parliament's defenders to foil a helicopter landing. Play!

A French photographer waved his hands in front of
me. "Please, sir," he asked in bad Russian. "A picture of you
for us?"

Smothered by smoke from the fires, my hand still
throbbing—me, Zorin, too old to be brave, given to bad
dreams, too nervous to suffer from any more dozing—gave
my permission between tunes. "Stand up, sir," he said,
making me move closer to a bonfire by the Parliament's
white steps, and generously sharing some vodka to wet my
mouth. "That's it, warm the body up." Click. I found
my pitch, and my audience. "Louder," Nadezdha said.
"Louder."

Click.

People listened to the music: lullabies, Ukrainian folk
songs, some Yiddish tunes my girls loved—"Dee . . . da, da,
dum, dum/Deedle, deedle, dum, dum . . . "—a few of
Bodikian's Armenian wedding marches, "Sweet Spring," a
song they used to sing in Leningrad during the siege, and
what I remembered (and embellished) from that British
singer who liked to imagine. Perfect pitch. "Not bad,
friend," a young man in faded battle fatigues, an Afghan
veteran, said. He slapped my shoulder and pointed around
us. "You take good care of them."

Click.

Someday, people will look at those photographs. They
will say that Zorin, a talented old Jew, made the morning
pass because he squashed fear with some music, and that
he was even heard within the Parliament building by those
who counted for something in this mess. Most of all, this

bugler (not that I believe a word of this bullshit) let some tunes battle the rumors that frightened many people still sore from the cold, wet night. "Shh, it's okay now," Nadezdha Yefimova told me when I had to stop to recover my wind. "Yeltsin is going to speak to us."

What do I remember? Yeltsin, red-faced and angry, the man we had come to protect with little more than the wet clothing on our bodies and a few Molotov cocktails, appeared in front of us beneath a huge Russian tricolor flag. "The conservative forces will not win," he told the cheering crowd. A famous poet threw his hands up in front of the loudspeaker, chanting something about Pushkin and Tolstoy being with us. A KGB colonel came next and begged his comrades who had joined the putschists "to stop" before it was too late. And the strongest one of the lot, the widow of the great Sakharov, a tiny woman with thick glasses and a deep voice, mentioned Gorbachev's name. "We cannot," she said, "let a bunch of bandits take over from the presidents of this country!"

"That's right," we screamed as we moved forward. "*Da, da, da!*"

"Too many speeches," Bodikian whispered in a fading voice from the other side of nowhere. "Come on, give the Siberian a tune, rabbi. Bust your balls for him."

And the only tune I could remember—the only one I could put my sore lips around and find enough breath to push out—was the final chorus of the *1812 Overture*.

"You've fucked 'em good now," someone said, just as my upper lip split apart, "real good, brother."

Nearby, the drunk carrying a portrait of the czar and a fancy Orthodox crucifix glowered at me as if I'd insulted his mother and everyone who came before her. "Believers!" he shouted, stumbling over broken boxes and mounds of trash. "Look carefully around you before you cheer."

Some, listening to the patriot, did.

Click.

"Rossiya, we've won!" a hundred thousand shouted. "Rossiya!"

12

You saw us, didn't you? It was Shabbes, a holy day. Inside the Orthodox church at the Vagankovskoye Cemetery, I moved forward along with the crowd. Holding my hat and bugle, I stood with Nadezdha Yefimova at the rear of the beautifully decorated church until the patriarch Aleksy finished chanting over the flag-draped coffins of the two heroes. Sweet-smelling smoke from the priest's beautiful silver censer, dangling at the end of a long chain, drifted over us.

While the patriarch bent and kissed the two coffins, the boys' relatives and friends held large photographs of the dead. Many people cried; some pounded their fists in tribute. "Beautiful boys," Nadezdha said. Then the patriarch nodded to his right, and the pallbearers carried the two coffins through the church and into the cemetery, toward the chosen place where a rabbi, a short man in a black coat, lowered his head by the freshly dug grave. Before he said the Kaddish, the rabbi carefully placed a white prayer shawl over the coffin of Ilya Krichevsky of blessed memory. Nadezdha Yefimova, my constant companion these past four days, held my hand and stroked my wrist when I, too, began to pray.

Now each of the dead had names chanted by a hundred thousand mourners: Dmitri Komar and Vladimir Usov, crushed to death, as we learned three days ago, by an armored vehicle on the Garden Ring Road, and Ilya Krichevsky, a young Jew, shot in the back of the head as he tried to attack a tank. The ones who murdered them, the eight coup leaders from a stinking regime, said Yeltsin before the funeral procession set off from our new Square of Free Russia, were "cockroaches in a jar." Standing on a parapet surrounded by his bodyguards, Boris Nikolaiyevich said the failed coup's victims were "heroes for all time." "Soviet heroes," a man shouted at the end of Yeltsin's speech. "Up yours!" answered a solitary voice from within the crowd. "They're Russia's heroes, you bastard communist."

Ten thousand, maybe more, squeezed into every square meter of the huge cemetery. The Moscow rabbi, unused to such crowds, swayed and wiped his forehead, his voice choking as if he might not remember all of the necessary words. And when he finished the simple prayer that I had said too many times in my life, a lone violinist, also a Jew, picked up his instrument and started to offer another kind of lament.

Suddenly, some twenty meters in front of us, in the space just beyond the rabbi and the violinist, I heard a clarinet's bittersweet sound. What to make of this? There were no other musicians close to the violinist, and the clarinet's tune sounded hollow, as if its melody had drifted in on the wind. The rabbi held out his hands, the crowd behind me pushed forward. The patriarch pointed.

Nadezdha Yefimova released my hand. "What does it mean?" she asked, pointing at someone ahead of us. "Is this what Jews do?"

I caught a partial glimpse of a large black hat trimmed in fur. Bobbing up and down like a floating mushroom to the clarinet's melody, the hat swayed from side to side. "A crazy man, maybe a relative," I said to Nadezdha. "It's nothing. Grief is grief."

But something about the clarinet's sound made the mourners move even closer, and I, taking babysteps with everyone else, strained to hear.

In the scraping of so many thousands of poorly made shoes on the gravel, the music—violinist's and clarinetist's—was lost for a few seconds. Then, just as the crowd moved to one side to get a better view, I recognized, in the hush that came for only a few seconds, the scratchy recorded music of a long-deceased Jew. "It's Fishbein from Minsk!" I said a little too loudly. "The great Hasidic musician Fishbein!"

"Who?" Nadezdha asked.

"A dead man," I answered, feeling a weakness in my sore knees. "He's dead!"

"Then he's risen from the grave," she said. "Look."

Perhaps I groaned too loudly, but what would you have done if you had seen an old Jew, wrapped in a tattered black coat beneath a hat two sizes too large for his narrow head, surrounded by a few thousand gentiles? With a flowing tallith hanging around his stooped shoulders, a portable phonograph in his arms (the late Fishbein's temporary home!), the old man somehow managed to dance atop some narrow slats nailed onto a wooden beer crate without upsetting the record. This time, I wasn't in the midst of a dream about poor Bodikian, God give him peace and a few more tricks in the other world. This time, ladies and gentlemen, I saw a real man toying with disaster.

Nadezdha, between sighs, said, "What's he holding up? What?"

"Fishbein," I stammered, not quite believing how the phonograph's scratchy sound carried over the crowd's murmuring, "or at least what's left of him."

In two minutes, maybe less, you sometimes endure a full life from one end to the other—a violinist plays, a Hasid jerks his body in time to a long-deceased clarinetist's music, people shove into one another for a closer look, and then, like the end of a lingering illness, it's over.

In the sudden silence that followed the conclusion of the violinist's sad music and Fishbein's sweet call to God, the mourners slowly began to back away toward the cemetery gate, surrounding the black hat. The old man, however, stayed on his tiny stage, frantically rewinding the Victrola's metal arm. Since his limbs were not twisted by an angry mob, maybe this is why I briefly saw him lift his head toward the sky as if to thank heaven.

"Berman!"

"Bugler," he answered. "Come over here and help a Jew."

I begged the pardon of scores of Russians as I pushed into the retreating crowd. People moved aside—the Red Sea parted, as it were—and I used my shoulders to nudge my way toward the tailor. "My God, Sasha!" I kept shouting each time I lost sight of him. "What is this? Are you hurt?"

I stumbled over feet, apologized, and righted myself. Nadezdha was somewhere behind me, a memory. The Victrola, cranked up to full strength, began to offer some more of Fishbein's clarinet. Although I couldn't see him, hearing was no problem.

"Berman?"

"Here, here," he cried as he lifted his arm and waved the tallith like a flag. "Over here."

You're right: What was I doing throwing myself back into the arms of this meshuggener? Now, as I recall my old anger, reason and justice should have ordered a good pop on the tailor's jaw, or at the very least a hard tug at the fool's lapels. Even better, a kick in the ass. But today's thoughts, as they say, never correct yesterday's stupidities. Once you're out in the open, there's little to be done; once you fall over fate's long tail, well. . . .

I lost my footing and, within a forest of legs, covered my head to avoid being trampled. I shouted. Someone offered a strong hand and a leg up. Then a helpful warning from a familiar voice. "Don't make so much noise, Simon Moskovich."

It was Oleshka the minesweeper, his paratrooper's tunic decorated with his old service medals from the Afghan horror. He supported me in his strong arms and added, "The rabbi here is telling a good story."

Rabbi?

Oleshka's ability to push and shove brought me to within inches of a group of young Russians, mostly students in jeans, whose musty, damp clothing and sour-smelling breath meant that they, too, had stood behind some barricades without knowing how everything would end. But it was Alexandr Davidowich, cradling the Victrola while he moved, wearing the black coat rescued from Olga Mikhailovna, who was now the center of attention. He looked, I noticed, somewhat heavier.

"I have been everywhere," he was saying as Oleshka, acting as bodyguard, made sure that no one upset the tailor's delicate balance. "We Jews have seen much . . . "

He was not the same man. Or, he was more than one man, or woman. Maybe the months of practice—of travel and loneliness, of clothing sewn and artifacts deposited behind glass cases, of being lost in the marrow of lives imagined and relived—had made Berman into what he now was: mourner and storyteller, history's tinker, dancer, and servant. Rabbi and teacher. Taking on the voices and the lives of the deceased who will never, ever appear in any book—not even this one—Alexandr Davidowich had, in voice and movement, become many people. He was what he was, so who was I to interfere? Who was I to break his concentration? Who was I to say, stop!

As I listened to him put together for these near-children who hovered around him the terrible details of a demented French marquis's murder of some of our own in that snowbound hut, I finally knew that he was sewing together— forgive me, but what better verb could I employ?—the past to the present. "This coat," he said, stroking the frayed lapels, "is a holy object. Do you see? Is it clear now? Will you remember?"

When Berman could talk no more, Oleshka gently nudged him off the crate and took charge of the Victrola. Berman took my hand and held me back. "Ah, my bugler is here with me again," he said without a word of explanation for past sins, all of which I had already forgiven.

Most of the crowd had finally parted. Some stragglers gathered around the nearby grave of Vysotsky and placed fresh flowers over the singer's modest plot, while others, this being a day to consider the dead, walked toward Sakharov's grave in the cemetery's new section. Seeing no danger in my accompanying his tailor, Oleshka was well ahead of us at the far end of the gravel path. Berman hobbled along, sometimes leaning against me for support. "Together we can maybe say a Kaddish for Ilya Krichevsky and a few others," he said, pointing to the area where the Moscow rabbi stood with nine or ten members of the boy's family. "Agreed?"

And so we did—for many, many people whose names are familiar to you.

Tatyana, I said to myself as we prayed together for God's grace. My lovely, lost Tatyana.

Berman motioned that we should go. Although I had a thousand questions to ask, I followed him down the path toward the cemetery's gate. As you understand, there are times for quiet.

Suddenly, I felt the tailor pull back on my sleeve.

"Look over there," he said, stopping before a large gravemarker. "They have no shame! Scum!"

Outside the wrought-iron gates, a few dozen black-shirted Pamyat hooligans, heads shaved, paraded in a circle. A short, squat Russian, whose belly hung over a shiny military belt, led their chanting. The louder they yelled, the more attention they drew to themselves with their placards and their czarist flags with the two-headed Romanov eagle. Soon, a small crowd gathered to watch. "Zionists out!" they shouted to a cadence marked by the short man. "No more Yids."

"We don't have to leave now," I told Berman. "We'll wait here."

Trapped by the crowd and the noisy demonstrators, unable to break through the circle because he was carrying the Victrola, Oleshka was waving us off. He kept pointing to a side gate. Then he began to argue with one of the blackshirts.

But Alexandr Davidowich, who seemed to be on the verge of an extraordinary insight, began fumbling with the buttons on his black coat. He leaned against the grave-marker and cleaned his spectacles. If he was frightened, he showed no visible sign. "They have shitty tailors," was all he would say as he studied those red throats tightened with rage and lubricated with cheap vodka. "Bad suits!"

"Yids out!"

I knew I was going to be sick.

At the cemetery gate the crowd grew. Oleshka and a few of the students who had recently stood close to Alexandr Davidowich were now involved in a shoving match with one of the Pamyat marchers. There were no militia officers in sight, but some television journalists and their cameramen were already working. Waiting.

"You know what they are?" Berman asked me.

"Yes."

"And what they want?"

"To make us disappear," I answered, feeling my stomach sink to my knees.

Berman nodded. I thought he was going to cry.

"We need to leave by the rear gate, Sasha," I said.

"No, bugler," he said, removing his spectacles. "We need to do something else."

Hiding from the shame, I turned away from Berman and retched behind a tall gravemarker. Who can control a nervous stomach with a life of its own? Not me. Not at my age. Impossible.

"No more pogromists!" Alexandr Davidowich shouted,

removing his black coat, beautiful hat, and dark trousers. "Not this time, not ever."

"Sasha, no!" I stammered when I saw what Berman wore beneath his top layer of clothing.

"Get on my back, Simka. I know I can carry you. Have faith, I've had some experience in schlepping sick Jews."

Then it hit me, a sudden, split-second click of the brain that croaked at me like an angry blackbird: "Look, you frightened schmuck, this is only a dream. Be still, let it play itself out and you'll wake up without hurting yourself."

Maybe this works in heaven, but not in Moscow, not when I was staring at Alexandr Davidowich in the striped prisoner's clothing he had once worn in the camps, a relic from history's asshole. A yellow triangle covered his breast and, just beneath it, his camp number. On his head, a slave's striped hat. His sleeves were rolled up to reveal the numbers burned into his flesh.

"One last time, Simka. Help a Jew."

Decide for me, Papa, I begged the air—before I grabbed ahold of the tailor and straddled his broad back.

"Maybe you know how to sing 'David, King of Israel?'" he asked, when my head rested on his shoulders.

"This one I know, Sasha."

Berman crossed his arms under my legs. A good tailor's hold.

"So now we can walk out of here, bugler. There's a good crowd to see us. Don't lose your grip . . . and don't forget anything."

Walking slowly at first until he was steady with the combined weights of me and the memory of another passenger, with Olga Mikhailovna's coat tucked inside his armpit, Alexandr Davidowich took a wide practice turn inside the cemetery. Some of the Pamyat filth noticed us and started to hoot.

"You're still with me?"

"Yes."

But I wasn't, and when we slowly approached the gate and the placards that waited for us, and my arms began to slip from his body, the tailor straightened up and I dismounted. "Please, my chest," I said as the pressure began to increase. "I can't do it."

"Then walk behind me and sing, Simka."

I spread my fingers for five minutes; then I touched my aching chest. "Ahh," he groaned as I slipped away from his hold. "You rest, how long could this take? Later, bugler, we'll talk about everything." He gave me his black coat, telling me to take good care of it until he returned, and then he took my shaky hand and kissed it.

I am taking care of that coat still, as I take care of his story.

"Please, Sasha," I said, clutching at the striped sleeve of his prisoner's uniform. "Don't go! Suffering we can do without."

"But who's suffering, my old friend? David is king of Israel!"

When Berman, in good voice, walked through the outer gate, singing about a Jewish king, or maybe mumbling the same psalms that gave the late Leo Gelbat a little peace of mind, the crowd lining both sides of the blackshirts let him pass. "It never happened," a Pamyat demonstrator suddenly laughed. He pointed at Berman's camp uniform. "They never died! It's a Yid's lie!" Someone else threw a stone. I ran to the gate just in time to see Berman cover his face and, without breaking stride, stagger into the center of the empty road.

"Sasha!"

One block away, his hood ornament centered on the man in the prisoner's uniform, with a clear view of his last important job, ex-KGB Captain Viktor Semyonovich Kostov—to whom no king was worth a shit in life or in dreams—pressed hard on the Zhiguli sedan's gas pedal.

Lawrence Rudner

"The photograph had a jolting effect upon me. It had something that I'd never seen before: a German soldier pointing a rifle at a mother holding a one-year-old child. It was the penultimate moment before her death. I must have stayed there an hour looking at the photograph. I was young enough, an adolescent, questioning, 'How could this happen?' "

—Lawrence Rudner, in a 1988 interview

Born in Detroit in 1947, Lawrence Sheldon Rudner held a doctorate in American Studies from Michigan State University. From 1978 to 1995 he taught journalism, world literature, and Holocaust literature at North Carolina State University. He traveled and taught extensively in eastern Europe, and was a Fulbright Fellow in Krakow in 1986 and 1987. In the early 1980s he began writing stories set in eastern Europe pursuing what he later called his "obsession . . . to reinvent some lost lives." His first novel, *The Magic We Do Here,* the story of a blond and blue-eyed Jew who survives the Holocaust by posing as a half-witted Polish farm laborer, has been called "a novel that is as heartbreaking as it is hauntingly beautiful." *Memory's Tailor* was finished in 1994, shortly before Rudner was diagnosed with cancer, of which he died in May of 1995.

The manuscript was edited for publication by Rudner's friend and literary executor John Kessel and University Press of Mississippi's fiction editor Susan Ketchin.